Some Passages
in the Life of

MR. ADAM BLAIR

Minister of the Gospel
at Cross-Meikle

—••✠ ✠✠ ✠••—

BY J. G. LOCKHART

with an Introduction by David Craig

EDINBURGH

©

EDINBURGH UNIVERSITY PRESS 1963
One George Square, Edinburgh 8

USA Agent: Aldine Publishing Company
64 East Van Buren Street,
Chicago 5, Illinois

Introduction

—••❊❳❳❁❱••—

In writing *Adam Blair* Lockhart did undoubtedly in-
tend with a large part of himself to tell a sober tale of a
sin and its due punishment, as a piece of life typical of
the old Scotland that had barely passed away. His
father, the minister of a Lanarkshire parish, used to tell
his son the true story of a minister deposed from his
charge as punishment for fornication. This was the
nucleus of *Adam Blair*. Many a case of the kind can be
found in the records of the General Assembly of the
Church of Scotland during the 18th century. They
take us into that world of severe moral sanctions that
Burns was revolting against in the majority of his finest
poems – 'The Twa Herds', 'The Ordination', 'The
Holy Fair', 'Holy Willie's Prayer.'

So the source of Lockhart's material was that pre-
industrial Scotland in which almost every value, belief, and social drive took a religious form and operated
inside the framework of the Kirk. But Lockhart, the
quick-minded young lawyer, at home in the literary
milieu of Regency Edinburgh, no longer himself in-
habited that 18th-century society. When he wrote *Adam
Blair* he had behind him a career at Oxford as an

v

Exhibitioner in Classics. It is not unlikely that his father (like the father of Reginald Dalton in the novel that followed *Adam Blair*) had given him *Pilgrim's Progress* and other godly books to read as a child. But at Balliol College he had been reading the novels of Boccaccio and Machiavelli, and he was one of the first literary men to admire Wordsworth and Byron. During his early days in Edinburgh, the quickening movement of the mass of the people into the towns, to a life of crammed streets and tenements, factory work, and political agitation, was transforming life and literature. The great stonemason-geologist Hugh Miller, an ardent Free-churchman, who moved from Easter Ross to Edinburgh a generation after Lockhart had lived there, observed that townsfolk no longer seemed even to have broken loose from religion – they had never known it at all.

Rapid social change made itself felt in literature as romanticism – the sensibility that feels experience as a flux of emotions. *Adam Blair*, for all its dutiful references to the old framework, nevertheless makes us feel the stir of a new feeling for life. The book is emotional in its essence. We do not mainly remember from it a scene with solidly real surroundings, a variety of people distinct in all their traits, a wider society visible, so to speak, close at hand. Rather we remember the distinctive emotional *timbre* – anguished bereavement dulled into quiet submissiveness, passion distraught because it has to fight with its own inhibitions, the sentiments of reverence, desire, remorse: all given in the eloquent

vi

abstractions of early Romantic prose, rather than in precise evocation of behaviour itself. Over this whole a colouring is thrown in the form of 'atmosphere': dark nights, which lend themselves to strange suggestions, are more typical of the book than daylight.

This atmosphere is shared with many a Victorian classic – *Jane Eyre* and *Wuthering Heights*, passage after passage in Dickens, the side of Disraeli's *Sybil* typified by 'the fair Religious' (Sybil herself) – and also, unfortunately, with MacPherson's pseudo-*Ossian*, although Lockhart's talent was fine enough to get a certain reality of emotional portrayal even from MacPherson's headlong verbiage. *Adam Blair* is thus one of the first pieces of Scottish literature in which we feel that the author is as much at home in the general British cultural climate as in the Scottish. Hence John Galt's remark to Lockhart (in a letter of 1822) that the novel shows 'neither vicar nor minister, but the workings of a man. It belongs to no age or country but to general human nature'.

Nevertheless the novel does belong (though in a new form) to the main Scottish tradition, for it shows a minister as the centre of gravity in his community. To John Maxwell, old crofter, senior elder, and Adam Blair's staunch stand-by in the neighbourhood, Adam is 'his Minister' – as we should say nowadays 'my doctor' or in America, so I am told, 'my analyst'. It was the minister above all who had to live the values and fight the moral bugbears of his society. This is what accounts for the psychological core of the novel and the matters that many of us must find hardest to enter into imaginatively – the appalling consequences that follow on Adam's adultery, the fatal and near-fatal illness, the utter social ostracism that descends on Adam and ruins his daughter's life.

The doubt we may well feel about the plausibility, and the justice, of this crisis in the novel was anticipated by the old *doyen* of Scottish literature, Henry Mackenzie, author of *The Man of Feeling* (1771), in the review of *Adam Blair* that he wrote in *Blackwood's Magazine* for March 1822. He knows that readers outside Scotland may hardly believe in 'that utter prostration of mind, and that long remorse, which are here so ably depicted'. But for him it is explained by 'the sanctity of the clerical character' which in Scotland is 'a part of the national belief and feeling'. Such a sin committed by a minister would, he says, give 'a shock to the whole moral and religious associations of every mind in the country'; if English readers thought Adam's penalties too severe, Scottish ones might well consider them too light.

This probably exaggerates in making out that Scottish piety was so unanimous and so highly-strung. Throughout the 18th century a goodly section of the Scottish people had inclined to an anti-clericalism, expressed passionately by Burns, that might well have found in a minister's downfall an occasion for derision and pungent propaganda. But this only restricts the application of Mackenzie's remarks. For it was most certainly true that the Scottish devotion to religion,

Kirk, and minister was still the essence of morality for great sections of the people. The fanaticism remembered from Knox's Reformation and from the days when the troops of the Anglo-Catholic English monarchy had hunted the Covenanters over the moors of the south-west had lasted on as a solemn and severe sense of Christian duties. *Adam Blair* is set in the 1750's. People could still retail first-hand memories of the heroic Covenanting ministers (as douce Davie Deans does in Scott's *The Heart of Midlothian*), and the new generation of ministers, milder and more genteel by far, actually had to warn their congregations against longing for the more stirring days when their religion had been persecuted. The Covenanting ministers had been 'more conspicuous as prophets than as pastors'* – more given to preaching fiery sermons than to supervising the morals of their parishioners. By the mid-18th century the Scottish religious zeal flowed very much into the supervision of morals. The restraint and suspicious vigilance that went into it were something we can now barely imagine. In Edinburgh (let alone the outlying towns and villages) the town Presbytery enacted and the Town Council enforced that no social visits should be paid on Sundays, for these were 'useless communications' on a day meant for higher things. 'Seizers' patrolled the streets to arrest people found there during Church service, and there was also a ban on 'idly gazing out of windows' which exposed you to the risk of

* W. L. Mathieson, *Church and Reform in Scotland* (Glasgow, 1916), 314.

ix

'beholding vanities abroad.' The iron fingers of the clergy had their grip on everything. Village girls could be physically examined by the local Kirk Session to find out which of them could be feeding a bastard child found dead or dying of exposure. The Session could also punish people for fornication or slander, and offenders could be made to sit on a stool for weeks in Church, wearing a coarse gown, in full view of the congregation. In *The Heart of Midlothian* Scott makes Jeanie Deans tell the Queen that women were so terri‑ fied of this public shaming that they often took refuge in that very concealment of their pregnancy which counted as a capital crime if the baby died.

The minister had to be in his own person the exemplar of this severe moral code, and in *The Wealth of Nations* (1776) Adam Smith says that the ministers' influence on the minds of the people was based on the real moral leadership that they gave. In time the code began to relax, and during a General Assembly of the Church held at about the time in which *Adam Blair* is set we find a minister of the Moderate (or liberal) party congratulating his brethren on having escaped from the rigour of the days when 'religion was so far driven, especially in ministers, that it was a principle they should not be conversible and should only be taken up upon serious things in common conversation.' But the struggle between broadmindedness and intolerance was to continue for some time yet. One of the most famous of the new liberal clergy was Alexander Carlyle, minister of Inveresk just east of Edinburgh, and he describes (in passages from his *Autobiography* and *Recollections* that apply to 1747) how his parishioners mistrusted him because he was 'too young, too full of levity, and too much addicted to the company of my superiors', because he 'danced frequently in a manner prohibited by the laws of the Church . . . wore my hat agee; and had been seen galloping through the Links one day between one and two o'clock.' This does not leave much that the minister *could* do or be, and Adam Blair's offence was no small fault of manners but the sin of adultery.

Such is the social experience that Lockhart had behind him in writing *Adam Blair*. But he did not deal with it *via* the painstaking description of 'manners' that had been the method of his immediate seniors in Scottish fiction, Walter Scott (who was to become his father-in-law) and John Galt. For some time Lockhart had planned a book of this kind. In 1814 he was writing to a college friend that he had in mind a novel which would be 'a receptacle of an immense quantity of anecdotes and observations I have made concerning the state of the Scotch, chiefly their clergy and elders. It is to me wonderful how the Scotch character has been neglected.' But before he could finish this project Scott's *Waverley* had appeared (1814), and Lockhart, fearing that 'the rush upon Scotland consequent to that popular work is such that mine is likely to be crushed among the row,' decided to let his own work 'sleep a year or two.' Perhaps his material went into his *Peter's Letters to his Kinsfolk* (1819), a book that challenges comparison with Cockburn's *Memorials* and *Journals* as the richest of all Scottish social memoirs. By this time, too, Galt's *Annals of the Parish* (1821) had appeared, and the vein of fiction-as-social-history must have seemed nearly worked out, especially to a young writer anxious to make his distinctive mark. By the 1820's the Romantic poetry will have sunk deeply into his sensibility, with the result that when he came to tell his old Scottish story, he did so in a manner vibrant with emotion.

The modern reader is bound to feel that the novelist's manner from Chapters XIII-XIX is hectically melodramatic, and these are the chapters in which Adam and Charlotte sleep together and dree the weird of it. No sooner have they sinned than Lockhart plunges them into a nightmare train of sufferings. Devils creep round them, they hesitate on the brink of suicide, hector each other quite in the manner of grand opera ('torment me not. . . . Shall the curse cling to me forever?'), and finally fall into the inevitable romantic prostration – fever, coma, and for one of them death. If Lockhart's readers did not query the plausibility of these consequences, it was because they were so attuned to the code which regarded the least 'irregularity,' or extra-marital passion, as an unspeakable crime.* The

* Some contemporary readers were scandalised that adultery should have been dealt with at all. Lockhart wrote to a friend on 20.3.1822: 'Adam Blair . . . has created a good deal of rumpus, and some of the low cattle here are saying, and printing, that it is fit for the same shelf with "Faublas".'

trouble is that it remains literally unspeakable in the novel – their love is never either shown or acknowledged – their 'fall' is followed in the first edition by a couplet of poetry and two rows of asterisks. Lockhart even has to make the pair drunk, as though to avoid facing the possibility that an unmarried couple might in all sanity have intercourse.

I am not implying that a novelist at that period should, or could, have presented love-making in the open modern way, or even with the brutal candour of the 18th century. What one expects is that the novelist should be perfectly clear-sighted about what he is presenting. Lockhart has brought his couple to the point of consummated passion, while suggesting scarcely one step in the growth of this strong feeling. In Chapter XII where Adam thinks over all that Charlotte has meant to him – 'long pleasant walks . . . interesting conversations . . . restoration of his own mental serenity . . . the charming, kind looks of Charlotte . . . her heroic resolution' – there is no word of anything even verging on acknowledged passion. This, it could be argued, is

---

It is noteworthy that for his next novel Lockhart was paid the large sum of 1000 guineas by Blackwood, twice the total payment for *Adam Blair*, presumably because of the 'rumpus.' After *Reginald Dalton* had proved anything but a sensation, Blackwood dropped to 400 guineas for the much more original *Matthew Wald*, a novel that mingles Presbyterian fanaticism with violent crime.

(See Andrew Lang, *Life and Letters of John Gibson Lockhart*, 1897, I, 295, 302; National Library of Scotland MS. 4010, 211; MS. 4012, 236.)

to present a man without enough self-knowledge to realise the feelings gathering force inside himself. But, as we read through the novel, it affects us rather as a sheer gap – a withholding of essentials on the part of the author. After the months of Platonic intimacy during which, evidently with no consciousness on their part, Charlotte has become virtually a wife-figure for Adam, the first of the clearly inevitable outbursts of passion between the two occurs, after Charlotte has rescued Adam and little Sarah from drowning. Her clothes are half torn off by the struggle in the water. Adam 'fell upon his knee close beside Charlotte and his child, and throwing one arm round each, he drew them both towards his bosom, and began to kiss them alternately, cheek, and brow, and lip, and neck, hastily and passionately, as if ignorant or careless that he was within sight of anyone.' Here, surely, we are bound to wonder: Is the scene credible? *could* the man, however distraught, conceivably have been so oblivious of bystanders and of all normal restraints as to kiss the woman in that way? Is the obliviousness not the author's – is he not, in spite of himself, coming out with such a moment as a kind of unconscious substitute for the frankly-acknowledged (though perhaps guilty) love that the reader nowadays will all along have regarded as asking to be presented?

Several pages later Lockhart might seem to be aware enough of the emotions involved: Adam's sleep on the night after the rescue is full of nightmares, dreams of exotic languor and heat, and also directly erotic images:

xiv

'Beautiful women's shapes, smiling eyes and burning blushes, darted in glimpses here and there from amidst the thickest of tumults.' Yet a little later again, as we have seen, Adam still does not say to himself, 'I love her' – we cannot even sense any strain of repression on his part. His nightmares, like the kissing after the rescue, seems rather to be a flickering into sight of something which for the most part has been allowed (by the novelist) to stay buried.

If there is evasion here, it has its counterpart in the direct suppressions that follow Adam's confession and penance. He is utterly humbled, 'silent, laborious, penitent, devout. . . . Seldom, except on the Sabbath day, did he for many months quit the narrow precincts of the field to which he had returned.' His former friends never come near him, Sarah never marries although she has 'ripened into womanhood' and become 'the most beautiful girl in that part of the country'. It is not that such an outcome is inconceivable in itself. Our most serious criticism is rather that Lockhart presents this outcome, in all confidence that his readers will approve, as the perfection of goodness and a supremely just moral consummation.

This kind of morals, setting the highest value on self-abnegation, repression, and self-sacrifice, is at the core of work after work as the 19th century goes on: think of Charlotte Brontë's *Jane Eyre* (1847), Nathaniel Hawthorne's *The Scarlet Letter* (1850), or George Eliot's 'Janet's Repentance' from *Scenes of Clerical Life* (1857). In *Jane Eyre* Rochester is married to a lunatic – we cannot but feel that it is no marriage, and that he, as a natural man, must seek another woman. But Charlotte Brontë could not face this: Jane and Rochester will come together, yes, but not until Rochester has been blinded in the very fire that rids him of his ghastly incubus. Like Lockhart, Charlotte Brontë has a flickering awareness of what she is suppressing: the blinded Rochester (who throughout has represented in a half-submerged way the force of real impulse) can even challenge Jane by saying she now wants to marry him only because she 'delights in sacrifice.' But Jane's reply, allowed to carry the moral of the book, is: 'I love you better now, when I can be really useful to you, than I did in your state of proud independence.' So the passionate meeting of equals in a marriage that could fulfil their whole natural selves is thwarted and side-tracked, and a repressed, maimed life is given the highest value.

George Eliot wrote in a letter about *Jane Eyre*: 'All self-sacrifice is good, but one would like it to be in a somewhat nobler cause than that of a diabolical law which chains a man soul and body to a putrefying carcase.' Yet she herself was not wholly immune to this morbid side of contemporary morality. Her *Scenes of Clerical Life* first appeared in *Blackwood's Magazine*, which was so careful to give the middle-class Victorians what they liked and what they liked and what was good for them. (Lockhart had been one of its principal contributors during the 1820's.) In the third *Scene*, the heroine, Janet, is married, like Rochester, to a monster – her husband is drunkard, bully, sadist. But just at the point when it looks as though the desperately-needed divorce may come about, the man is stricken with *delirium tremens*, and his sufferings so renew Janet's devotion to him that she nurses him selflessly until his death. Her whole situation and capacity for emotion, like Adam's or Charlotte's in *Adam Blair*, cry out for a partner, and, like them, she gets one only for the author to keep the relationship at a level either buried or else sublimated into a thin substitute for the real thing. Janet's real love is the curate Transome. But he is tuberculous. In so many 19th-century works, if you are good you are 'not long for this world'; the more virtuous, the more sickly. The pair acknowledge their love once, after the husband's death and shortly before the curate's, and Janet then faces the rest of her life as 'a solemn service of gratitude and patient effort.' It is as though George Eliot, like Charlotte Brontë and Lockhart, wants us to feel that such resignation to a deprived life is somehow *supremely good*, that this kind of martyred saintliness raises human moral capacities to their highest level.

This notion had been strong in Christian belief for centuries. It is the morals of the downtrodden – mankind despairing of social justice and helpless against a Nature he could control so little. All these novelists emphasise Christian values: Adam with his minister's responsibilities; Rochester 'bending his sightless eyes to the earth' and praying to 'my Redeemer to give me strength to lead henceforth a purer life than I have done hitherto'; Transome telling Janet that when he himself had been wicked in his student days, a friend had 'made it clear to me that the only preparation for coming to Christ and partaking of his salvation, was that very sense of guilt and helplessness which was weighing me down.' We are readier nowadays to ask why a life repressed, curtailed, or trodden into submissiveness should be a better life than one that is fulfilled and thriving in itself. Mrs Leavis points out in her most searching history of this strange moral tradition that Victorian fiction, masterpieces and cheap novels alike, was steeped in 'the attitudes formed round the words "noble" and "pure," and the idea of self-sacrifice for its own sake.' She analyses a case from the old best-seller Florence Barclay (whose novel *The Rosary* can still be found on the bedside tables of old-fashioned boarding houses) in which a man regards it as 'sacrilege' for a daughter to criticise her mother even if she has deserved it, and remarks that this is typical of the way 'in which an ideal that directly conflicts with experience is none the less quite gratuitously given moral support.' *

Such was the popular literary atmosphere that still tinged the emotions of millions early in this century. It is significant of the real perplexities involved that the greatest successor of the 19th-century tradition in fiction, D. H. Lawrence, should have done – should have been forced to do – more than any other writer to free morals from the old cowering negatives and self-denials. In Lawrence, ultimate encounters between men and women re-emerge into the light of a full artistic pre-

* Q. D. Leavis, *Fiction and the Reading Public* (1932), 245, 326.

sentation. They had been shunned by the writers, with scarcely an exception, for over a century. Lawrence, as we know from a letter to Donald Carswell in 1927, disliked Lockhart for the censorious righteousness of his attitude to Burns in the *Life* he wrote of him in 1828, and it is not surprising to find that Lawrence repeatedly criticised the line of fiction that has been followed out above. In the essay called 'The Novel' (from *Reflections on the Death of a Porcupine*, 1925) he develops the notion that 'nearly all great novelists have a didactic purpose, otherwise a philosophy, directly opposite to their passional inspiration.' His key instance is a novel that, like *Adam Blair*, concerns adultery – Tolstoy's *Anna Karenina*. In a few straight sentences we have the nub of the matter:

Vronsky sinned, did he? But also the sinning was a consummation devoutly to be wished. The novel makes that obvious: in spite of old Leo Tolstoy. There you have the greatness of the novel itself. It won't *let* you tell didactic lies, and put them over. Nobody in the world is anything but delighted when Vronsky gets Anna.

What Lawrence opposes above all is submission to a principle that we have to will ourselves to believe – that does not emerge from the real needs of our natures. This to my mind is a key problem in *Adam Blair*. Adam, raised again to the ministry, has to rebuke penitent sinners from the pulpit, 'but he never failed to commence his address to the penitent before him, by reminding him, and all present, of his own sin and its consequences.' One is driven to wonder how such self-mortification was humanly possible. Could a man be so subdued as to act as a living object-lesson his whole life long, meek and uncomplaining? Would the ego not revolt at all, through some kind of self-hatred or hatred of the community?

It may be that in those communities the religious code was so unquestioned that sheer dutifulness was all-powerful and wholly permeated the man. The Kirk had the extraordinary authority described already. Unfortunately, contemporary records are not insighted enough to reveal what kind of psychological toll was taken. Burns and his friend Gavin Hamilton in their Ayrshire village loathed the machinery of spying, admonishing, and public shaming, and this was typical of the popular anti-clericalism. Some dialect stories by the Glasgow town-crier Dougal Graham give us vivid records of life at the period of *Adam Blair*, and in his 'Jockey and Maggy's Courtship' an old woman rages at 'Whigry,' or Presbyterian puritanism, which made no provision for bastard children but simply punished the parents (as long as they were poor and not gentle-men): 'a' your mortifying o' your members, and a' your repenting-stools; a wheen papist rites an rotten cere-monies, fashing fouks wi' sack gowns, and buttock-malls,* an' I dinna ken what.' This, however, is simple war between the Kirk Session and those who refuse to knuckle under. In *Adam Blair* the sinner does to all appearances submit humbly to the Kirk discipline,

* Fines for fornication imposed by the Kirk Session.

and it would have taken a writer of rather more urgent imagination than Lockhart to follow through these complexities on which his subject actually borders.

What these novelists as a group seem to represent in the collective consciousness of their class at that time is moral conscience that has hypertrophied and become so over-susceptible that it is forced compulsively into the most harrowing ordeals. I suggest that this is indeed what was happening; conscience was the strongest element surviving from the old religious culture, now that the less tenable things (Calvinist predestination, the literal truth of the Bible, the unquestioned authority of minister and Kirk Session, superstition of various kinds – Dougal Graham's characters actually fear Satan will jump out at them) were losing their power over the freer minds. The American critic Yvor Winters makes in his *Maule's Curse* (1938) a classic analysis of this process as it took place in New England and conditioned her novelists from Hawthorne* to Henry James. In the similar culture of Scotland, or the Nonconformist England that produced George Eliot, conscience emerged as an overweening faculty operating more and more on the individual's more private experiences as people grew less part of a closed church community, less aware of a Power 'up there' to worship, less interested in technical problems of theology and more

---

* Hawthorne's finest novel, *The Scarlet Letter*, is in many ways strikingly akin to *Adam Blair*: this comparison is dealt with at length in David Craig, *Scottish Literature and the Scottish People* (1961), 174-8.

oriented on the real life of which theology had been the fantastic projection.

Lockhart's own generation was notable for a drift away from formal religion. In Scotland, James and John Stuart Mill, Thomas Carlyle, the great surgeon and anatomist William Hunter had all paused at the brink of the ministry and turned away. Their counterparts in England were such men as Matthew Arnold, the poet Clough, and Leslie Stephen. But the mental habit of anxiously weighing and testing one's actions in the light of an 'ultimate' value long outlived the religious cult with which it had originally been bound up. The peculiar quality of *Adam Blair* – its raw material rooted in old Presbyterian Scotland but the doing of it permeated with the rather worried emotionality of the Romantic frame of mind – is due, I suggest, to its position at this stage in the re-absorption of religious feelings and ideas into the general atmosphere of our culture.

This still does not explain why such a consciousness prevailed and even re-intensified itself at just this period. Where Fielding could deal with a seduction, elopement, or rape with crude lightheartedness, or else as a vehicle for a perfunctory moral, for the Victorian or an immediate predecessor like Lockhart it must all be veiled – less definite, less straightforward, more felt. We say 'Victorian' or 'Regency.' But why did this deep change occur? It can hardly have been 'spontaneous' – occurring in the human psyche on its own.

The major changes in material and social life during

the period that formed the first 19th-century generations included such things as the swelling affluence of people engaged in trade and the rapidly increasing numbers of such people. This class had also become (as is attested by so many of the 18th-century records of periodicals, circulating libraries, etc.) the dominant section of the public for fiction. And the life of this class was more and more one in which 'appearances had to be kept up' – the material means for keeping them up (linens and cottons, china and glassware for the table, capital to build houses and imposing meeting-places) were multiplying year by year. Suburbs grew up round the towns, at a decent distance from the working-class slums, and tradesmen ceased to live above their work or to share tenements with either workers or noblemen. The Scottish middle-class was expanding fast on the overseas trade opened to Scotland as a result of the Union with England, and on the increase of internal trade due to the mechanisation of textiles, the rise in consumption, and hence of shopkeeping. Lockhart himself has left us, in *Peter's Letters to his Kinsfolk*, some of the very best contemporary descriptions of this class. He describes in graphic first-hand detail the merchant families of Glasgow, a 'very large number' of whom aimed at spending their profits on land and taking 'their place in the great body of British gentry, with as much propriety as any that elevate themselves to that most enviable of all human conditions.' These were the Glaswegians most akin to the Edinburgh bourgeoisie in their mindfulness of aristocracy and close ties with the land (the type of Bailie Nicol Jarvie in Scott's *Rob Roy*). It was Edinburgh that had been the cradle of Scottish literature since the start of the 18th century, and Edinburgh was at this time deliberately building a *polite* society – clean markets, capital punishment executed in decent privacy, merchants doing their business in a dignified Exchange instead of in pubs or on the streets, and a proper segregation of the classes both in hostelries and in the city sections where they lived.

Such a transformation in the way of life couldn't but affect people in their intimate living. Robert Chambers tells us in a note to his *Scottish Song* (1829) that courting had quite changed. Formerly, young people, poor or well-off, had sauntered together in the meadows, parks, and fields that fringed the town. But as the half-wild grassland was built over, as the New Town laid out its formal parks, as more and more folk from the middle-class and upwards felt that 'in their position' their behaviour must be irreproachable, courting was transformed. Now only 'artizans and serving-girls' went together in the meadows. He dates the change from thirty years before – that is, the time when the ideal of civic dignity, a studious expunging of all that could be thought uncouth, had become dominant.

Such changes were at work in Boston and London as well as Edinburgh and Glasgow. It may seem a far cry from the expansion of business to the shrinking yet intense sensibilities of the Brontës and the rest. Yet it cannot be doubted that, in culture generally, bourgeoisification was the root change from which most else flowed. Dickens, with his piercing social insight, saw the connection perfectly well; he fixed it in one of his best symbols, Podsnappery, the sacred principle of never 'bringing a blush to the cheek of the young person,' an attitude that spread outwards (as *Our Mutual Friend* shows) from the newly-rich above all. The novelists I have discussed are typical of those who were at least emotionally honest enough to feel, and record, the pangs of repression that were bound to result.

Lockhart scarcely had the deep current of imaginative power that makes a man work as an artist to the end of his days. Yet *Adam Blair* and *Matthew Wald* are sufficiently charged with life to make us regret the works that 'might' have come. *Matthew Wald*, his fourth novel, came two years after *Adam Blair*, in 1824, and turned out to be his last. The next year he left Scotland for London, to edit the *Quarterly Review*, and there he spent the rest of his life. So he was pulled south on that cultural drift which emptied Scotland of every kind of talent – craftsmanly and technical, intellectual, political – in his and the succeeding generations. Is he yet another case, like David Wilkie the painter, Allan Cunningham the poet, John Galt and Thomas Carlyle, of an artist who could have continued to tap his most personal, imaginatively fruitful levels of experience only if he had stayed close to its native sources?

DAVID CRAIG

MR. ADAM BLAIR

Chapter

I

—••༺༻••—

Seldom has the earth held a couple of human beings so happy in each other as were Mr Adam Blair and his wife. They had been united very early in love, and early in wedlock. Ten years had passed over their heads since their hands were joined together; and during all that time their heart-strings had never once vibrated in discord. Their pleasures had been the same, and these innocent; their sorrows had been all in common; and their hours of affliction had, even more than their hours of enjoyment, tended to knit them together. Of four children whom God had given them, three had been taken speedily away; – one girl only, the first pledge of their love, had been spared to them. She was now a beautiful fair-haired creature, of eight years old. In her rested the tenderness and the living delight of both; yet, often at the fall of evening would they walk out hand in hand with their bright-eyed child, and shed together tears, to her mysterious, over the small grassy mounds in the adjoining village cemetery, beneath which the lost blossoms of their affection had been buried.

Adam Blair had had his share of human suffering; but hitherto the bitter cup had always contained sweetness at the close of the draught. The oil and the balm had flowed plentifully for every wound, and his spirit was not only unbroken, but composed, happy, cheerful, 'with sober cheer.' The afflictions that had been sent to him had kept him calm; and all men said that he was an humble, but none that he was a dejected Christian. What the secret errors of his spirit might have been, it is not for us to guess. But he was destined to undergo severer chastenings; and who shall doubt that there was cause enough for the uplifting of the rod of love?

After the death of the last of these three infants, Mrs Blair dried her tears, and endeavoured to attend as usual to all the duties of her household. But the serenity of her temper had been tinged with a shade of grief which she could not dispel; and although she smiled upon her husband, it was with pale lips and melancholy eyes that she did so. If there were moments in which all her sorrows were forgotten, these were few and transitory. Her husband subdued himself that he might constrain her; he talked with her in a tone that was manly as well as tender; he talked like a Christian as well as a father; he caressed his remaining child, and twined the fingers of the mother's hand among her flowing ringlets; he hoped the best; he hoped even to the last. But if it be true that love often lends keenness to the eye, it is not less true that the sight of affection is sometimes the slowest and the

2

dimmest of all; and he had kept striving to nourish his hopes, and striving successfully too, for many months after it had been once a common remark among the kind-hearted people of Cross-Meikle, that 'the Minister's wife, poor body, would never hold up her head again.'

And, in truth, it was as they said. It may be, the seated disease of the mind, by slow but sure degrees, communicated its poison to the body; at all events, the frame, like the inhabiting spirit, soon exhibited all the features of decay. The long melancholy summer passed away, and the songs of the harvest reapers were heard in the surrounding fields; while all, from day to day, was becoming darker and darker within the Manse of Cross-Meikle. Worn to a shadow – pale as ashes – feeble as a child – the dying mother had, for many weeks, been unable to quit her chamber; and the long-hoping husband at last felt his spirit faint within him; for even he perceived that the hour of separation could not much farther be deferred. He watched – he prayed by her bedside – he strove even yet to smile and to speak of hope, but his lips trembled as he spake; and neither he nor his wife were deceived, for their thoughts were the same, and years of love had taught them too well all the secrets of each other's looks as well as hearts.

Nobody witnessed their last parting; the room was darkened, and no one was within it but themselves and their child, who sat by the bed-side, weeping in silence she knew not wherefore – for of death she knew little,

3

except the terrible name; and her father had as yet been, if not brave enough to shed no tears, at least strong enough to conceal them. – Silently and gently was the pure spirit released from its clay; but manly groans were, for the first time, heard above the sobs and wailings of the infant; and the listening household shrunk back from the door, for they knew that the blow had been stricken; and the voice of humble sympathy feared to make itself be heard in the sanctuary of such affliction. The village doctor arrived just at that moment; he listened for a few seconds, and being satisfied that all was over, he also turned away. His horse had been fastened to the hook by the Manse door; he drew out the bridle, and led the animal softly over the turf, but did not mount again until he had far passed the outskirts of the green.

Perhaps an hour might have passed before Mr Blair opened the window of the room in which his wife had died. His footstep had been heard for some time hurriedly traversing and re-traversing the floor; but at last he stopped where the nearly fastened shutters of the window admitted but one broken line of light into the chamber. He threw everything open with a bold hand, and the uplifting of the window produced a degree of noise, to the like of which the house had for some time been unaccustomed; he looked out, and saw the external world bright before him, with all the rich colourings of a September evening. The sun had just sunk behind the distant screen of the Argyll and Dumbartonshire hills; the outline of huge Benlomond glowed like a blood-red jewel against the wide golden sky beyond; a thick and hazy cloud of mist had gathered over the rich valleys to the westward, through which, here and there, some far-off bending of the river flashed for a moment in a streak of reflected crimson; near at hand, the tall elms that surround the village churchyard stood, with all their brown leaves whispering in the faint breeze of the twilight; a fine herd of cattle were passing along the neighbouring 'green loaning,' in a long deliberate line; the hum of the village sent an occasional echo through the intervening hedge-rows; all was quiet and beautiful above and below; the earth seemed to be clothed all over with sights and sounds of serenity; and the sky, deepening into darker and darker blue overhead, shewed the earliest of its stars intensely twinkling, as if ready to harbinger or welcome the coming moon.

The widowed man gazed for some minutes in silence upon the glorious calm of nature, and then turned with a sudden start to the side of the room where the wife of his bosom had so lately breathed; – he saw the pale dead face; the black ringlets parted on the brow; the marble hand extended upon the sheet; the unclosed glassy eyes; and the little girl leaning towards her mother in a gaze of half-horrified bewilderment; the tears dried up in their young fountains, by the instinctive awe of life in the immediate atmosphere and presence of death. He drew near to the couch – grasped the cold hand, and cried, 'Oh God! Oh God!' – a shriek, not a prayer; he closed the stiffening eye-lids over the soft but ghastly orbs; kissed the brow, the cheek, the lips, the bosom, and then rushed down the stairs, and away out, bare-headed, into the fields, before any one could stop him, or ask whither he was going.

There is an old thick grove of pines almost immediately behind the house; and after staring about him for a moment on the green, he leapt hastily over the little brook that skirts it, and plunged within the shade of the trees. The breeze was rustling the black boughs high over his head, and whistling along the bare ground beneath him. He rushed he knew not whither, on and on, between those naked brown trunks, till he was in the heart of the wood; and there, at last, he tossed himself down on his back among the withered fern leaves and mouldering fir-cones. Here every thing accorded with the gloom of a sick and shuddering soul, and he lay in a sort of savage stupor, half-exulting, as the wind moaned and sighed through the darkness about him, in the depth (as he thought, the *utmost* depth) of abandonment and misery. Long-restrained, long-vanquished passions took their turn to storm within him – fierce thoughts chased each other through his bosom – sullen dead despair came to banish or to drown them – mournful gleams of tenderness melted all his spirit for a moment, and then made room again for the strong graspings of horror. Doubt hung over him like some long-laid spectre risen again from a roaring sea, to freeze and to torture – Faith, like a stooping angel, blew the shadow aside, but the unsubstantial vapour grew together again into form, and stood within sight a phantom that would not be dismissed. All the past things of life floated be-

6

fore him, distinct in their lineaments, yet twined together, the darkest and the gayest, into a sort of union,
that made them all appear alike dark. The mother, that
had nursed his years of infancy – the father, whose hairs
he had long before laid in the grave – sisters, brothers,
friends, all dead and buried – the angel forms of his
own early-ravished offspring – all crowded round and
round him, and then rushing away, seemed to bear from
him, as a prize and a trophy, the pale image of his expiring wife. Again SHE returned, and she alone was
present with him – not the pale expiring wife, but the
young radiant woman – blushing, trembling, smiling,
panting on his bosom, whispering to him all her hopes,
and fears, and pride, and love, and tenderness, and
meekness, like a bride; and then again all would be
black as night. He would start up and gaze around,
and see nothing but the sepulchral gloom of the wood
and hear nothing but the cold blasts among the leaves.
In a moment, it seemed as if years and years had intervened since he had become a widower. Every thing
looked distant, chill, remote, uncertain, cut off from
him as if for ages, by the impassable wide gulph of
death. Down he lay again, and covering his face with
his hands, struggled to overcome the strength of delu-
sions, with which all his soul was surrounded. Now
boiling with passions, now calm as the dead, fearing,
hoping, doubting, believing, lamenting, praying, and
cursing – yes, cursing all in succession. – Oh! who can
tell in one brief hour what ages of agony may roll over
one bruised human spirit!

7

The storm of desolation was followed by a lowering state of repose. He lay insensible alike to all things, stretched out at all his length, with his eyes fixed in a stupid stedfastness upon one great massy branch that hung over him – his bloodless lips fastened together, as if they had been glued – his limbs like things entirely destitute of life and motion – every thing about him cold, stiff, and senseless. Minute after minute passed heavily away as in a dream – hour after hour rolled un-heeded into the abyss – the stars twinkled through the pine-tops, and disappeared – the moon arose in her glory, rode through the clear autumn heaven, and van-ished – and all alike unnoted by the prostrate widower. He only, in whose hand are all times, and all seasons, and all the workings of the spirit of man, can know what was and was not done within, during this space of apparent blankness. Not in dreams alone, it may be, does the soul work unconsciously, and exert all or many of its noblest powers. But these things are of the mys-teries which human eyes cannot penetrate, and into which we should not be presumptuous enough to peer with all our blinding imbecility about us.

Adam Blair came forth from among the fir-trees in the grey light of the morning, walked leisurely and calmly several times round the garden-green which lay immediately in front of his house, then lifted the latch for himself, and glided with light and hasty footsteps up stairs to the room, where, for some weeks past, he had been accustomed to occupy a solitary bed. The wakeful servants heard him shut his door behind him; one of

them having gone out anxiously, had traced him to his
privacy, but none of them had ventured to think of disturbing it. Until he had come back, not one of them
thought of going to bed. Now, however, they did so,
and the house of sorrow was all over silent.

Chapter

2

···‹⋅›⋅···

It was the custom of the house, that a servant rung a bell every morning at eight o'clock, to assemble all the family for prayers. That morning the old man, whose common duty this was, did not venture to perform it; but not many minutes had elapsed beyond the accustomed hour, ere the bell was rung, and all, so soon as it was heard, entered the parlour with their Bibles in their hands. When they came in they found that Mr Blair had already taken his seat, and had the book lying open upon the table before him. Little Sarah was sitting on her stool close beside him, and his left hand rested upon her shoulder, while the right was occupied in turning over the leaves of the Bible. The child's eyes were red, but she too was composed; she too was handling her book, and turning over its leaves. As for Mr Blair, he did not look up when he heard his servants enter, but as soon as they had taken their seats, he uttered his usual preliminary petition much in his usual manner, and

then proceeded to read aloud the lines of the 121st
Psalm,

> 'I to the hills will lift mine eyes
> From whence doth come mine aid,' &c.

in a tone of serenity and firmness, that filled the hearts of
those who heard him with a mixed sentiment of surprise and veneration – surprise at the strength exhibited,
and veneration for that deep sway of religious feelings,
by which, as they rightly judged, such strength in weakness had been produced. They had not witnessed the
struggle, but they guessed something of what had been;
and they, simple as they were, had sense enough and
wisdom enough to revere the faith which had passed
through such fires, to come forth purified, not tarnished.
After the Psalm had been sung, he read the fourteenth
chapter of the Gospel according to St John, and concluded with a prayer, such as none, most surely, but a
sorely chastened heart could have conceived, although
throughout the whole of it there was no express allusion
to the particular situation of the person by whom it was
uttered. Once or twice the voice faultered, but he soon
recovered himself; and when the service was over, and
all had once more arisen from their knees, I believe the
countenance of the young bereaved Minister bore fewer
traces of trouble than any other countenance in the
room.

Even in the house of sorrow, the ordinary matters of
life go on, for the most part, in their ordinary course;
and I will confess, that to me this has always appeared
to be one of the most truly affecting things in the world.

The cloth is laid, the meal is prepared, the bottle is brought up from the cellar, the family sit around the table – all these affairs go on just as duly the day that the mistress or the master of a family is dead, as any other day in the year. Grief, even the sincerest and deepest grief, occupies, after all, when the first triumph of its energies is over, no more than a place in the background. The front of life is as smooth as ever.

All this was so within the Manse of Cross-Meikle; of course still more so round about its walls. Servants passed to and fro about the occupations of the house, inquiring friends and acquaintances came and went, the little motherless girl was seen from time to time busied in the garden among the few lingering flowers of the autumn. Mr Blair himself was not visible to any but his own family, and to them only at the hours when the family were accustomed to be together. At other times he was in his chamber alone, or with his orphan by his side – the accustomed volumes lying about him – to the eye the same quiet, grave man, or nearly so, that he had been a week or a month before. The closed windows of the chamber in which the body lay, furnished the only outward and visible sign that death was in the house.

Mr Blair was sitting by himself on the evening of the third day; apparently he had been reading, but the light had deserted him, and his book had been laid down on the table near him, when the door of his room was opened, and some one, as if hesitating to go farther, stood just within the threshold, with his finger on the handle of the door. Mr Blair did not observe, for a minute or two, that the door of his room had been opened, but at last his eye happened to travel in that direction, and he perceived that John Maxwell, one who had for many years been the oldest among the elders of his parish, was come to visit him in his affliction.

'Come in, John,' said he; 'so old a friend may come at any time; I am glad to see you – sit down, John;' and in saying so, he had taken the worthy man by the hand, and was leading him towards the seat from which he himself had just arisen.

'The Lord is gracious, Mr Blair – the Lord is very gracious. It is HE that giveth, and it is HE that taketh away. Blessed be his holy name! Oh, sir, I thought the Lord would never surely leave your father's son, and I see he has not left you.'

The old man meant to speak words of comfort, but ere he had done, his voice failed him, and the tears were gushing over his cheeks as he looked in his young minister's face, and wrung the hand that had been extended to him. It was no wonder, surely, that the afflicted man sympathized with his comforter, or that some minutes had elapsed before either of them was in any condition to renew the conversation.

Nor shall we trouble the reader with any needless detail of it. Let it be sufficient to know, that on the part of Mr Blair, it was all that could become any man afflicted as he was, and much more than could have been expected from so young a sufferer as he, while John Maxwell shewed himself worthy of holding the rank he did in the church of Christ. The minister and the elder laid their hearts open to each other; they wept, they prayed, and they took sweet counsel together. John had been more than once nerved, softened, and renerved again, ere he at length took courage to whisper into Mr Blair's ear, that *his presence was wanted in the chamber.* Mr Blair understood perfectly what John meant. He arose at once, and walked towards the place where his wife's remains were about to be closed up for ever from all human view.

It is the rule in Scotland, that no male, except it be a husband, a father, or a brother, can be permitted to remain in the room while the coffin-lid is screwed down upon a female corpse. John Maxwell attended his minister to the door, therefore, but no farther. Within, three or four village matrons only, and the female servants of the family, were assembled. Mr Blair entered, and found them in the midst of all the fearful paraphernalia with which it was (and is) the custom of Scotland to deepen the gloom of the most sad of all possible occasions. Well as he was acquainted with all the habitudes of his country-folks, he had never before brought fully home to his imagination all that now met his view. The knots, the ribbons, the cushions, the satin, the tinsel – all that melancholy glitter turned his soul sick within him, and once more he yielded; not, however, as before, nor to the same enemies. Sadness, weariness, heartsickness – these were now his visitants. He stood pale and feeble, while the tears flowed over his cheeks in utter silence. One of the old women thought that a sight of his wife's face might bring him, through emotion, to himself again, and she lifted the veil. But even this was of no use, and to no purpose. The man was altogether unnerved – the strong-souled Adam Blair was in that hour a weanling, and he wept on as silently, and not a whit more bitterly than before. They led him, unresisting, to his room; he allowed himself, for the first time of his life, to be undressed by hands other than his own. After he had been put to bed, John Maxwell stood over against him for some minutes, saying, 'Wae's me, wae's me.' He then commanded all the rest to retire, and, kneeling by the bedside, began to pray aloud in the old sublime simplicity of the true village worthies of Scotland. The priest felt in his soul the efficacious piety of the elder of Israel.

'Good night, John Maxwell.'

'God bless you – God strengthen you!' and so they parted.

The next day, no worldly work was done in the parish of Cross-Meikle. At twelve o'clock the church-bell began to toll, and the friends of Mr Blair were seen walking slowly in twos and threes along the green lanes which lead towards the Church and Manse; while the rest, assembling in the burying-ground, awaited the forthcoming of the mournful procession. Such as had been particularly invited, entered the house. One by one they were ushered into the parlour of the Manse, and not one approached it without something like a feeling of fear. But that feeling was dispelled in a moment: Mr Blair stood in the midst of the apartment with a face of

15

such calmness and composure as if he had been the only man there that day whose business it was not to receive comfort, but to give it. To each of the guests who entered the room he went up separately, and extended his hand in silence. Not one word was uttered by any one.

Each took his station; and then, a salver of wine having been handed round, Mr Blair himself called upon the eldest of his brother clergymen present to ask a blessing. It is in that form, that the funeral prayer of the Scottish ceremonial is announced and uttered. The person called upon to pronounce it on this occasion, was by no means one who had lived on any very particular terms of intimacy with Mr Blair; neither was he any great favourite among the country people of the neighbourhood. He bore, in general, the character of a dry, sarcastic sort of man, and, being very old, was personally little known, except among the immediate circle of his own friends and connexions. Yet not one that heard Dr Muir pray that day, would have wished the duty to have fallen into other hands. The old man had himself experienced the sorrows of life, and he spake like one who was about to go down into the grave, leaning on the only arm in which strength lies.

It was a touching spectacle to see the churchyard when the procession entered it. Old and young stood around unbonnetted, and few dry eyes were turned on Mr Blair when he took his station at the head of the opened grave. The clods, as they rattled down, sent a shudder to every bosom, and when the spade was heard clapping the replaced sod into its form, every one turned

16

away his eyes, lest his presence should be felt as an intrusion on the anguish of the minister. He, on his part, endured it wonderfully; but the dead mother had been laid down by the side of her dead children, and perhaps, at that moment, he was too humble to repine at their reunion. He uncovered and bowed himself over the grave when the last turf was beat down, and then, leaning on the arm of John Maxwell, walked back slowly through the silent rows of his people to the solitude of his Manse.

After he was out of sight, not a few of them drew near to contemplate the new-made grave, and the old were not slow to retrace the memory of those of the same family who had heretofore been committed to the same dust. On the wall of the church, immediately adjoining a large marble tablet had been affixed, to record the pious labours of Mr Blair's father, who preceded him in the charge of that parish; and most of those who were present could still recall with distinctness the image of the good old man, and the grave tones of his voice in exhortation. But there was a green headstone there, rudely fashioned, and most rudely sculptured, to which their fingers were pointed with feelings of yet loftier veneration. That stone marked the spot where Mr Blair's grandfather was laid – a simple peasant of the parish – one whose time on earth had been abridged in consequence of what he had done and suffered in days when God's chosen race, and the true patriots of our country, were hunted up and down like the beasts of the field – when the citizen of a Christian land durst not sing a psalm in the wilderness, without the risk of being hewn into pieces by the sword of some godless slave. They who are acquainted with Scotland – above all, with the west of Scotland – cannot be ignorant of the reverence which is still cherished for *the seed of the martyrs.* Such feelings were more widely spread, and more intensely felt, in former times than, I am sorry to say, they are now. It was to them, in no small degree, that Adam Blair was indebted for the deep affection with which his person and all his concerns were, and always had been, regarded by the people of his parish. To their love he had 'titles manifold,' but not the least was his being the grandson and namesake of old Adam Blair, who had fought against bloody Clavers and the butcher Dalyell, at Bothwell-bridge, and endured torture, without shrinking, in the presence of *false Lauderdale.*

Chapter

3

—••≺❊≻••—

Nobody, after that day, ever heard Mr Blair mention
his wife's name. A little picture of her in crayon, which
had been painted when she was a very young girl, had
hitherto hung over the mantle-piece in the parlour, but
it was now removed into the room where he slept, and
placed opposite to the foot of her bed. The most of her
books were taken from the room in which she died,
and arranged in the same apartment; and after all this
had been done, he was never known to enter that fatal
chamber. For some time before Mrs Blair's death, the
duty of teaching young Sarah to read and write had de-
volved upon him – and in this duty he continued to
exert himself. After dinner, the child seldom left the
room in which he sat, till it was time for her to retire to
rest. He read to her, he talked to her, he listened to all
her little stories, and took a part in all her little occupations. But though he had been used to take much delight in hearing her sing before, he was never heard now
to bid her try either *The bonnie wee crowden doo,* or *Bird
Marjory,* or *The Earl of Bothwell's wife,* or any of the

other favourite ballads of that part of the country. Sometimes, indeed, when the girl was singing to herself in her chamber, he would stand listening to her for a few seconds behind the door, but she never knew herself to be singing in her father's hearing, unless when she joined her voice close beside his knee in the domestic psalmody. The servants remarked all this, and said it was no wonder, for little Sarah's singing put one very much in mind of her mother, when she used to be merry, in the first years of her marriage, by the fireside.

Some of those, however, who had less opportunity of understanding the character and feelings of the man, were sufficiently inclined to put quite another sort of construction on many parts of Mr Blair's conduct and demeanour the winter after this calamity befel him. There are such a number of people in the world who cannot conceive of affliction apart from the images of white handkerchiefs, long weepers, and black sealingwax, that it is no great wonder this should have been so. Of all this class of observances Mr Blair was somewhat negligent; of many of them he did not even know that any such things existed: – and, accordingly, to give one instance in place of fifty, the Presbytery to which Mr Blair belonged, had not met above three or four times, before – some one remarking that Mr Blair had not yet made his appearance among them since his wife's death – another of the reverend brethren made answer in rather a sneering sort of tone, that the minister of CrossMeikle had, it was likely, work enough upon his hands, if he designed, as was said about Semplehaugh, 'to fill up the vacancy' before summer. I am sorry to say, that this sarcasm was uttered by the same Dr Muir, whose very different behaviour on the day of Mrs Blair's funeral I have already noticed. But the truth is, the Doctor had taken it a little amiss, that Mr Blair had omitted to send an answer to a long letter of condolence which he had despatched to Cross-Meikle the morning after that sorrowful day; and was, moreover, somewhat displeased to find that he had been seen often on horseback, and even known to spend the New Year's-day at the house of Semplehaugh – while, as yet, he had not once made his appearance at the Manse of Cambuslee. The last part of his speech was not probably intended to be taken as if uttered with any serious meaning; but Dr Muir was never sorry to have an opportunity of cracking a joke at the expence of the worthy Lady Dowager of Semplehaugh, (the widow of the gentleman who had been patron of both his parish and Mr Blair's,) in whose good graces he was pleased to imagine, that he himself had been rather on the decline ever since Mr Blair had become minister of Cross-Meikle. But a man who has the reputation of being a joker, is generally, in his own person, a pretty favourite subject of jokes. And, accordingly, no sooner had Dr Muir left the room in which the Presbytery dinner took place, than Mr Robertson cocked his spectacles with an air of great sagacity, and told Mr Allan that he shrewdly suspected Miss Anne Muir would have no objection to become little Sarah Blair's step-mother. At which joke Mr Allan laughed very heartily, and Mr Robertson was exceedingly flattered to find his joke took so well, not being at all aware that Mr Allan knew perfectly well that he, Mr Robertson, had paid his addresses to Dr Muir's well‑portioned daughter about eighteen months before, – and withal, received such an answer as rendered it not very likely he should ever think of renewing them.

Now, all these parsonic jokes were fair enough in their way, with the exception of Dr Muir's ill‑natured hint about the old Lady of Semplehaugh. There was not an elderly lady in the whole county, against whom such a sarcasm could have been directed with less rea‑ son. She was a most excellent woman. As wife, mother, and mistress of a family, she had always conducted her‑ self in the most irreproachable manner possible. She was a sincere devout Christian, and though she had a very tender regard for Mr Blair, both for his father's sake and for his own, I believe she would just as soon have thought of marrying the venerable Dr Muir himself as her young minister.

Mrs Semple was one of that (once numerous) class of ladies in Scotland, who, virtuous and religious, and every way estimable as they may be, do a great many things as if they believed the stomach to be by far the most important part in the whole construction of every human being. For instance, if she heard of a long absent son or brother returning to any family in the village, her first speech was sure to be – 'Poor bodies, poor bodies, I'm very glad to hear it, I'm very heartily glad to hear it. I hope they'll have something comfortable in the house – It would be a burning shame if they had not a good supper the night;' and the end of her speech would in all probability be a whisper to her butler – 'Thomas, take down the cauld pye to John Anderson's, wi' my compliments – and say, I'm very glad to hear their calland's come back – and stay, Thomas, since ye're about it, ye may as weel tak some o' yon finnan haddocks, and a bottle or twa of your ale wi' you too' – after which she would resume her usual tone, and say once or twice over again, 'Poor John Anderson! it would be a crying sin if they had naething but parritch on sic a night for their suppers!'

In cases of affliction, Mrs Semple's sympathy was most commonly expressed in the same sort of substantial method; and accordingly, for some time before Mrs Blair's death, the Semplehaugh errandboy very seldom rode to the posttown (which he always did once a week for the newspapers,) without having some can of jelly, or fricassee of chickens, or string of trouts, or something or other, which the good lady thought the sick woman might fancy, to be dropt from his basket in passing the Manse. The day before the funeral, she sent off, in the same fashion, a dozen of Madeira and a piece of cake, saying – 'Poor Mr Adam, I'm sure my heart's wae when I think on him. I'm sure it's not for him to be gaun down to the cellar, and giving out wine at sic a time as this, and it would not be decent if there was nothing comfortable to be set before his company. He'll have meikle need o' a glass o' wine himsel, poor man, when he comes hame again.' – In short, there was no end with her to such attentions as she conceived might be acceptable;

23

and little as most of these might be in accordance with the real necessities of Mr Blair's situation, it would have been a poor sign of him if he had not felt, and, in due time, expressed his sense of the kindness from which, he well knew, all of them proceeded. The affectionate interest she displayed in regard to little Sarah, was a favour for which he might well feel deeper, if not sincerer gratefulness. Indeed, Mrs Semple had all along conducted herself in the most friendly, or rather, in the most *motherly* manner. And Mr Blair, be his faults what they might, (and, no doubt, they were many,) was not a man whose heart ever tasted the baseness that recoils from the sense of obligation. He might be a proud man in some things; but he had no pride about him that ever warred with gratitude.

It may be very true, notwithstanding all that has been said, that – excellent woman, and sincere Christian, and universally benevolent, as the Lady Semplehaugh most unquestionably was – she might not improbably have shewn fewer marks of attention to Mr Blair, had he been an ill-favoured old man, instead of being what every body must have acknowledged him to be, a very handsome young one. It may perhaps be mere frailty which makes both men and women, the best and the wisest of them, acknowledge at times by their looks and actions at the least, if not by their words, the power and effect of personal comeliness; but if it be a frailty, it is certainly a very common one, and has been so in all ages of the world, and will probably continue to be so, as long as human creatures shall be fashioned in soul and body as they are and have been. And indeed, although in so doing she followed a rule of somewhat less general acceptance, Mrs Semple herself had no scruple about confessing that she liked Mr Blair so much the better, and took so much the warmer interest about all his concerns, because he was an exceedingly comely and amiable-looking young man. Even his sermons, she said it openly enough, would have had less effect upon her, had his countenance been a less expressive index and expositor of his ideas; and perhaps she might have fancied it to become so, had he only exchanged his own fine raven hair for the most reverent-looking periwig in the country. It is wonderful with what ease the female fancy can at all times discover likenesses among the objects of their liking; and accordingly, Mrs Semple had not unfrequently furnished a little amusement to her old friends, by asking if they did not perceive some cast of resemblance between the bonny young minister (so she called him) and her own deceased husband. [But she had never, we may suppose, put such a question to Dr Muir; otherwise, in all probability, he might have been tempted to entertain his brethren at the Presbytery dinner with rather a different strain of wit.]

Many weeks, therefore, had not elapsed before Mr Blair went up to Semplehaugh-house, (or, as the country people more commonly called it, the Castletown,) to pay his respects to this old friend and patroness of his family. It has already been noticed, that the attentions of the old lady to his orphan girl were in a particular manner pleasing to him; and, indeed, he would neither have been a very kind, nor a very considerate father, if this had not been so. It was impossible for him, when he had acquired some power of reflecting calmly on all that had happened, not to perceive, that, in case he himself should be carried off early in life, as his beloved wife had been, the friendship of such a person as Mrs Semple might come to be of the utmost consequence in every way to the welfare of his child; and he therefore considered himself as bound, by the duty of a parent, to give little Sarah every opportunity of being as much as might be under the eye of the good lady; while, at the same time, he was not at all insensible to the immediate advantages which his own mind might be likely to derive from mingling in such society as the mansion-house afforded. There was no other family of any rank or worldly consequence in the parish, nor any one in its immediate vicinity, with which he had formed habits of the same sort of early intimacy and mutual attachment. Tenderly beloved as he was by the humbler members of his own flock, and freely as he was accustomed to mingle with them on all occasions, there were times, and, of course, many times, in which his mind felt the want of some more intellectual sort of intercourse than was to be expected at that period among people in their situation; and there was no place where he was, at least, so likely to meet with the supply of this mental want, as beneath the roof of Semplehaugh. Having suppressed within himself, to the utmost of his power, the first unruliness of his passionate grief, he was wise enough to know, that, though every great work of the spirit must be the work of solitude, the solitary exertions of the spirit must always be apt to flag and languish, unless recourse be had at fit intervals to those social stimulants which the Author of our nature has formed the strongest of us to need, and enabled the weakest of us to relish. And Mr Blair acted as he thought it was his duty to act, although indeed, in the then shattered condition of his mind, it often required a considerable struggle and exertion before he could bring himself to do so.

Now, although several such struggles had already been successfully made, it certainly was with undiminished reluctance that he set out on New Year's-day with his daughter towards Semplehaugh. He had dined there almost every New Year's-day since he could recollect any thing; and but that day the year before, his wife had accompanied him in all the innocent gaiety of youth and the season. He would much rather have staid at home; and yet, when he looked round him in the morning, and saw his loss in every object that met his view, there were moments when he shrunk from the prospect of spending the day and the long winter evening, that used to be so happy at that time of the year, in solitude. He could not bear neither to think of his poor little girl being condemned to sit by a single melancholy man's chair, when all the village was sure to be sending forth sounds of mirth and festivity. The end of it therefore was, that Mrs Semple's annual invitation was complied with; and taking Sarah in his hand, he began, ere the beautiful clear frosty day had lost its brightness, to walk along the well-known path by the river-side. The orphan, clad, as she of course was, all in her deepest mourning, did not trip at her father's side past the door of one cottage, without receiving some pitying benediction from its affectionate tenants. How different from the joyous and hearty salutations which they had received the last time they trode together the same path on the same errand!

The sun had almost gone down in the west before they reached the long dark avenue which leads to the old house, and the rooks were already cawing loudly among the bleak branches of the tall leafless beeches. After walking for a quarter of a mile beneath the gloom of those venerable trees, the white turrets and blazing windows of the hospitable mansion were cheering objects even in the eyes of Mr Blair, and he entered the light and lofty chamber, where Mrs Semple received her company, with feelings, in spite of all that had come and gone, more approaching to a temperate species of elevation, than he had perhaps experienced ever since the day of his great calamity. The good old lady herself was in spirits of considerable buoyancy; for her son, who had been absent for more than two years, had come home that morning unexpectedly, and the whole house was filled with visible exhilaration by the presence of the young Laird. Mr Blair, who refused his sympathy to no feelings of an innocent nature, would have thought himself a bad man, if he had not done his utmost to shew that he shared the happiness of his best and oldest friends upon such an occasion as this; and he had power enough over himself to receive the grave but cordial salutation of Mr Semple in a way that surprised him, and filled the heart of his mother with new delight.

There was a considerable party that day at Semple-haugh – Mr Spens of Spenstarvit, a gentleman nearly connected with the family, who lived about ten miles off, and his two beautiful daughters – Miss Ogilvie, a fine, cheerful old spinster, from Glasgow – the blithe Laird of Croscobie and his literary lady, and a variety of country neighbours besides. The huge rifted fir-trunks sent a roaring blaze up the chimney; the old massive tankards and salvers glittered on the sideboards; the venison smoked upon the table; and the claret flowed abundantly to the healths of the season. Mr Blair looked round him, and could not help participating in the genial feelings visible on every countenance that met his view. From time to time, indeed, he betrayed in his manner something of that abstraction of thought with which those who have ever had misery seated at the roots of their hearts are acquainted, and the appearance of which furnishes at times so much amusement to the thoughtless people of this world. But, upon the whole, this was a cheerful evening, and the widowed minister partook in its cheerfulness. The conversation of the young Laird, who had spent the greater part of the last year in foreign countries, furnished new topics of attention and discussion. The kindliness of manner universal in the company, had a soothing effect upon the only wounded mind that was there; for the feeling of human kindness is, after all, not the feeblest reconciler to the ways and doings of this feeble and imperfect existence.

If any thing threw an occasional damp upon the general enjoyment of the day, it was the presence of a person whom I have not yet named, and who was the only one present that could be said to be a stranger in the circle of Semplehaugh-House. This was Mr Semple's tutor, who had been on the continent along with him, a smart, and rather pompous-looking young man, of the name of Jamieson, who, having performed the important exploit of a *grand tour*, had perhaps thought himself entitled to assume more of the external appearances of a man of the world than was, or indeed is yet, common among the probationers of the Scottish Church – and even to hold his head a good deal above such a plain parish priest of the old school, as he rightly supposed the minister of Cross-Meikle to be. Mr Blair, who had never in his life aspired to ape the fashions of a class to which he did not conceive himself to belong, was always in his own character, and therefore always in his own place. The *hauteur* which peeped through the great superficial civility of Mr Jamieson's address in conversing with him, did not, however, simple man as he was, escape his observation. Now, Mr Blair was, at that time, even less likely than he commonly was, to resent, with any feelings of bitterness, any injury of any sort received at the hands of any man; but it must be confessed, that mental troubles do not unfrequently irritate the surface, at least, of the meekest disposition; and it is certain, that he would have retired to his chamber that night in a serener mood, if no Mr Jamieson had been in the company, to tell long stories about the superiority of

30

some preachers he had met with in England, over any he had yet heard in the pulpits of Scotland; the superior decency of the Episcopal ritual, and some other topics of the same sort, which it is seldom, under any circum/stances, a very agreeable thing for any clergyman of the Presbyterian church to hear discussed. The manner of the young man displeased him even more than the sub/jects he chose to speak about; and altogether, Mr Blair was not disposed to consider Mr Jamieson as any great acquisition to the society of his parishioners.

All this, however, was a very secondary matter. The evening was a very happy evening, and Mr Blair had a share in its enjoyment a hundred times greater than he could have dreamt himself capable of, when he rose from his bed that morning. Healthful excitation of spirits was naturally followed by healthful repose; and Mr Blair, after having conducted the devotions of the numerous and attentive household, slept better that night than he had done for many, many long weeks before. He returned next day to the Manse, his little girl dancing every now and then before him on the path, and exhibiting to every acquaintance they met the finely bound little book which Mrs Semple had given her for her Christmas/box. A merry party were busy *curling* on the ice, as he crossed the bridge, and he paused for some minutes, contemplating, almost with his old in/terest, the state and progress of the game.

Such was the New Year's/day dinner at Semple/haugh, which had been so unkindly alluded to at the Presbytery dinner.

Chapter

4

—••⫶⫶••—

Shortly after the commencement of the New Year, the good Lady of Semplehaugh and her family removed to Edinburgh, where it was their custom to spend a considerable part of every winter season. Their departure deprived Mr Blair of a cheerful society, in which he mingled at least once a-week, and of many little occasional attentions and incidents which served to break and diversify the even and uniform tenor of his retired existence. The day on which he was to pay a visit at the mansion-house, was a thing to be looked forward to before it came, and to be looked back upon after it had passed. Above all, it was a thing to be continually talked about by little Sarah; and, in short, the want of it formed a blank in the domestic calendar of Cross-Meikle.

The winter, moreover, had set in with more than usual severity. Drifted snow deepened all the roads in the neighbourhood, and rendered them quite impassable, or very nearly so, for several weeks in succession;

and the profuse thaw which followed, made matters little better in a country where the soil consists, in so great a measure, of wet and heavy clay. To travel about to any distance in the midst of such a season, was a thing quite out of the question with Mr Blair, and nearly as much so with the few friends who remained in his neighbourhood during that part of the year. The gay, the busy, the active, had all fled to the cities; and those who stayed were people who stayed only because they could not bear to be absent from their own homes, or preferred solitude to society. Except an occasional call from some brother of the cloth, and the everyday intercourse of his own humbler parishioners, Mr Blair had therefore little to disturb or vary the course of his own solitary life and meditations. It is no wonder that his melancholy sat down upon him every day more and more heavily in such a state of things as this; and that the more heavy it became, his resolution to struggle with it grew so much the fainter and the feebler. The dark and gloomy skies by day, and the ghostly howlings of the winds about his lonely walls by night, harmonized with, and increased the oppression of his spirits; – all the dismal sights and sounds of benumbed Nature afforded nutriment to his grief – for the contemplation of dreary things was felt, in that diseased state of the mind, to constitute a sort of morbid luxury; and a sick fantasy was nothing loth to exert its feverish and fitful energies in brooding over and blending together the unseen troubles of a bleeding heart, and the too congenial images of external desolation.

It is probable, that Mr Blair's mind might have soon learned to assume a different tone, had he happened to have his residence in a city, instead of a thinly-peopled country parish. Grief, such as his, shrinks at first from the busy aspects of man and the world; but human nature will have its way, and the soul cannot long shut itself against the impressions of the bodily senses. The man of the city, besides, can scarcely keep himself unemployed, even if he have a mind to do so. The work of the world is about him, and he must take his share in it. New sights force themselves upon the eye, and new duties and occupations upon the hands; if new pleasures come not, new distresses will – to push the old sorrow from its seat, to replace it for a season, to make room for it again, it may be, – but not to make room for it such as it was in its first undisturbed and entire possession of the spirit.

The Sabbath, with its various duties and requirements, broke, in some measure, the torpor of Mr Blair's melancholy. When that day came round, he was compelled to bestow more attention upon his personal appearance – and even this was not without its salutary effect. But, what was of infinitely greater importance, he was compelled to exert his faculties. In spite of himself, the sight of the Christian congregation stimulated his spirit; the sound of their simple psalmody sent a trumpet to his heart; and when he rose to lead the prayers of his people, the ancient fervour of his devout and affectionate soul kindled the whole man, and shone out clearly once more from amidst the weary mists in which they had been smothered and obscured. Such temporary elevations were, however, but too frequently followed by the reaction of the more besetting influences. Often would some good old man of the congregation linger at the porch, that he might have an opportunity of whispering some humble word of comfort or gratulation to his minister, after having heard from his lips some noble and energetic strain of eloquence, which naturally appeared to him to indicate the approach, at least, of better days; but when he came forth, and stood among them all within sight of his wife's sepulchre, the gloom returned in a moment, the enthusiasm vanished from his eyes, the transitory glow deserted his hollow cheek; and the heart sunk again within every kind bosom, when it was seen with how slow and listless steps the unhappy young man paced his way over the broad pavement of tombstones, back towards his solitary dwelling.

There was no one who took a deeper concern in the visibly melancholy condition of his minister, than old John Maxwell the elder, whose name we have already had occasion to mention more than once; and the delicacy with which he testified his feelings was such, as those who have lived among the peasantry of most other countries would not have witnessed without some astonishment. No noisy expressions of sympathy, no well-meant offences against the sacred dignity of sorrow, ever proceeded from him. His quiet looks, his grave and fatherly smiles, his minute acts of kindliness, would have done honour to a heart refined by all that the most

cultivated men are pleased to reckon the most potent in,
struments of human refinement. He came often to the
Manse, but he never came without an errand that might
prevent his visit from appearing to be nothing but a
visit. At one time, it would be that he had some slips
of sweet,briar, which he wished Mr Blair would permit
him to put in the hedge about the garden – at another
time, his pockets were full of flower,roots – and a third
time, his daughter,in,law had thought the Minister
might not have a 'caller egg' for his breakfast at this time
of year; and she had just made a point of it, that he
should take a walk over with a basket of them. The
minister knew John, and felt all his kindness; but John
returned to his farm, and he to his desolate chamber –
where Young's Night Thoughts, or the Book of Job,
lay open on the table, rather, it may be, to be looked at
than to be read. While his daughter sat and prattled by
him, the soothing influence of young and innocent
looks could not fail from time to time to make itself felt;
nay, there wanted not moments when the light voice of
infancy had power to chase sorrow almost entirely from
a father's heart. But at night, after Sarah had gone to
bed, there was a long interval of uninterrupted hopeless,
ness. Often would he permit the fire and candles to go
out unnoticed, and sit musing in darkness and in silence,
beside the cold hearth that had once been used to shine
so brightly beneath the eyes of a light,hearted circle. At
other times he would throw open the window, and lean
over it for hours and hours, listening to the sulky ravings
of the midnight tempest, or watching the pale uncertain

36

stars, as they drifted hither and thither, like the lights of storm-tost vessels, over the troubled bosom of their lurid and angry sea of clouds.

One evening as John Maxwell, his son, and his son's wife, (for this was the whole of his family then resident with him), were sitting round the fire together, after the hour of their domestic worship, the conversation happened to turn more seriously, and at greater length than it had ever before done, upon the minister and his unhappy situation. – 'Oh! my bairns,' said the old man, 'what I have seen of poor Mr Adam in his affliction, has often, and very often, made me think of the goodness of Providence to all ranks of men, and how equally good and evil are mixed in the cups of all. I was not quite so young as Mr Blair is when my Marion was ta'en from me – but I think I may say, my Marion had been as dear to me as any wife ever was to any husband; and I'm sure, when I look back to the time of her death, and think of all that she had been to me, and all that I had been to her, if I may say sae, I cannot think by what means I was strengthened. But now, that I have seen what has come upon our minister, some things that used just then to seem to me among the hardest parts of my lot – I can scarcely help thanking my Maker for these very things, and wishing that Mr Blair were in a way to fall in with the like. Grieved and oppressed as I was, I could not be idle – I could not sit all day in the house with nothing but my book to take me up – I was obliged to rise with the cock and guide the plough – I behoved to mount my horse and ride to the town –

I had bargains to make and fulfil – I was a busy man as I had been used to be – when the night came I was wearied, and I could not but sleep. Now, look ye, poor Mr Adam, if it be not on the Sundays and Saturdays, he has seldom any thing to do that he may not put off till a more convenient season. Take my word for it, if he had had two hundred acres on his hand instead of yon poor, starved, useless glebe, Mr Blair would have been a different sort of man ere now, than what he's like to be for many a day yet. But, oh! my bairns, let us never forget that all these things are ordered from above. Re member who it is that has said, "Men groan from out the city, and the soul of the wounded crieth out: yet God layeth not folly to them." Let us all hope that our good minister may soon be himself again. It is a dark Provi dence to us that has laid him in the dust; but is it not written, "Behold, happy is the man whom God cor recteth: therefore, despise not thou the chastening of the Almighty. For HE maketh sore and bindeth up: he woundeth, and his hands make whole."'

The young people looked upon each other while the worthy man was speaking in this way, and thoughts crowded over the minds of both, sufficient to prevent them from following his argument to its close. But John himself went to his bed that night, more deeply troubled about his minister than perhaps he had ever yet been; and when he rose in the morning, the same subject was still uppermost in his mind.

It so happened, that John had occasion just about that time to send a dozen or two of kain fowl – ducks and turkeys – into Edinburgh, for the use of Mrs Semple; and, as usual, he had to write a letter to his lady along with the basket which contained them. To write a letter – above all, to write a letter to Lady Semplehaugh, was a matter of no trivial importance with such a man as John Maxwell; therefore, one whole morning was set apart for the concocting of it. In the course of writing and meditating how to write it, it struck John that he might very well fill up a part of the necessary two pages with some account of the state of things at the Manse of Cross-Meikle; and little as he was accustomed to the use of his pen, the simple and sincere feelings of the man were expressed in such a manner, that this portion of his letter did not fail to produce a very strong effect, when it was read by the worthy lady to whom it was addressed. All the time that Mrs Semple was engaged in reading John Maxwell's absurd-looking, three-cornered epistle, she kept saying over and over to herself, in a sort of distinct and audible whisper, 'Oh sirs! Oh sirs! poor man, poor man!' – in a way that indicated to those that were present, and who were intimate with Mrs Semple, the communication of some very distressing and painful piece of intelligence.

About a week after this letter was received in Edinburgh by Mrs Semple of Semplehaugh, little Sarah came into her father's library one forenoon, with a face full of importance, to tell him that the Hamilton carrier had stopped at the Manse, 'with a meikle meikle kist frae Edinburgh.' The 'meikle meikle kist frae Edinburgh,' turned out to be a box about two feet long, by ten inches broad, containing a new volume of Sermons by Dr Doddridge; a bundle of the Idlers, which were, that winter, in the course of publication in London; an East India *hunch* – six yards of black poplin, with trimmings to suit – and, at the bottom, below all these weightier articles, two letters for Mr Blair, with a copy of one of which we shall presently favour the reader. The epistle which we do not think it quite necessary for us to insert in this place, was addressed in the stiff, but still beautiful, antique hand-writing of Mrs Semple. It contained only the expression of a multitude of good wishes and affectionate inquiries; while it was reserved for a postscript to explain that the poplin was designed for a frock to Sarah Blair, and that the Buffalo's hunch was reckoned the best thing in the world for a breakfast relish.

The other letter was in a hand-writing with which Mr Blair had, at one period of his life, been sufficiently familiar, but which he had not had any opportunity of seeing for several years past. It ran as follows: –

'Dear Sir,
'Having been for near four weeks in Scotland, you may think it very strange that I have not taken an earlier opportunity of saying, *what I hope, indeed, I need scarcely say*, that I have heard with feelings of the *sincerest* sorrow, of the *great* blow with which it has pleased God to visit you, (I may add myself,) and of expressing, at the same time, my hope, that you are and may be strengthened for the supporting thereof. Since we saw each other last,

many, *many* things have happened which could little have been expected by either uf us; and I believe I may add, that in that time I have had *my own full share* of the sorrows of this *world*. I trust your *dear little girl* is as well as I can *wish*, and that she is *really* your comfort, which I am *sure* she *must* be.

'Mrs Semple has been so good as to ask me to spend *next summer* with her at Semplehaugh, and I have accepted of her *kind invitation*, although, I am sure, there are many things which must render that beautiful part of the country a *melancholy quarter* for *me*. But Mr Campbell not being expected home for better than a twelvemonth, and some of my own friends being out of the way, I was really, till Lady Semplehaugh spoke to me, something *at a loss* where I should be during the summer season now ensuing. Dear Mr Blair, this town is full of *gaieties* and *diversions*, from which I can scarcely keep myself *quite disengaged*, although I was never less disposed for *such things*. Now it has occurred to me, that perhaps you might bear with the company of an *old* and *sincere* friend (though she has been much out of her duty, and *is sensible of that*, for some time past,) for the six or seven weeks that must pass before the time of Lady Semplehaugh's *removing to the country* comes round. If it be *perfectly convenient*, I shall, therefore, set out for Glasgow next *Monday*, and be with you at Cross Meikle *on the following day* – but if there be any thing to render this visit anywise *unacceptable* at the *present moment*, I am *sure* you know me *too well*, at least I would *fain* hope so, to have *any scruple* about saying so. God bless you, dear SIR, and *yours*, says your affectionate cousin, and

    'Very humble servant,
       'Charlotte Campbell.
 '*Edinburgh, Feb.* 3, 1758.

'P. S. – Direct to me, care of Mrs Martha Bell of Bellstown, Libberton's Wynd.

   '*To the Rev. Mr Adam Blair, Minister
   of the Gospel at Cross-Meikle.*'

Chapter

5

—••✲)✕(✲••—

Mr Blair was not a little surprised by the receipt of this letter, and by the intelligence it conveyed. Mrs Camp, bell, though a very near relation, and, in former times, a most intimate friend and companion of his late wife, had not exchanged any sort of communication with him, or any part of his family, for nearly nine years, and having heard of her sometime before as being perma, nently resident in the Low Countries, he had given up, in a great measure, any notion of ever seeing or even hearing from her any more. At times, indeed, during the fatal illness of his wife, it had occurred to him how much both he and she might have been the better of having under their roof some such active, and affection, ate, and cheerful inmate as Charlotte Bell was when she spent some three months with them at Cross, Meikle in the first year of their marriage. But various circum, stances had occurred in the intervening space, which prevented him from ever wishing seriously for the return of Charlotte herself to the domestic circle of which she

43

had then formed the life and the ornament. At the same time, after all that passed, he could not now see once more her well-known hand-writing, without having many kindly feelings again called up in his mind – and after thinking over the matter a great part of the night, the result was, that Mr Blair felt some pain in the idea of being disturbed by the presence of any six-weeks visitor whatever, but was, on the whole, as much disposed to receive such a visit from Mrs Campbell, as from any other person of her sex who happened to occur to his recollection; besides, the letter was received on Friday, and as the lady was to leave Edinburgh on Monday morning, there was no time left for any farther epistolary communication on the subject. That she would arrive at Cross-Meikle on the day she had mentioned, was therefore certain; and Mr Blair's only business was to prepare his house and himself, as well as circumstances would permit, for her reception.

But the reader may naturally expect that we should explain some of these hasty allusions, by giving a slight sketch of Mrs Campbell and her history. And we have no objections to do so, but it must be as briefly as possible.

Charlotte Bell, then, was the daughter of a grave and much-respected Clerk to the Signet, a maternal uncle of the late Mrs Blair – in whose house Isabel Gray (for that was her maiden name,) had spent two or three winters at the time when Adam Blair was prosecuting his studies at the College of Edinburgh. It was in Mr Bell's house that Adam was first introduced to Isabel Gray, and it was not long until the passion which afterwards united these young people for life, betrayed itself sufficiently to the lynx eyes of the crafty old writer. His daughter, however, (for such things *may* occur, even among women, when they are very young,) did not for some time quite make up her mind whether Mr Blair's attentions were meant for herself, or for her cousin; and I believe few people who knew the family, and were accustomed to see them all together, had much doubt but that the handsome young theologian might have made a pretty easy prize of either of the fair kinswomen he might have chosen to woo. It is not impossible, therefore, that Miss Charlotte felt some momentary touch of disappointment when the true object of his fancy was first discovered; but she was a warm-hearted, high-spirited girl; – and if such were really the case, it could be no wonder that she should have had either generosity enough altogether to dismiss, or pride enough altogether to conceal her less genial feelings, on an occasion in every other point of view so well calculated to give pleasure to a girl of her years.

She became the friend and confidant of these lovers. During the happy days of courtship, she sat beside them, smiling with the innocent waggishness of a kind sister. She acted as bridesmaid at the wedding, and, as has already been said, took up her abode for some of the first months of their married life beneath the humble and cheerful roof of the Manse of Cross-Meikle. Frank and open in her manners – candid, even to a fault, it may be – cordial, affectionate, light of heart, and buoyant in spirits – and unwearied in glee – the beautiful

45

black-eyed Charlotte Bell was, in those merry days, the delight of every body that saw her –

'Friends in all the old she met, and lovers in the young.'

Whoever knew her then, would have been sorry to think it possible that she should be any thing but a happy wife and mother in her time; but such was not the destiny that awaited Charlotte Bell.

On returning to Edinburgh, from her visit to the family at Cross-Meikle, she found that her father had been so fortunate as to increase his clientage very considerably during the summer, and had begun to be and to seem a greater man than heretofore. Several new rows of green boxes – those external symptoms of a Scottish attorney's prosperity – had been added to the standing furniture of his business-room, and the appearance of the other parts of the house had been a good deal improved at the same time. Mr Bell entertained more company, and lived, in short, in much better style than he had been used to do; and Miss Charlotte was nothing loth to lend a helping hand in doing all the honours of a now flourishing establishment. It is true, that even in Mr Bell's humblest days, the gay young aspirants of the bar did not hesitate sometimes to accept his invitations – acting, in this respect, no doubt, upon the same profound views of wisdom and prudence that have since been so admirably embodied in that excellent 'Song upon the Mystery of Huggery.' But now there was no end to his suppers, and no suppers could be more *recherchés*. The result of all this was, that nobody was more admired that winter in the northern metropolis than the charming Miss Bell, the accomplished heiress-apparent of all this old writer's wealth. Young writers thought of partnership – young advocates of fees – many thought of the black eyes, and more of the rich succession; and the old ladies laid wagers of ribbons and gloves, that Charlotte would change her name ere the season came to an end.

And she did so – but not in the way her friends could have wished, or her enemies expected – (for, good-natured as she was, she had wit and beauty, and the prospect of wealth, and dozens of beaux – and she could not want enemies.) Among the young men who had dangled for several gay weeks in her train, was one so young, that every body but herself thought and spoke of him as a boy. He was English, and of good family, and had been sent to Edinburgh for a winter, by way of putting off the time until there should be rooms vacant for his accommodation at Trinity, Cambridge – on the books of which college his name had already been entered. This young gentleman fell in love with Miss Bell; and although, when he first told her so, she was inclined to laugh at him – for in truth he was very young, – the end of it was, that he prevailed upon her to elope with him one night, at the conclusion of a very pleasant, quiet, little ball, which had exhibited every charm that any ball can exhibit, and among the rest, a capital supper, served up with plenty of mulled sherry, about two o'clock in the morning, – the said supper constituting, in the opinion of some present, though the last, not the least among the ball's claims to approbation. An hour or two had elapsed before Mr Bell learned what had happened, and the raging sire was in hot pursuit on the Carlisle road, not many minutes afterwards. On reaching the second stage, however, his progress was arrested by means of a very clever expedient, the imagination of which was entirely Miss Charlotte's. That young lady, finding just eight horses in the stable, had clapt four of them to her chaise, and made a couple of post-boys ride on to Hawick before her with the rest of the cattle. Mr Bell stormed like a fury when he discovered the state of things consequent upon this ingenious device; but no fresh horses were to be got, for love or money, within several miles of the inn, and those he had been travelling with were entirely done up. The Clerk to the Signet therefore gave up the quest of his romantic damsel, ate a hearty breakfast at Selkirk, and returned very leisurely to Edinburgh, where he next day exhibited in public a composure of face and manner that greatly astonished many of his acquaintances, displeased some of them, and gratified a few.

The mystery was explained very satisfactorily about a week afterwards, when it became known that Mr Bell had invited a party of friends to dinner, and introduced to them a comely body who did the honours of his table, by the style and title of Mrs Bell the second – His acquaintance with this person, and indeed his intimacy with her, were at the same time announced to be of some little standing, by the appearance of three or four pretty boys and girls, who addressed the lady at the head of the table as mamma, and bestowed a name of equal tenderness upon the respectable senior at the foot of it. At this party, although most people could not help connecting it in some measure with Miss Charlotte's elopement, no allusion whatever was made to that distressing occurrence. On the contrary, nobody mentioned either Mr Beauchamp Arden or his lady, more than if there had never been any such persons in the world; and here is a circumstance which does, I think, very great honour to the delicacy and politeness of the jolly-faced bachelors and heart-whole widowers, who that day surrounded Mr Bell's 'festive board.'

Mr and Mrs Beauchamp Arden, by the time this dinner took place in the Lawn-market, had spent five days in the then unhackneyed fairy-land of the Cumberland lakes, and become as heartily weary of the sight of the real meres and mountains as the keenest anti-laker of our own day has of the sound of their names. They skirted Furness, crossed the sands to Lancaster, regained the great road, and were soon in the heart of London. Noise, tumult, glare, produced on Charlotte the same sort of effect which, when visible in the demeanour of a masculine being, is sometimes by the malicious attributed to the influence of Champagne, and for three weeks once more she thought herself the happiest woman in the world. But at the end of the month, several new and not less melancholy facts were forced upon her knowledge.

First, Mr Arden's father had announced his resolution never to give his son a shilling unless he got rid of the Scotch Bourgeoise, who had been cunning enough to take him in.

[Old Bell, by the way, had written to old Arden in a strain of high indignation about the marriage; but this only made matters worse by convincing him more thoroughly than ever that the W. S. had had his finger in the pye.]

Secondly, Mr Beauchamp Arden had confessed that, both of the fathers being thus untractable, he saw no feasible prospect of being able to raise the wind for himself.

Thirdly, Mr Beauchamp Arden's handsome countenance was capable of expressing some feelings, the appearance of which was far from adding to its comeliness; and fourthly and lastly, the gay lady *sometimes* doubted, when she looked back to the careless gaiety, and ease, and abundance of her father's house, whether, after all, *Charlotte Bell* might not raise a spirit as well as *Charlotte Arden*.

Several months of mingled ennui and care terminated in an unexpected catastrophe. Mr Beauchamp Arden was missed at home, and his wife discovered, after a very painful search and investigation, that a certain Signora Boracci, one of the *prima donnas* of the Opera, had been so kind as to give him a seat in the corner of her carriage to Paris.

The first rage of Charlotte nobody need attempt to describe; but the affliction of a lovely woman is seldom left without the offer, at least, of consolation, and the deserted Mrs Arden did not always sigh in solitude.

The particulars of her mode of life, during some eighteen or twenty months after the disappearance of her boy-bridegroom, have never reached me. At the end of about that period, Mrs Arden's beautiful face was seen as beautiful as ever upon the streets of Edinburgh. But let it not be imagined that she had gone thither for the sake of soliciting the lost favour of her father: Charlotte had a spirit above that. Her true attraction to Scotland was that excellent institution the Commissary Court – an institution to which many have been, and more have wished to be, obliged in our own time. From that demi-reverent judicature Mrs Arden soon procured a sentence of divorce against the swain of the Boracci, and the same day on which that sentence was signed, the hated name of Arden was dropped for ever. It made way for an appellation as ancient, and more noble; for Charlotte was forthwith announced in the Caledonian Mercury, as having bestowed her fair hand upon one of that numerous division of the human species which may be shortly and accurately described as answering to the name of Captain Campbell.

The Captain Campbell of Charlotte was, in almost every respect, unlike the curly-headed boy who had preceded him in her good graces. He was a thick-made, square-built, sturdy Highlander, with what are commonly called heather-legs, (*Anglice*, bandy). His nose had been blown up a good deal by snuff and brandy, or both; his eyes were keen grey; his hair, eye-brows, and whiskers, bristly red; his bob-major dressed *à merveille;* and his Dutch uniform fine as fivepence.

Captain Campbell, being the second son of one of the first families in Argyll, had, of course, begun the world with a pair of bare legs, and ten guineas. He had entered into the service of their High Mightinesses, and risen by degrees to the high rank (that of Lieutenant) which he now occupied. Nevertheless, in the course of some West India services, the shrewd man of Morven had contrived to feather his nest; and if the possession of several thousand pounds entitles a military man to style himself Captain, there is every reason to believe that his proper designation, as well as his usual one, was Captain Campbell. With money in his purse, the gallant hero had returned to Britain for the double purpose of providing himself with a wife and an estate. He was introduced to Mrs Arden at a gay party in Kensington Gardens. He heard all her long and touching story in a romantic hour, among

————'woods and alleys green,'

and the result was, that Captain Campbell and Mrs B. Arden set off next day for Scotland, and remained in Edinburgh together, until the above mentioned interlocutor of the Consistorial Court of that legal city was pronounced and ratified *more solenni*.

Fortune seemed to smile upon Captain Campbell; for he met with an estate to his fancy, about as soon as he had done with a wife to his fancy. A picturesque, rather than profitable domain, on the shores of his own dear Loch-Fine, received the weary conqueror, 'curru descendentem Teutonico,' and he took very solemn possession of a grand castle, containing a parlour, a bedroom, a garret, a closet, and a barn. To this imagined Otranto Mrs Campbell approached with glistening eyes, and a beating heart; while the Captain leaned back in the herringboat, and snuffed pinch on pinch, as who should say, 'What think ye of that?'

In three years or less, neither the Captain nor the lady thought any thing about it, except that it was a raw, cold, shell of a house, with not one rational neighbour within thirty miles. Mrs Campbell had seen Garrick, Quin, and Mrs Bellamy; she had been at balls and masquerades, at fashionable places of all sorts, from the circus to the chapel. She languished for the city, and she soon learned to hate LochFine. Forgive her want of taste, for she shared but the defect of Dr Samuel Johnson and Madame de Stael.

The Captain, on his part, saw his money sunk in land, which produced little or no return; and this alone was enough to make his weatherbeaten countenance gradually mingle a shade of sulkiness with its original colourings of resolution and firmness. Besides, in the long evenings, charmingly as Mrs Campbell sung, and deliciously as her fair round fingers could touch the strings of the guitar, it was a thing rather to be blamed than wondered at, that the Captain sometimes remembered, with feelings of regret, the jovial messroom of the Scots regiment, and the good cheer of the Hogan Mogans. Visions of longsmoked pipes, and longemptied bottles, rose up before him in dim and shadowy procession, and Captain Campbell paid a touching tribute to the sensibility of his nature, when he requested to have his respectable name put once more on the full-pay list of the distinguished corps to which he belonged. To be brief, Mr and Mrs Campbell had gone over to Holland, and joined the gallant Scots at Dordrecht, where, or whereabouts, they and the regiment had remained for several years in a state of very glorious inaction.

While the Campbells were in Argyllshire, obvious reasons had prevented the Blairs from soliciting the visit, which the Campbells had never offered. Their departure for the continent had all the appearance of being a final one; and Charlotte, not to mince matters, was suspected of deserving to be forgotten, and was in a fair way to be so by her friends in Scotland.

The progress of this oblivious disposition was once more interrupted by the personal appearance of the comely Mrs Campbell. On first arriving in Edinburgh, she gave out among those of her ancient friends with whom she was still in the habit of communicating, that she had preceded the Captain, in order to arrange matters in the Highlands for his reception; and that when he should have joined her, which in the course of a few months she expected him to do, they might both be considered as at last restored for ever to old Scotland. It was at the house of one of those friends, that she chanced one evening to meet with Mrs Semple, with whom, on a former occasion, (I allude to her visit at Cross-Meikle) she had formed some acquaintance. It was natural for Mrs Semple to dwell at great length on the melancholy accounts she had received about Mr Blair, listened to as she knew herself to be by a near relation of the wife, whose death had produced an effect of such lasting and profound depression upon that strong, manly, and cultivated mind. It was, at the least, not unnatural for Mrs Campbell to say, after hearing such a story, that she had a great mind to go out to Cross-Meikle, and try to soothe the affliction of her old friend's affectionate husband. And, finally, Mrs Semple could not hear Mrs Campbell talk of going to Cross-Meikle Manse, without taking the opportunity of saying, that she hoped she would be so kind as to spare a week or two to Semplehaugh-House.

The letter which we have already quoted was written by Mrs Campbell on the day immediately following that on which she had the honour of meeting the Lady of Semplehaugh, and the letter came in the same parcel with that excellent person's presents to the minister and his daughter, simply because, in those days the letter of a Scottish lady regularly, although perversely enough, preferred any other method of travelling to that furnished under the provisions of the Post-Office Act.

Chapter
6

—•••ЄӠЄЗ•••—

When Tuesday [1] came, everything had been duly prepared for Mrs Campbell's reception: the household,
long unused to any extraordinary exertions, had exerted
themselves with gladness, and all things without and
within the Manse of Cross-Meikle had assumed an air
of life and occupation, such as for many months they
had not been called upon to exhibit. The day itself was
one of those bright days which about the middle of
April announce the long-looked-for opening of the
Scottish spring. The sky was clear blue, with here and
there grey drifting clouds that passed and repassed upon
the breath of a stirring but balmy breeze: the sharp green
leaves enlivened once more the hedges about the garden;
the early crocus shewed its virgin blossom; the air played
light and elastic round every freshening branch and
bough, and the small birds twittered cheerily once more
from the eaves and copses. Mr Blair, as he came forth beneath the brightening honeysuckles that twined around

[1] Corrected to 'Saturday' in 2nd ed.

and over the lowly porch of his dwelling, could not resist feeling and partaking for a moment, the genial atmosphere and influences of renovated nature. He stood for some minutes, enjoying the surrounding gladness of all things, and said to himself, 'Yes, this is once more a gay spring morning; well, poor Charlotte will see Cross-Meikle looking just like what it used to do, when we were all younger and happier people than we are now.'

The distance from Glasgow is such, that it was natural for him to expect Mrs Campbell's arrival early in the day; and after the forenoon had passed, it was still thought impossible but that she must come before dinner. Dinner was deferred from hour to hour, and at last served up, but still she came not; and Mr Blair, when he perceived that the twilight was thickening apace, began at last to feel some perplexity, and almost to think that Mrs Campbell would not come that night at all. Little Sarah sat with the tea things set forth upon the table before her, and the kettle humming by the fire, while he stood at the window, looking forth every now and then towards the darkened village lane, and listening to the undulations of the breeze, in every sudden rise of which he fancied himself to catch at length the distant rattling of wheels.

The night closed, and all expectations being at last given up, the family were assembled in the usual manner for the purposes of social devotion. The psalm had been sung, the chapter read, and the prayer commenced, when a carriage stopt at the door of the Manse unheard and unheeded. Mrs Campbell alighting and entering the house, heard Mr Blair's voice, and immediately comprehended what was going forward. She gently opened the door of the well-known parlour, and stepping in, knelt down beside one of the servants, – all so quietly, that Mr Blair, being at the other end of the room with his back turned towards the door, and, of course, deeply occupied with his devotional duty, had not the least suspicion of what had happened.

He continued, therefore, to go on with his prayer as if no stranger had been hearing it; and perhaps the effect of what he uttered might have been less powerful, had he been speaking in the knowledge of her presence. More powerful, under any circumstances, it could scarcely have been; for his mild, subdued, chastened spirit, poured itself forth in free, unrestrained, gushing earnestness, and all the humble aspirations of the man rose to, and were overshadowed in, the sublimity of his religion. The voice of affliction was retoned in that sacred moment, and trembled with all the fervid eagerness of unbroken faith, while the affections of a father, a guardian, and a priest, flowed forth all together in one full, soft, and soothing stream of supplication.

He, who after being brought up in a house where the ancient Scottish system of family worship was regularly followed, has wandered abroad in the world, and lived among people ignorant, careless, or scornful of such things; and then, perhaps, returned after a lapse of many years to the paternal fire-side, there to witness once more those old and venerable observances of village piety, the effect of which has probably never entirely departed from his mind, however little their salutary influence might, at times, be visible on the surface of his conversation and his conduct – such a man, and, I am sure, there must be many such, will have no difficulty in sympathizing with the emotions which rose and struggled within Mrs Campbell's heart, while she listened to this evening service of Cross-Meikle Manse. She, indeed, had not enjoyed the happiness of being born and reared beneath the shadow of habitual godliness; but she had, in her early days, been often domesticated for a time in pious families, and above all, she had spent the last of her truly happy summers under the roof of her cousin and Mr Blair. Throughout all the years of wandering that had intervened – amidst her gaieties and revellings, her follies and her frailties, – the picture of those quiet and gladsome summer months had remained – obscured but not obliterated – at the bottom of her heart; and not seldom, when sleep brought the luxury which waking thoughts durst not harbour, had her dreaming fancy recalled all the fresh calmness of that happy and innocent life – the sweet sounds of its Christian psalm, and the grave simplicity of its domestic prayers.

In the old Norman and Spanish romances, we have often read of juggling fiends, demons, and sorcerers, being scared in the very moment of temptation or of torture, by some sudden gleam of the moon or the stars beaming upon the symbolic cross-hilt of a warrior's sword, or by some casual, or even unconscious ejaculation of the name of St Denis, or the Virgin. How often may not the too real sorceries of unhallowed pleasure, the fiends of human passion, and the demons of crime, have been arrested or turned aside from their work of evil, by the apparently fortuitous upspringing of some image of ancestral piety within a Scottish mind – a mind astray, but not lost! There are some readers who may smile at such things; but I speak what I feel to be true, and wherever there is truth, there must also be wisdom.

Mr Blair rose from his knee, and was made aware of her being in the room, by Sarah pulling his skirts, and saying, 'Papa, papa, you're no seeing the lady.' He had scarcely time to give more than a look, ere Mrs Campbell had rushed into his arms. He held her back, and gazing upon her once familiar features, altered, as they of course were, in the lapse of ten long years of an eventful history, he could scarcely, for the first moment, believe that it was indeed the same Charlotte whom he had known. He had heard enough of changes in her – and he had witnessed changes enough in every thing about him; but her image had remained on his memory as it was first imprinted, and it had not occurred to him that he was to see any thing but the same rosy cheeks and sparkling laughing eyes, which all men liked to look upon in the young and virgin days of Charlotte Bell. Instead of that bright personification of maiden loveliness and maiden glee, a pale face met his view – a pale, thoughtful, melancholy face – a faint serious smile struggling upon the surface of a pair of white and quivering lips – cheeks fallen in upon the bone – and soft eyes streaming with irrepressible tears. A thousand,

and a thousand thoughts rushed into his mind, and gladly would he have suffered his tears to have their way also, and mingled his whole soul with hers in one agony of lamentation. But eyes were upon him, and he commanded himself. The water stood in his eyes, but was not permitted to overflow the sockets. After a moment, he could say, 'God bless you, Charlotte!' in a scarcely faltering voice; and saluting her like a long-parted brother, he turned to his child, and bade Sarah come near to be kissed by one that must not be reckoned a stranger at Cross-Meikle. Sarah drew back and blushed, but Mrs Campbell caught her up, and folding her to her bosom, rained a shower of mingled tears and kisses upon the face and neck of the beautiful orphan, who, in her turn, was not slow to weep, for company's sake, although she could have but little understanding of the emotions for the turbulence of which Mrs Campbell had found a vent in tears.

Mr Blair interrupted this passionate scene by desiring the child to conduct Mrs Campbell to her apartment, and went out himself to see that her luggage was properly taken care of. After a little interval, they all met at the supper-table, where a few kind words were said from time to time; but, on the whole, there was silence. Neither could look at the other without seeing dim eyes; and although both strove to speak freely, and to seem easy, the struggle was by no means very successfully maintained. As soon as the things had been removed, Mr Blair rose from his seat, and said that he could not think of her sitting up any longer that night, after having gone through so much fatigue. He forgot that Mrs Campbell had travelled but a few miles: but she had no inclination to prolong moments that had already been too painful, or to say anything that might tend to prolong them.

The room to which Mrs Campbell was conducted was the same which she had occupied when formerly at Cross-Meikle. It had afterwards become the apartment of Mr and Mrs Blair; and was the same which had remained unoccupied ever since the time of Mrs Blair's death. These circumstances were of course unknown to Mrs Campbell; and it was not likely that any one should communicate them to her immediately on her arrival.

Chapter
7

—••❊ ❳❲ ❊••—

It was not without a very strange mixture of feelings
that Mrs Campbell, when left to her solitude, looked
round the little airy bed-chamber in which, in former
times, light slumbers and pleasant dreams had so often
soothed her maiden pillow. In all respects, the room
was exactly as she had left it ten years before. The bed
stood on the same spot; and its white dimity curtains had
preserved all the neatness of their appearance, while a
cheerful fire-light shewed the walls, still covered with
the same little prints and drawings with which she and
Isobel had taken so much pleasure in adorning them.
A piece of needlework, on which the fingers of them
both had been exercised when they were girls at school
together in Edinburgh, hung in the centre, over the
chimney-piece, and displayed all its fine flowers, and
leaves, and hieroglyphical emblems, in their original
shapes, though the worsted had become a little tarnished and dimmed in the colouring. The same Bible
and Psalm-book lay on the dressing-table, and there

was not one tall, long-backed cherrywood chair in the room but was an old acquaintance. She seated herself, half undressed, in the familiar corner by the fire-place, and gazed round and round her, till her mind was quite bewildered with the long trains of minute images and remembrances that arose one out of another, and flitted like so many dreams over her mind. There is a charm in such reveries that nothing can entirely destroy; and so, though her musings were melancholy enough in the main, there was a sort of romantic influence mingled in their airy texture, which soothed, in some measure, a heart naturally of great sensibility; and perhaps it might almost have been said, that excited and exerted memory made up to itself, in the consciousness of its energies, for the substantial gloominess of too many of the objects which those very energies had recalled from long oblivion.

She rose from her seat in a mood of pensiveness rather than of sorrow, and walked towards the window, which, almost without knowing what she was about, she threw open, and looked out upon one of the finest moonlight nights that ever adorned the most delightful season of the Scottish year. Her half-sickly mind was in a vein for indulging all its fancies; and the first thought that struck her, was to go out and visit the grave of Isobel Gray. She wrapped her long white dressing-gown about her, and, gathering up her loosened tresses, tied her shawl round her head, and tripped down the stairs as softly as she could. In those days, nobody in the country parts of Scotland ever thought of locking doors and bolting windows at night; so Mrs Campbell found herself in a moment upon the little piece of open turf which lay in front of the Manse, and all this without the least suspicion that her motions could have disturbed one ear in the house.

Charlotte walked rapidly over the green towards the stile by which the inhabitants of Cross-Meikle Manse have their easiest and most private access to the church-yard, and found the stile, and every thing about it, quite in their old place and condition. A row of very ancient and gigantic elms and willows skirts on that side the edge of the cemetery; and her resolution was, it must be owned, a little shaken, when she found herself beneath their broad black shadow; but she looked back, and saw the Manse bright in the moonshine; and perceiving that all was in like manner quite light in the churchyard itself beyond, she plucked up her courage again, and crossed the stile very quickly. Having fairly entered the precincts, she would have been much ashamed of herself to have turned back; and on the whole, she proceeded along the path with steps firmer than perhaps some even of my male readers might have been able to command, if *quite alone*, at such an hour, and in such a situation.

It must be confessed, however, that if any churchyard be likely to be trodden by unhesitating steps at the witching hour of night, it is that into which Mrs Campbell had made her way. Although surrounded, for the most part, with dark and venerable trees, it is in itself an open and spacious place, with nothing gloomy about it, except what no churchyard can be without, – affording free access to God's light, which shines as fairly on graves as on cradles, if men will permit it to do so. It has nothing of the affected and fantastic gaiety which the romantic damsels of Paris admire in the cemetery of the Père la Chaise; for although Scottish peasants fear death like other men, they have never had the ingenuity to think of rendering the approach of death less terrible, by associating it with the ideas of hyacinth beds, treillages of clematis, and trim thickets of lilac and laburnum. Neither has it the soul-filling majesty of your great old English burial ground, spread out beneath the shadow of some towering minster – a majesty in the presence of which the fears of human feebleness may sometimes be supposed to shrink into nothing – before which frailty may gain strength from the very sense of littleness. The simple livers of Cross-Meikle are contented with humbler images round the resting-place of their forefathers, but it exhibits nothing of that sorrowful and dismal aspect which we must all in general connect with the notion of a Scottish *kirkyard*. The flat tombstones lie in the clear light of sun and moon, and the green sod is refreshed by the visitings of the healthful breezes. Careful eyes watch the receptacles of lowly worth, and no atmosphere of needless desolation oppresses the spirits of those who walk over the ground, beneath which they know they are one day to be laid.

The church itself, which stands near the western limit of the burial-ground, is one of the few fine old ecclesiastical edifices that are still to be found in the country districts of Scotland. It is a small, but an exquisitely beautiful specimen of the earliest and simplest style of Gothic architecture, having no richness of minute decoration, but perfectly graceful in its outlines, and chaste in its whole effect. The original roof of stone still remains entire, although there is room enough between some shattered layers, for the support of wallflowers, ivy, and hawthorn bushes, and here and there a little crooked apple-tree has even contrived to find way for its roots, and hangs forth its blossoms and fruit over some projecting groin or parapet. Altogether in a country where few of those buildings remain otherwise than in a state of ruin, Cross-Meikle Kirk is well entitled to be visited with considerable attention. And although, to be sure, such matters were little thought of by people of taste and cultivation (for that is the fashionable phrase,) in the days of Adam Blair, the natural good feelings of the peasantry of that parish had always led them to be not a little proud of their fine 'grand auld Kirk.'

It was, as I have already mentioned, close beneath the wall of the church that the Blairs had their burying-place, and Mrs Campbell easily found her way once more to the conspicuous tablet placed above the remains of Mr Blair's father. It was exactly as it had been; but below it, three small heaps of turf disposed in the same line, and one quite new tombstone farther out from the church-buttresses, indicated the havoc of the short years that had passed over her head. Having found what she had come in quest of, Mrs Campbell was in no haste to exhaust its contemplation. She did not try to read the whole of the inscription – She saw, HERE LIES MRS ISOBEL GRAY – and these words were quite enough for her; and she sat down, at once, upon the edge of the large stone, with the composure which awe can lend to sorrow in the immediate presence of the departed. She was not of what is commonly called a superstitious turn of mind: – the buoyancy of her original character and disposition, and the very circumstance of her being where she now was, may sufficiently attest that she was not so; but we are all superstitious, and ideas forced themselves upon her after she had taken her seat on her friend's grave, which she strove to dispel and banish, but with which a stronger mind, in a similar situation, might have struggled as vainly as hers did. She gazed abroad upon the calm, breathless surface of the field of sepulchres, with eyes which would fain have seen nothing, but which could not for one moment escape from the fascination that fixed them; and she could hear her own heart beat in her bosom amidst a silence which she shrunk from disturbing even by her breathing. The real stamina of her mind were such, however, that her imagination was able to keep rid of any strong or palpable delusion; and after a little time, she had almost entirely recovered her self-possession.

When she had in some measure done so, there were other thoughts enough that gathered themselves round her, and these of power to dispute even the supremacy of the deep stirrings of human superstition. By degrees, she forgot all the wide dominion of death, and con-centered her imaginations upon the individual stone by which she was sitting. She wept not, however; it was with perfect calmness that she reflected on all the innu-merable images and feelings of those long past days, in which Isobel Gray had been the sister of her young bosom. It was not until she had begun to turn from them, to the memory of the very different sort of days that had followed; and to retrace, in the presence of her friend's peaceful dust, all the long mingled tissue of her own follies, faults, and sufferings, and troubles, that Charlotte's womanly weakness burst forth in its bitter-ness, and the voice of repentant misery was heard to pierce the ear of Night, as it brooded over the burial-ground. Sighs and passionate sobs burst together un-checked and unresisted, and the bruised heart poured out all its luxury of tears. – She lifted her eyes to the moon and the stars, and the beautiful heavens, and her eye spake reproachfully to their beauty. 'Why, oh why are ye, eternal bright eyes, not shining on my grave – on my repose? Isobel loved, and was loved, and was happy! I loved, and was never loved again! I sought refuge where the foolish seek it, and I found what they find. Oh, why was I not the wife of Blair! One year – not ten long blessed years – would have been enough for me, and I should have slept sweetly where I knew his eyes would every day rest upon my grave! Ye cold, cruel stars, when shall I be laid at rest beneath your beams!'

In the progress of all this, Mrs Campbell had so entirely forgotten the recent fears of her situation, that she had uttered several sentences aloud – or, at least, some incoherent ejaculations sufficiently expressive of the thoughts that were labouring in her breast – when she was suddenly arrested in the midst of all these melancholy wanderings of the imagination, by the touch of a human hand laid gently upon her shoulder – which, by the way, she had, in her forgetfulness of all immediate things, permitted to become quite bare. She started with a shudder, and then forcing her eyes to look steadily, saw that it was Blair himself who had intruded on her privacy. The first thought which flashed over her brain was, that he had been long there, and heard enough to make him acquainted with things, in regard to which she had never even dreamt it was possible she could do otherwise than carry them unrevealed with her to the grave. But she had strength enough, even at that moment, to gaze steadfastly upon his face, and the innocent mixture of surprise and sorrow depicted on all its features, restored to her, after the lapse of a few silent moments, the possession of something that, for the first time in her life, she had felt the possibility, and almost the pang of losing.

The truth of the matter is, that Blair, on entering his bed-room that night, had felt himself but little inclined to sleep; for his spirits, as we may easily suppose, had been in no ordinary degree confused and agitated. After going to bed, he had striven to lead his thoughts into some more soothing channel; but, at last, finding it quite impossible for him to do without assistance, he had risen again, re-lighted his candle, and taken a book into his bed with him, which he hoped might give a new direction to his ideas, and so prepare him for the needed embrace of sleep. Homer was the book he had happened to light upon, and his hand had perhaps unconsciously turned over the leaves to that part of the Odyssey, in which the interview between Ulysses and his mother's shade, in the nether world, is described with so many exquisite touches of simple and sublime pathos.

There was something in the first lines his eye chanced to rest upon so charming in itself, and, at the same time, so much in unison with the species of feelings on which his own mind had been dwelling, that although he had meant at first to read but for a little while, he had gone on turning page after page, till he had become completely interested and occupied, and could not think of stopping. Although Mr Blair was by no means a profound Grecian, he had mastered Homer early in his youth; and having no great library near him, far less any easy access to the literary novelties of the day, he had continued from year to year to read Homer, both because he was sensible that he ought not to lose what he had once gained, and because, without affectation, there was no book in his possession he had more delight in reading. Unlike most other men, the Odyssey was always with him a greater favourite than the Iliad – and this had been the case of late more than ever; for the buoyant and active spirits of the world prefer battles and other displays of the vigour of human life; but a mind, sobered by religion and affliction, might well be supposed to find greater pleasure in contemplating those images which the great poet himself, when grown old, had most delighted to dwell upon – images of a more domestic and softened character – illustrations, for the most part, of the deeper and more elemental workings of our nature – the declining majesty, rather than the hot noon-tide power of the sun of genius. The sorrowful, and at the same time calm and grave strain of that inimitable portion of his favourite poem, had therefore been exerting a salutary and composing influence upon his mind, all the time that poor Mrs Campbell was giving way to her own troubled meditations in the room immediately adjoining to his bed-chamber. And having come to the end of the book, he was just about to extinguish his light again, and once more court slumber, when he heard, in the breathless stillness of the hour, a neighbouring door gently opened, and immediately afterwards the step of a light foot on the stair-case.

His first idea was of little Sarah, for none of his servants slept on that floor; but he knew Sarah's footstep so well, that, after listening a moment, he was satisfied it was not she. He was sure it must be his guest; and when he had ascertained that the person, whoever it was, had left the house, it flashed upon him (for troubled spirits have many sympathies) that Charlotte had gone out to enjoy the fine moonlight night, and soothe herself with the freshness of the air. If of old she might have done so (and she had often done the like) in the mere wantonness of exuberant gaiety or luxury of girlish romance, – why should she not do the same thing now to relieve the bosom of its weight? The end was, that he himself had begun to slip on some of his clothes, while these things were passing over his mind; and that he was very soon out upon the green, where the moonlight shewed him distinctly on the dewy grass the mark of Charlotte's neat little footsteps. He followed them, and traced them to the stile. There he divined the object of her wandering, and he was in no mood either to disturb her privacy, or to chide her for her yielding-ness. He therefore passed the stile, simply from a sort of feeling that it was his duty to watch over Charlotte, and the apprehension that, in her visibly perturbed and shaken state of mind, some foolish little fancy might take hold of her, and perhaps render the assistance of masculine nerves desirable. Beneath the shadow of those great elm-trees he could linger unobserved, and without interrupting what he had no right to interrupt, be at hand to lend his assistance, in case any assistance should turn out to be required. There was a flutter on his own spirits at the moment, produced, no doubt, by the suddenness and unexpected nature of these little incidents, that prevented him from feeling almost any thing of what even he might probably have felt in that place any other night in the year; yet no man is likely to stand in the black shade of old sighing trees, looking out upon a church-yard at midnight, without some little sensations of unquiet; and he surely, of all men,

73

could have no reason to be ashamed of some such visitings there.

After a few minutes, his eye at last caught a glimpse
of Charlotte's figure, where she was sitting on the tombstone. He had come to see Charlotte, and it was *there* he
looked to find her. Yet now, when he saw a female
form clothed all in white, bent over his wife's grave at
that hour, and bent in motionless silence, he might be
forgiven for allowing one superstitious dream to heave
his bosom for a moment. He gazed and gazed, and was
aware of his folly, and shook it from him, or supposed
himself to do so. The effect, nevertheless, was such, that
he stood quite rooted to the spot, as if he had been fas-
cinated by the presence and vision of something not of
this world.

But when Charlotte raised herself up, and, clasping
and wringing her hands, made the echoes of all that
desolate place resound with the voice of agony not to be
mistaken, a crowd of far different feelings forced themselves into his manly and affectionate mind. It was then
that Blair stepped forth fearlessly from the shaded nook
in which he had been standing, and walked towards
the weeping woman with a firm step over the graves.
The feelings of a brother and a friend were blended with
those of a Christian and a priest, and being witness to
misery, it was his business by all these titles to soothe it,
even though it were by partaking it.

But the touch of Blair's hand upon Charlotte's neck,
and still more, something already alluded to, had effectually disturbed the tenor of her meditations.

'Dear Charlotte,' said he, 'why is this? Why *here*, and *now*, and *thus*? It is not so that we should receive what God sends, Charlotte. We must struggle, else we cannot overcome.'

He said these words calmly, for the sight of another's emotion had with him, and has with many, the effect of giving that which some people might imagine it more likely to take away; and she, in her turn, was as calm as if she had undergone nothing of all that fervid agitation. 'Adam,' said she, 'forgive me; I am a poor silly creature.'

'Come away, Charlotte,' said Blair, 'we have been long enough here.' And so saying, he drew her cold arm within his, and she leaned all her weight upon it, like one that was faint and weary, but otherwise walked well and firmly by his side. The presence of kindness had not come in vain to sorrow; and when they had reached the Manse, and entered their chambers again, I believe both of them felt the better for all that had happened. Nay, I believe it might be said with safety, that softer and more soothing slumbers than came to both of them that night, had not, for a long while, visited the pillow of either.

Chapter

8

It is said by a writer, whose celebrity, perhaps, does no great honour to the feelings of human nature, that, let a man die amidst ever so many lamentations, if he could rise from the grave again after the lapse of a few years, or even months, his re-appearance would not be found to be productive of unmingled satisfaction among the friends who had wept over his closing grave. There is much wickedness in this satirical remark, and certainly a great deal of exaggeration; nevertheless, there is perhaps some foundation for it in the truth. This much, at least, we must all have observed, that friends who have been long absent from each other, however they may have lamented their separation, do very seldom, on meeting again, experience all that pleasure which they themselves had expected to derive from being restored to the society of each other. The reason I take to be a very simple one; namely, that however close may have been the intimacy of former days, those who come together again after being long asunder, never do come together the same persons that they parted. In spite of every thing, new events have passed over either head; new thoughts, new feelings have left their traces in either bosom: the sorrows of one have not been sympathised with: the joys of another have not been partaken: the mind of each has been occupied, in by far the greater part of its depth, with things of which the other has no knowledge, and can form no guess: and after the first tumult of rekindled affection is over, the melancholy truth forces itself upon those most reluctant to admit it, that the internal man suffers changes no less surely than the external; and that the mental eye regards remote objects in a way as fallacious as the corporeal; –

> Fallunt nos oculi, vagique sensus
> Oppressâ ratione mentiuntur,
> Nam turris prope quæ quadrata surgit,
> Attritis procul angulis rotatur.

And, in like manner, he who, being far off, has been thought of as if he had remained what he was ere he went away, no sooner approaches us once more, than we discover how fondly imagination has been playing with the materials of memory. Nay, when there has been room and leisure for a little pause of reflection, the consciousness of changes within one's own mind becomes so strong, that very many men are apt to give their friends, in such a situation, credit for having been changed during the period of absence – in a measure not less but greater than they really have been.

Adam Blair was too good a man either to have

many secrets or many suspicions; yet the sort of coldness to which these feelings lead all men, was not imperceptible in his demeanour towards his guest, after she had spent a few days under his roof. There were many subjects on which she was evidently unwilling to speak – and, above all, she seemed to labour with great difficulties whenever the natural course of conversation would have led her to speak of the things that had befallen herself during the last years of her absence from Scotland. Blair was not by nature a curious man, but he was so very kind, that this species of reserve could not fail to chill him at times; and, on the whole, though little occasions were every now and then occurring on which every thing like reserve seemed to be quite forgotten on both sides – these, after all, were but exceptions to a general rule. The painful character of the subjects on which his own meditations chiefly rested, made him feel that open speaking and concealment of nothing, would, on his part, be cruel at the best; – and Mrs Campbell had, no doubt, her painful thoughts also. Their intercourse, then, was invariably kind and affectionate; but it was no longer the same thing as when, in early and untroubled days, Adam Blair and Charlotte Bell were used to sit together, like a brother and a sister, in the presence of her who was a sister to the one, and more than a sister to the other.

To restore the full confidence of long-broken sympathy, was here, as it probably always is, the work of time and of trifles. Yet nobody who was in the habit of seeing Mr Blair could doubt, that from the date of Mrs

Campbell's arrival at Cross-Meikle, his condition had been gradually, but surely tending towards improvement. The obligations inspired by the duties of hospitality had visibly furnished a stimulus to his mind. Society and conversation had exerted their usual influences, and the whole aspect and demeanour of the man had, ere long, lost that shade of undisturbed and settled heaviness, which indicates to the watchful eye of kindness, the sickly luxuries of a spirit wasting all its energies in brooding over the dark places of remembrance. This, it may be supposed, was more particularly a matter of constant and thankful remark among Mr Blair's worthy country folks. Deeply as they all respected both the man and his affliction, it is not to be denied that some of them had been occasionally inclined to find fault with the extent to which he carried his indulgence of sorrow. The old bedridden peasant, whose solitude had been enlivened, whose faith had been strengthened, whose feelings had all been soothed by the frequent visits of an affectionate minister, felt the comparative rareness of those visits as an additional infliction of calamity; and sometimes, the natural querulousness of age, and suffering, and desertion, would have its way. Younger people, again, who had met and resisted griefs of the same species with those to which Mr Blair had been exposed, did not all of them think so wisely and so deeply as we have seen John Maxwell did; but, on the contrary, were apt to consider the leisure and superior information of their minister as reasons why he should have been less likely, than they themselves had been, to give way to the enervating influences of a cherished distress. The arrival of Mrs Campbell was associated by all these people, with the notions of strengthened zeal and discharged duty on the part of Mr Blair; while such were the frankness of her manners among themselves, her readiness to give all sort of assistance in cases of necessity or of suffering, and the kindness of all her conduct in every situation wherein they had any opportunity of contemplating it, that it would indeed have been very wonderful had the lady not become, which she really did, the greatest possible favourite among those good villagers.

But, perhaps, there was no part of Mrs Campbell's behaviour which tended so much to secure for her the affection of these humble neighbours, as her own unwearied attention to little Sarah Blair. In all her walks, in all her visits to their cottages, this child was made her constant companion. Tripping by her side, or clinging to her hand, alike in her moments of glee, and in those tinged with more sobriety, it was evident to every eye, that Sarah's young heart beat once more in that security, which the presence of a mother diffuses over the breast of childhood.

Nor is it to be doubted, that this unwearied kindness to his child, was one of the surest of avenues to the heart of such a father as Mr Blair. Such an appeal to his affectionate dispositions was irresistible; and not the less so, surely, because it was made in the most modest and unaffected manner in the world. I believe an artful woman, who had cared nothing for Sarah, might have easily deceived Mr Blair, by feigning to love her; but there was no need for feigning here. For the sake of her own innocent beauty alone, the girl would have been dear to Mrs Campbell; but had Sarah been as plain a child as she really was a lovely one, Charlotte would still have loved her well, because she was the orphan of Isobel Gray, and the child of Blair. Moreover, Charlotte, though twice married, had never been a mother; and now, in that deep well which nature has placed in every womanly breast – and that, I believe, so deeply, that it can never be exhausted – the sweet waters of motherly affection rose freely at the call. A heart that had not been over-generously dealt withal, was still full of the capacity of tenderness; and poor Charlotte, whose warmer affections had been but unfortunately placed, felt more delight than she was perhaps aware of, in the idea of pouring out love upon an infant bosom, where there was no reason to fear the influences of those ungrateful passions which had hitherto disappointed or betrayed her; or which, at least, she blamed for having done so. Sarah, therefore, grew dearer and dearer to her from day to day; and that affection, which from the first had been a luxury, became much more so as it was returned. Those whose spleen has been boldly stirred by the probings of calamity, above all, of that worst calamity, human ingratitude, will appreciate the soothing effect of which that long-forgotten luxury of loving and being loved might naturally be productive in such a breast as Mrs Campbell's. The sense of it did indeed soften and soothe her in many ways; but, most of all, by filling, or rather seeming to fill, the place of some other feelings, the existence of which has already been sufficiently hinted to the sagacious reader.

One strong sympathy does more for bringing two strongly-feeling minds together, than can ever be effected between minds of the common order, by the most perfect accordance of opinion as to all the matters about which common-place minds are ever busied, – as one breath of the furnace will do more for uniting two pieces of kindred metal, than all the strings and knots in the world. Their common sorrow for the death of Isobel, and their common affection for Sarah, were not long, therefore, in producing feelings of mutual confidence and reliance between Blair and Mrs Campbell, such as could not fail to overpower, in a very great measure, those adverse influences, in themselves rather of negative than of positive quality, which have been already described as somewhat checking the genial flow of their intercourse during the first days of their renewed acquaintance.

It is not less true, that there are minds, some of the strongest attachments of which may be ultimately referred, not to original identity, but to original diversity of opinion, if not of character. Perhaps not a few of the attachments which arise between persons of the different sexes may, in one point of view, be considered as falling under this principle more than any other; but there can at least be no doubt, that it has its share in almost all of them. And it is quite the same in attachments of a less passionate description. The chief friend of the hard-hearted, indomitable Luther, was the mild and gentle Melancthon, who must necessarily have regarded almost every subject in a way totally unlike his. The divine Plato was not so great a favourite with Socrates as his fellow-disciple, the brilliant, headstrong, luxurious Alcibiades. Charles V preferred Peloux to Alva; and Samuel Johnson liked James Boswell better than Edmund Burke. Queen Elizabeth's favourites were not the Raleighs, but the Essexes; and her fairer rival was not ruined for a Surry, but for a Darnley. Madame de Stael married Rocca, not Schlegel. The friendships of such men as Swift and Gay, and Rousseau and Hume, must evidently have originated, in like manner, from circumstances of difference rather than of similarity in feeling and character; and, above all, in opinion. But indeed, Homer, the great master of human nature, has sketched his Achilles and Patroclus quite upon this principle.

Now, there was one great subject on which Blair and Mrs Campbell thought so very differently, that at first sight one might have imagined it alone sufficient to repel them from each other. – I mean that of religion; and yet the discussions to which their differences of opinion as to this matter gave rise, had perhaps more effect in levelling the barriers which at first kept their spirits apart, than even those strong sympathies of the affections, of which I have already spoken. Mrs Campbell had been a wanderer in the world, and an unfortunate one; and although neither the irritations to which her own mind had been exposed, nor the tone of the company into which she had been too often thrown, had been sufficient to banish altogether the original impressions of a mind, trained as Scottish minds were in those days uniformly trained; yet neither of these unfortunate influences had been entirely neutralized by the safeguards she had brought to their first encounter. I do not propose to lead my reader into a theological dissertation; but I may just mention, that Mrs Campbell's own misfortunes, which she still considered as for the most part unmerited, had at times darkened her confidence; and that the light and sarcastic mockeries of heartless men, even although heard at the moment with any thing rather than approbation, had not always failed to leave some traces of their venom behind them. Mrs Campbell was far from being an infidel, – but there were moments in which she could scarcely be said to be a believer; – and at all times, when she spoke upon topics of a religious nature, expressions escaped her which gave pain to the unsullied purity of Blair's religious feelings.

The pain with which Mr Blair heard the expression of such sentiments from Mrs Campbell was, however, and indeed it could not be otherwise, a totally different sort of feeling from the pain with which he should have listened to sentiments in anything like the same strain from a person of the other sex, and who had enjoyed the advantages of another kind of education. What *she* said seemed to be nothing but what she could not help saying, without being guilty of a species of unworthy dishonesty in the course of conversation with one whom

it was plain she regarded as a most sincere and affectionate friend. It was evident that she knew what she said
must give him pain, and that she said it with reluctance
and pain to herself on that account; but it was not less
evident that her soul abhorred the idea of receiving a
confidence unmerited, and that she uttered what she
did utter simply from her scorn of deceit, or of anything
that might do the work of deceit. Besides, the sources of
her delusion were apparent, and the pain created by
knowledge of the effect could never be separated from
the pity created by knowledge of the cause. Had Mr
Blair happened to fall into the society of a sharp-witted,
cold-blooded man of the world, capable of throwing
out infidel hints and insinuations in the mere wantonness of an unrestrained spirit, and this either in utter
scorn of the feelings of others, or in utter indifference to
them, I believe there is no man in whom indignation
would have risen higher, or who would have expressed
his indignation with more withering power than Mr
Blair. – But this was not an occasion to call forth any
of the angry feelings of such a man as he was. A tran-
sient pulse of horror was touched the first time the idea
flashed upon him of Charlotte Bell having wandered
from the faith of her Redeemer; but this was secret, and
the only feelings he did not conceal – those of sorrow,
regret, and, above all, of gentle pity – were the only ones
which his mild spirit harboured, after that first momentary pang had gone by.

As a man, it was his nature to pity the errors of a
woman, and as a priest it was his duty to amend them;

and perhaps the most powerful and salutary stimulant which could have been applied to such a mind as his in such a situation as this, was furnished by the strong sense with which the obligations of this sacred duty rose upon him as he pondered, in his retirement, over the melancholy truth which had thus been forced upon his observation. To soothe the heart that had been visited by so many baleful fevers of passion – to calm and confirm the understanding which had been shaken amidst the tempests of the world – to rebuild the faith that had been shattered – to restore the hopes that had been blighted – and to renew, in all its parts, the health-ful tone of a mind which had originally been meant for health and the happiness of health – these were the ob-jects to which his soul, in the silence of meditation, devoted all her energies, and to which he henceforth applied himself, not indeed with any visible demonstra-tion of zeal, but with a quiet and affectionate persever-ance much more worthy of himself, and much more likely to secure the attainment of the truly sublime pur-pose he had in view. It is not for the writer of this story to follow Blair into the secret exercises of his sacred calling, nor is it necessary to suggest doubts to the pre-sent generation, by telling how the doubts of their fore-fathers were subdued. It is enough for me to say, that nothing passed between Blair and Mrs Campbell but what has passed a thousand and a thousand times be-tween a fervid and a learned minister of God's word, and a feeble, but not a scornful stranger to the mysteries of our faith. The apparent result was such as never fails to take place when knowledge and faith on the one hand, and ignorance and doubt on the other, meet each other fairly and on fair grounds. The unpretending simplicity with which Mr Blair expounded the subjects that had formed the study of his life, did not lead his pupil (for such she was) to distrust either the depth of his study, or the sincerity of his conviction. Religion is a part of our nature, and Mrs Campbell's nature, with all her faults and errors, was entire in her bosom: Her feelings, soothed by the presence of sympathy, and originally too warm for the purposes of the sceptic, rejoiced in running back into the old channels. Her constant observation of the blessed effects of religion in the person and family, and among the flock of Mr. Blair, lent the best of all commentaries to the doctrines she heard explained, and revived gradually all the genial aspirations which, even in her worst days, had never entirely deserted her bosom. Without any affected exclamations, any violent professions, any confident or presumptuous declarations, Mr Blair was satisfied that the good work had prospered, surely though slowly, in his hands. If some momentary feelings of exultation, such as man should never feel, might occasionally pass through his mind, – if he thanked his God too rashly, and even then gave not to God all the glory, – the man most unlikely to fall into Blair's errors, will, I take leave to think, be the first and the readiest to excuse them.

Meanwhile, under the influence of new and continued excitements of so many different sorts, and all powerful in their kind, the mental lethargy into which

Mr Blair had for a long time sunk, had gradually been shaken off, and the whole outward appearance of the man bore testimony to the blessed alteration which the state of his spirits had been undergoing. Once more the humble hearth of the Manse had resumed its air of sober cheerfulness, and often, after Sarah had retired to her early repose, would Blair and Mrs Campbell sit up hour after hour together, engaged in conversation, which, on whatever subject it turned, had so many charms for both, that neither were willing to think of its termination. The deep and serious subjects to which I have already alluded, paved the way, imperceptibly, for other topics of a nature less solemn indeed, but too profoundly interesting to the one of them not to command the warmest sympathy and attention of the other. Woman, however chilled and reserved by the first sense of strangeness, is, by nature, communicative: it is her fate to lean upon man; and to man she is never slow to tell her griefs, when she is once sure that her griefs are to be listened to, not by the ear of harshness, nor with the gesture of cavil, but gently, kindly, warmly, as it becomes man ever to listen to woman. The openness of communication which had taken place in regard to one set of subjects, led to a similar openness as to others; and, by degrees, all the long story of Charlotte's miseries – as much, at least, as any woman could tell to any man of such a story – had been told over and over again to Blair, under circumstances which might have rendered a less affecting story sufficiently dangerous to a man more feebly guarded than he was. There is not, nor ever

88

was, a man in the world having the common feelings of a man, who could have heard such a story with indifference – and Charlotte had all the power to tell it as it ought to have been told. Her eyes were suffused with heaviness and gloom, and her cheek burned, as she narrated the early treacheries of the boy Arden, for it was evident that she could not, without shame of the deepest dye, retrace the folly of her own girlish behaviour – the green enthusiasm which had buoyed her up while she was floating, with her eyes open, to abandonment and scorn – the glowing heart of hearts which she had laid bare to the breath of insult – the confidence which had grown like a gourd, only that, like a gourd, the next day's sun might see it withered to the inmost fibre, and every broad green leaf already mouldering into the dust of derision. – Her countenance recovered its calmness as she went on, but her voice, although it shook not, sunk as low as ever did the intense whisper of hatred. 'I toiled for him,' said she, (it was of Campbell she spoke) – 'I toiled for him – I banished myself for his sake – I made myself his drudge, his slave, his victim. I had been bred in abundance, and he was not poor; yet, because he chose it should be so, I lived as if I had never known what plenty was. – But what was this? – What would I have cared for this had I been requited with affection? – I would have starved myself, – yes, Adam Blair, I would have starved myself, and gladly too, could I have been sure of one kind look – one tender kiss, Adam, when the night closed in upon my misery. But no – things went on from worse to worse, and to all I submitted. I left Scotland – a weary hateful Scotland it was *then* to me – and I went to Holland, and we were gay, and my husband's face was lighted up, except only when his eyes fell upon mine. Oh, Adam, why should I tell you the weary tale over again? Suspicion, black, false, detestable suspicion – blacker and falser it was than ever the devils made hell or found it – suspicion, distrust, scorn, – these are the bitter ingredients that have at last made my cup run over. Adam, if I have borne any part of all these last miseries well, it is you I have to thank for doing so. I have breathed more freely, dear Adam, since I came back to your shelter: any body else would have refused such shelter to such a creature as me. I have had many faults, but I trust I have never been an ungrateful creature. Pray for me, dear Adam, I have much need of your prayers.'

Once more they shed sympathetic tears, and once more they parted.

Chapter

9

— ••⟨•⟩⟨•⟩•• —

Pass over the few short weeks of a spring, which, on the whole, we may call cheerful, since it followed so dark a winter, and imagine to yourselves the beautiful region all around Cross-Meikle, clothed once more in the richness and pomp of summer in 'the leafy month of June.' The skies are all over bright, dark, sultry blue, without a single cloud; the trees seem to be loaded and bowed down with the luxuriance of their foliage; the shadows lie black beneath them upon the fervid turf; the brook leaves half its rocky channel bare to the sun, but slumbers clear as some large translucent gem within the deep green pool which it never has deserted. All nature pants beneath the sense of her own excessive beauty, and a still low chorus of universal delight is breathed from the surface of all living and inanimate things into the ear of noon.

It was on such a day that Blair proposed to Mrs Campbell that they should take Sarah along with them, and walk over to Semplehaugh, to pay their respects to

the good old lady, whose arrival, (from accicental circumstances, deferred longer than was usual,) had taken
place the day before, and been announced the same
evening, by a message of kind inquiries to the inhabitants of the Manse. Mrs Campbell smiled her consent,
and the child, bounding with childish glee, was soon
ready to run on the way before them, and open every little
gate they had to pass, in their walk through the fields,
ere they came up to it. They walked slowly, and were
sure never to pass a clump of old shady trees, without
lingering in the coolness for a few minutes; yet the distance was not great, and it seemed as if they had scarcely
begun their journey ere it was ended.

Mrs Semple did not conceal the pleasure she felt in
observing the great improvement that had taken place
in the external appearance and bearing of Mr Blair,
since she parted from him about the beginning of the
year. The accounts she had heard of him in the interim,
had prepared her for seeing him even thinner, and paler,
and graver, than he had been then; and this added not a
little to the agreeableness of the surprise with which she
saw how it really was with him now. Grave, indeed, he
still was; but Adam Blair had never, from a boy, been
any other than grave; and if he was somewhat graver
now than he had been at the same beautiful season two
years before, such slight alterations might easily elude
the unscrutinizing eye of such a person as Mrs Semple.
He was no longer either leaner or paler than he had
usually been in former times, and there were matters in
regard to which there certainly was much less likeli-

hood of the good old lady's being mistaken. His cheek had recovered all its brown, his nerves seemed to be re-strung, his step was firm, his eye had thrown off the cloud beneath which its fires had languished, and the manly comeliness of Blair was as perfect as it ever had been. Indeed, an additional tinge of gravity was not likely to have taken any thing away, either from the grace of his movements, or from the beauty of that dark and noble cast of countenance.

The change which a few weeks had been sufficient to produce in the appearance of Mrs Campbell, was scarcely less remarkable, although of this, also, Mr Blair had no adequate notion, until his attention was called to it by Mrs Semple. The hollow cheek and dim eye, which struck him so much at their first meeting, had gradually, but very gradually, filled up and brightened under the influence of a quiet, sober life, affectionate so-ciety, and innocent occupations; and Mrs Campbell, though she could no longer boast the sylph-like shape, and sparkling maidenly vivacity of Charlotte Bell, was one of the finest women imaginable. Her form, although with somewhat of a matron-like air, had preserved its outline as perfect as it was at bright seventeen; – her full arms were rounded with all that delicate firmness which Albano delighted to represent in his triumphant Sea-nymphs; – the clear brown of her cheek had banished its once steady roses, but that did not prevent an occa-sional flush of crimson from being visible; – if the curls of her hair were not quite so silky and slender, they were darker and richer, and more luxuriant than they ever had been; – and a slight heaviness about the lids, did not diminish the effect of her beautiful black liquid eyes, whenever they ceased to be downcast. It was the fashion of the day to wear two or three long ringlets of hair down on the shoulder, and never did glossier ringlets float upon a fairer bosom than hers. There was an intermixture of pensiveness and natural glee in her aspect and in her manners, which few women could have denied to be singular, and which, I believe, no man would have hesitated to pronounce singularly interesting. Altogether, if Titian had seen Charlotte, he would have made a point of painting her portrait; and his only difficulty would have been, whether to have made her a companion to the most radiant of his Ariadnes, or to the most lovely of his Magdalenes.

Dr Muir's daughter, a celebrated rural beauty, and, as has already been mentioned, something of an heiress to boot, had been spending some weeks in Edinburgh with Mrs Semple, and had returned to the country in her carriage, and the old Doctor was already at Semplehaugh to receive his fair daughter, and conduct her home to Cambuslee. Miss Muir was, at that time, in full possession of all the charms of fresh nineteen; she had the rosiest of cheeks, the brightest of eyes, and the brownest of curls, and the whole of her smiling face sparkled continually with the conscious exuberance of girlish high spirits. Nevertheless, from the moment that Mrs Campbell entered the room, there was no one, unless perhaps we except the young lady herself and her proud father, who did not acknowledge the presence of superior fascinations. Even Mr Jamieson, the tutor, who had been paying great court to Anne Muir while in Edinburgh, could with difficulty keep his eyes off the beautiful stranger; – he sat gazing, and gazing, and could scarcely be persuaded that this was the identical Mrs Campbell, whose pale and emaciated appearance had struck him so much when he met her two months before in Libberton's Wynd. The young Laird him-self was indefatigable in his attentions; – while the old Lady, who, having no plainish daughter of her own, was always delighted with the sight of a handsome young woman, looked now at Miss Muir, and now at Mrs Campbell, and could not help whispering to Mr Blair: – 'My certie, I think it would have ta'en a' the King's Assembly could do to match these twa bonny faces; but Mrs Campbell's the bonniest of the twa; – indeed, Mr Adam, she's picket up in an extraordinary manner since she came out to Cross-Meikle. There's no denying that there's something very reviving in the air about this part of the country. Poor thing, I dare say she's been meikle the better of regular hours, and plenty o' milk diet. There's nae young body ever thrives in big towns. Oh, sirs! your racketings and junketings does nobody good but the haberdashery folk and the con-fectioners.'

Mrs Semple insisted that the whole party should re-main to dinner, saying that Cross-Meikle was but a step off, and that there was a fine early moon to light the Doc-tor and Miss Muir home to Cambuslee; and they con-sented; for, in truth, there was no one whose invitations it was so difficult to resist as Mrs Semple's. In the mean-time, it was proposed, that they should all take a walk in the garden, which the good Lady herself had not had an opportunity of visiting since her return, and in which, at all times, a great share of her pleasure lay. From one of the windows of the drawing-room in which they were assembled, a low flight of steps led down to the green mossy terrace which extends all along the back part of the house; and in a few minutes the whole party were walking beneath the shade of those fine old sycamores which still skirt the edge of that broad walk, and lean their mighty branches far over, shedding their leaves and blossoms right down upon the dark face of the river which winds through the glen a hundred feet below.

The garden itself consisted in those days of a succes-sion of narrow terraces, constructed upon a less precipi-tous part of the river bank, at the eastern extremity of this shaded walk; – and, by the way, 'it may be doubted,' (as Mr Macleod says in *The Absentee*,) whether that old terraced garden, with its connecting flight of steps, its venerable bowers of yew and holly, and its gigantic hedges of beech, was not a finer thing, after all, than the modern garden of Semplehaugh, situated about half a mile from the house, and inclosed within four high brick walls, and much celebrated, for some good ten miles round, by reason of its magnificent succession of hot-houses, and the superior flavour of its grapes and pine apples. In like manner, 'it may be doubted,' whether the bank between the river and the old mansion-house has been at all improved, by the processes of levelling, clearing, and smoothing it has undergone, and the substitution of a few occasional patches of laurel and privet, for the rich masses of dark foliage which then waved in the breeze, and threw many a congenial sweep of shadow upon the deep and silent pools beneath. But these changes were probably considered indispensable at the time when the late Laird had the fortune to become bit with that Gothic fever which seems to be establishing itself as an endemic among us, and conceived the grand idea of concealing the old, irregular, manywindowed mansion of his forefathers, beneath that heavy and elaborate casework of sculptured freestone, which has served there, as elsewhere, the double purpose of conferring upon a good old *Scottish hallhouse* the dignity of a PRIORY, and the comfort of a DUNGEON.

It so happened, that for some time in their progress through this oldfashioned garden ground, Mrs Semple walked between Mr Blair and Mrs Campbell, while Dr Muir, his daughter, the young Laird, and Sarah, moved somewhat in advance before them. The old Lady stopped to examine every bed of flowers, and having plucked a knot of beautiful hyacinths, she gave one or two to Mrs Campbell, and desired Mr Blair to follow Miss Muir, and present her with the remainder of the nosegay. Mr Blair obeyed; and while he was doing as he had been bidden, Mrs Semple took occasion to entertain Mrs Campbell with a variety of eulogies both on him and on Miss Anne Muir.

'O, Mrs Campbell,' said she, 'what a change has

been wrought in our poor friend these few short weeks, since I told you how John Maxwell wrote a haill letter about the melancholy condition he was in! He was getting his spirits up as well as could have been expected, we all thought, so long as this family continued in the country; but the dull, cauld, wet winter, kept him in to his Manse, and he had nobody wi' him to make it the cheerful place it had used to be; and day after day he was drooping and drooping, till the poor folk round about thought he would just follow the same gait his wife had gaen, and never see out the simmer. It was a blessed thought your coming out to him; every creature that kens him is sensible his restoration is entirely owing to your being with him. O dear, ye'll maybe think me a heartless woman for what I'm going to say; but really, Mrs Campbell, when I think how young he is, and how he sinks in the lonely way that he cannot avoid being in so great a part of every year, it has often occurred to me, that it would be a happy circumstance if he would make up his mind to marry again. Now this is a thing, Mrs Campbell, that I'm sure ye'll no suspect I would ever have mentioned, be not to such a friend of his and his family as yourself; but the summer will soon be blawn by again, and ye'll, no doubt, have other duties to attend to, and we'll be back to Edinburgh as usual, and I greatly dread the thought of what may come o'er him when he's left once more to himself. Nay, for that matter, if he once begin to go down again, he'll maybe be worse than ever, after being refreshed and revived, as we may a' see and say he has been by your kind company. Since I've come upon this topic, my dear Mrs Campbell, I may just as weel speak out my mind at ance. A year will soon have gone past, and I wish from my heart Mr Blair would fancy Annie Muir there; she's been wi' me in the town these eight weeks, and a sweeter-tempered, more cheerful, pleasant, obliging, heartsome lassie, I never met with. I weel ken that nae love can ever be like a first love; but oh! mem, it's folks' duty to struggle with the evils of our condition; and Mr Blair is not in the same kind of situation that he would have been in, had he been left at the head of a large family, wi' every thing astir round about him. He has naething but yon puir bit lassie, little Sarah, and I'm sure she has as meikle reason as he has to wish for such a change. Annie Muir must be allowed to be a very comely young woman – she's no such a beauty as poor Mrs Blair was at her time of life, (weel I mind her weel-faured sonsy face, when she came first to Cross-Meikle,) but she's a bonny lassie – a very bonny lassie; do you no think sae, Mrs Campbell? And I'll take it upon me to say, that the Doctor, honest man, would have no objection to the connexion. – Na, hoot, Mrs Campbell, I doubt ye're no heeding what I've been saying. Do you not allow her to be a comely young body?'

'Her? – Whom?' said Charlotte; 'O, I beg your pardon, ma'am, it was Miss Muir you were speaking of; I beg your pardon a thousand times, I think she's very well – very well indeed. Perhaps, if she had seen a little more of the world, it might have done her air no harm;

but considering every thing, I perfectly agree with you. I think Miss Muir is really very well – exceedingly well indeed. I have no doubt she's very much admired in the country.'

'Indeed is she,' replied the Dowager, rather tartly, 'and in the town too, Mrs Campbell. There's young Mr Fairholm the Advocate, he did nothing but dance after her early and late. I'm sure I've often thought his business maun hae been sairly neglected. And what's mair, there was Major Spankie, him that's to be heir to auld Glenspankie, and is very weel to do as it is already. At the last Assembly we were at, I promise you he danced a hornpipe wi' her, forbye a *minuet de la cour*, and a wheen reels after supper. Annie Muir might haud her head high enough, if she were like some folk; but she's a modest lassie, and I'm sure she'll never covet ony thing aboon her own proper condition; though, let me tell you, the Doctor has been forty-four years minister of Cambuslee, and Cambuslee's another kind of stipend frae the like of Cross-Meikle here, and he's ay been a quiet living, canny, careful carle; and, my word, I'se warrant Annie Muir will hae a braw little penny to her tocher, Mrs Campbell. Do you no think now, mem, it would be a very proper connexion?'

'No, ma'am,' answered Mrs Campbell, her face flushing with sudden crimson, 'no, ma'am, I assure you, I think no such matters, and I assure you it is the last proposal I should have expected to hear from one who knows Mr Blair so well as you do. What! marry Adam Blair to the first pair of red cheeks and blue eyes that happen to cross his path, and this, forsooth, because he is alone, and a sufferer from solitude! Would it make *him* feel less solitary to have fifty pretty faces like *that* staring round it like so many painted Cupids' heads on a picture frame? I trust Adam Blair knows himself better, and that Miss Muir will lose no time in arranging her affairs, either with Mr Fairholm the Advocate, or young Glenspankie, or somebody else that will suit her better, and, take my word for it, make her a happier woman in the long run. – Mrs Semple,' she added, in a quieter and more serious tone of voice, 'I have seen something of human life in my day, more perhaps than it is good for any woman to see if she can help it; but depend upon it, that if there be one curse that has come to earth as the crow flies, and with all the poisonous steam of hell hot about it, it is that of an ILL-ASSORTED MARRIAGE.'

'An ill-assorted marriage!' quoth the old lady, with an air of great surprise; – 'I protest, Mrs Campbell, I cannot pretend just to follow you. You go on, mem, at a wonderful rate when once you begin. One would have supposed that something very horrible had been mentioned, mem. I believe there are few young lairds on Clydeside that would turn up their noses at Annie Muir, in the way that you seem to think the minister of Cross-Meikle should do, mem. Different people have different ways of considering things, mem; but I confess I am something at a loss, – I confess ye dinna just take me with you, Mrs Campbell.'

'It is no matter,' said Charlotte; 'and yet,' she continued, after a moment's pause, 'I don't see why I should not speak my mind as honestly as you have yours. Mr Blair is a man of a strong mind, and of strong feelings. He loved his wife, and how could he do otherwise when she adored him as she did! and yet even his wife – even my poor dear Isobel – even she perhaps was not what Adam Blair's wife should have been. His talents are as powerful as his passions. My God! what a lover, what a husband would he not have been, had he fallen in with one moulded, soul as well as heart, in the same cast with himself!'

'Mrs Campbell,' whispered Mrs Semple, 'my opinion is, that all this now is nothing but romantic palavers. My woman, God does not scrimp his creatures of happiness the way you fancy – there could not be a happier couple——'

She was interrupted by a piercing scream from Mrs Campbell, who instantly rushed from her side, dashed down through among the brushwood which clothed the bank of the stream, and had disappeared from her view before she had the least suspicion of what had taken her away. The old lady followed her steps as nimbly as she could, but it was not an easy matter for her to force her way through the entanglements of the copse, and a minute or two had elapsed ere she gained the brink of the river. A heavy plunge in the water reached her ear before she gained it, and the sudden sense of something terrible was so strong as to prevent her from being able to cry out, although not to arrest her progress. The first object that met her view was a man's hat floating close past her on the surface of the stream, and a hasty glance upwards shewed her, the moment after, Mr Blair struggling deep in the pool with his daughter in his arms, and Mrs Campbell wading rapidly towards them, with her arms stretched out to their utmost extent, and her long black hair already dipping into the water every time she advanced a step farther from the shore. The old lady stood completely immovable, petrified with fear, unable either to stir head or foot, or even to utter a single exclamation for help, shaking all over, as feeble as an infant. Her eyes remained fixed on the water, as if by some horrible fascination, and she saw every thing with that sort of painful, helpless, clearness of vision, of which we have all been sensible in a shocking dream. She saw Mr Blair struggling fiercely, encumbered with the load of his child, the child herself with wide eyes staring round and round, and now and then sobbing audibly; she saw that his steps were, every instant, tottering more and more; – and, at last, a plunge and a cry – and, for a moment, they both sunk entirely under the water. The next moment Mrs Campbell had seized Mr Blair by the hair of the head, and was dragging him at the full stretch of her arm, him and his child together, back into the shallow part of the stream; – a mist covered her eyes, everything swam indistinctly before her; she sunk down upon the turf in a reeling stupor, and remained totally blind and insensible until long after the whole was at an end.

When she awoke from this kind of swoon into

which she had fallen, the old lady found herself in the arms of her son, who was sitting on the grass by her side, and laving water upon her face and neck. A little way off, Mr Blair was standing upright, dripping all over from head to foot, while Mrs Campbell, of course equally wet, seemed to be entirely occupied with little Sarah, who was sitting panting at her feet, and sobbing as if her heart would break. Mrs Campbell was on her knees, stooping over the child, soothing and caressing her with whispers and kisses, and apparently quite unconscious either of what she herself had undergone, or of the state in which her exertions had left her person. Her hair, as we have already seen, had been flung loose at the beginning; – she had lost her shawl, her neckkerchief, her cap, all the lighter parts of her dress, in the progress of the struggle; and, in short, she was now as thinly and as moistly clad as any goddess or nymph of the sea that ever Guido drew, or Flaxman modelled. Mr Blair, who had stood for a moment with his arms folded upon his breast, as if half bewildered with so many sudden transitions, now fell upon his knees close beside Charlotte and his child, and throwing one arm round each, he drew them both towards his bosom, and began to kiss them alternately, cheek, and brow, and lip, and neck, hastily and passionately, as if ignorant or careless that they were within sight of any one. He paused for a moment, and casting his eyes upwards, ejaculated some brief syllables of thanksgiving – and then stooping again, imprinted a hundred fervid kisses more, until Charlotte, tearing herself out of his embrace,

and pushing him away from her, fixed her eyes stedfastly upon his countenance, and began to shake and
tremble all over, as if now, for the first time, she had become sensible to the peril through which they all had
passed. She gazed, and gazed with suffusing eyes, and
pale lips, fixed immovable as if by some freezing spell,
and then flinging herself forwards into his bosom, began to weep, sob, scream, and laugh, all in a breath, like
a maniac. By slow degrees, her agony exhausted itself;
then, gathering herself up again, she sat with downcast
eyes, silent tears pouring over her cheeks, and parting
the wet curls from off her forehead with her quivering
fingers.

Mrs Semple now drew near, and after whispering
something to Dr Muir and her son, about Mrs Campbell's appearance, and the propriety of retiring, and desiring Miss Muir to take little Sarah in her arms, she
herself raised Mrs Campbell gently from the ground,
and began to lead her along the walk towards the upper
part of the garden. At first Mrs Campbell walked
rather firmly, leaning partly on Mr Blair, and partly on
the old lady, and they were making progress very considerably more than might have been expected. But ere
long her limbs seemed to fail altogether, and she would
have sunk once more to the ground, had not Blair
caught her, and supported her in his arms. He hesitated
for a moment; but Mrs Semple motioned to him what
he must do, and so he lifted her like a child. She sat in
his arms with her flowing ringlets hanging down over
his face, and her hands about his neck; and he, feeble

as he had seemed to be but a few minutes before, walked with a steady, though not a swift step, beneath his burden.

When they reached the house, they found that beds were already prepared by the directions of Mr Semple, who had run home before the rest of the party. Charlotte and the child were conveyed both into the same apartment, where Mrs Semple and her maids immediately began to undress them, and to chafe their limbs with hot wine, after the most approved fashion in all similar cases. The room was soon darkened, and nobody but the good dowager herself remained to watch over their repose.

As for Mr Blair, he was soon equipped in a suit of the young squire's clothes; but he did not leave the room in which he had shifted his dress until the great bell had been twice rung; after which he was summoned to dinner more effectually by a visit of the old butler himself.

About two hours might have passed in the interim, and a great part of that time he was observed sitting in the same posture by the window, which, by the way, commanded a fine view of the garden terraces, the bright river far down among the trees, and the waving bank of copse-wood on the opposite side of the glen.

Chapter
10

————·•★)(★•·————

There is always some little awkwardness perceptible in the demeanour of people, when, after partaking in, or even perhaps witnessing, a scene of great excitement, they meet each other for the first time, under circum⸗stances of perfect security and repose. This sort of em⸗barrassment was sufficiently observable even in the good dowager of Semplehaugh and her other guests; but it was very strikingly so in Mr Blair and Mrs Camp⸗bell, when they found themselves together that day in the dining⸗room.

Perhaps their appearance was much more noticed by the rest of the company, in consequence of their being clad, both of them, in other peoples' clothes; and, as it happened, in a style of dress very different from what either of them were usually accustomed to wear. Mr Blair had put on a suit of Mr Semple's, made in the ordinary fashion of the time; but, of course, in colour and in every other particular, unlike his own clerical garb. It was a plain suit of brown kerseymere, with but a very slight edging of silver, and it fitted his shape very well; but this, together with the substitution of a rich lace cravat for a linen stock, was enough to alter him so much, that, I believe, had none of them actually known who he was, he might have passed any one of the party in the streets of Edinburgh or Glasgow without any great risk of being recognized for the minister of Cross-Meikle. Mrs Campbell, on the other hand, after bursting one or two pairs of silk sleeves for Miss Muir, had been compelled to content herself with what the wardrobe of the dowager afforded, and you may believe that she began to rummage among the drawers that were laid open for her inspection with very slender hopes of finding any thing quite worthy of her wearing. After turning over an infinitude of black and grey dresses, she had recourse to an enormous chest, in which Mrs Semple kept those articles of gayer attire, the use of which she had discontinued ever since the death of her husband: (for in those days, the reader must know, Scottish widows and Scottish grandmothers were not a whit ashamed of being dressed like widows and grandmothers:) Here, there was no lack of splendour at least – here was heap on heap, and layer on layer –

> 'The velvet, smooth and rich, display'd
> Beneath its fret-work of brocade:
> The long luxurious fardingale
> Of damask dark, or satin pale:
> And all on end with silver set,
> The thin transparent tabbinet.'

Mrs Campbell's only difficulty was to find something not over conspicuous, (for even then the rage for costly glare in dress had begun to be something on the decline) and she, in the end, made selection of a petticoat and train of pale green satin, wrought over with silken fleurs-de-lis of the same colour, as the most modest set of garments this repository of discarded finery afforded. Her thick tresses were still too moist for being worn uncovered, and none of Mrs Semple's ancient head-dresses were such as she could venture to display; so she tied a veil of white lace round her head, in something of the same sort of style which one still sees retained in the costume of the Parisian Grisettes. Nor, on the whole, did this borrowed attire do any very essential injury to Mrs Campbell's appearance; for the truth is, that it is no easy matter for a young woman to make herself look old by wearing an old woman's habiliments, any more than for an old woman to make herself pass for a girl by dressing herself like one. On the contrary, I believe the general impression of the company was, that although Mrs Campbell was one of the finest women imaginable, when she arrived at Semplehaugh that day, in the full flush of health and exercise; she was a lovelier creature now, in spite both of the paleness of her face, and the old-fashioned green garb, which, no doubt, tended to make her appear even paler than she was. The effects of the violent agitations she had undergone were visible enough in a sort of flutter of the nerves, which she in vain endeavoured to conceal, and in many little changes of her complexion. For although she kept her eyes very downcast for the most part, whenever she lifted them up and met the glance of any of the gentle-men, a slight blush would just cross her cheek and brow, and then leave them as pale as before – as you may have seen in some fine winter evening a snow-covered hill catch and reflect some soft crimson gleam of the setting sun, and then lie, after a moment, as white as ever against the sky. They, however, suspected the cause of her confusion, and they were polite enough to do all they could to spare it; Mr Blair alone was either less knowing or less well-bred than the rest, for he could scarcely keep his eye off her for a moment, although every time her eyes met his, her look grew more down-cast, and her blush deeper in its glow. But, to say the truth, Mr Blair himself had almost as much the look of embarrassment as the lady. Like her he felt himself a stranger in a strange garb; and although he was natur-ally a graceful man in his demeanour, and would have become any dress well had he been accustomed to it, it is not to be denied, that the sight of a clergyman evi-dently ill at ease in a lay attire, produced an occasional smile, which was by no means the likeliest thing in the whole world to restore what part of his self-posses-sion had been lost or shaken. Besides, whatever other causes of confusion had influenced Mrs Campbell's mind, we may fairly imagine that they might also be, in some degree, partaken on this occasion by Mr Blair.

The old lady, with all her disposition for talking, had *tact* enough to feel that she would be doing nobody a service by introducing the subject of the morning's accident. She kept off it therefore, and indeed gave it the go-by rather sharply, when it was once slightly broached by Miss Anne Muir. But the old Doctor, who was deafish, and never more so than when he disapproved of what was said, would not understand any of Mrs Semple's considerate hints, and kept up, during the greater part of dinner, a sort of running under-chorus of remarks and interrogations, and exclamations, every one of which added something to the painful state of Mrs Campbell's sensations. The great praises he lavished on herself were, above all, extremely disagreeable to her; and, upon the whole, I believe no lady was ever more glad to leave a dinner-table set in a roar by a party of jolly sportsmen, in the incipient glories of inebriety, than she was to quit that respectable board, surrounded as it was, by as sober and decent a company as could well have been brought together in the same room. And, indeed, so intent was the worthy old Doctor on his theme, that I suspect the lady might have found it almost as difficult a matter to escape from his *prose*, as ever any poor stunned damsel did to get away from the melodious verse of 'Bright god Cupid,' or 'Little Frank was belabouring a broken-down hack,' – or

> 'At five in the morning, by most of the clocks,
> We rode from Kilruddery in quest of a fox.' ——

Mrs Semple, however, very luckily for her, was one of those ladies who would have thought it about as strange a thing to witness two circulations of the bottle

111

after the cloth was removed, as to see the sun rise and set twice within the four-and-twenty hours. The female part of the company, therefore, withdrew very early to the drawing-room; and it was not long after their retiring ere a message was brought to Mr Blair to signify that Mrs Campbell, finding herself not very well, Mrs Semple had ordered the carriage to take her home to Cross-Meikle, and that she would be ready to set off if he pleased, in few minutes.

I have said it was not long before this message was whispered into Mr Blair's ear; but, nevertheless, there had, in the interim, been room enough for the bottle to make its circuit rather more frequently than Mr Blair was much in the habit of witnessing. Mr Semple liked a free glass, as most of the gentlemen of that day did; and Dr Muir, though he never tasted anything but simple element when he dined with his family at home, was not a man to take offence at a little occasional relaxation of those very rigid rules of abstemiousness to which he in general conformed. Mr Blair had probably never been touched with liquor in his life, or, at least, not for many years, nor did he drink as much wine now as would have made the smallest impression on most men of his standing; yet the little he did take, although it caused no visible change in his appearance or manner, was enough, in the state in which his nerves were, to produce a slight degree of internal elevation. The first sensations of awkwardness and embarrassment having gone by, his mind was at leisure to dwell upon the happy termination of the perilous accident which had occurred; and, the feelings natural at such a moment being heightened by the genial influences of the wine he had swallowed, he was assuredly in a temper for regarding all things about him with the utmost benignity and complaisance, when he stepped into the carriage after his daughter, and the common preserver of his own life and hers.

Mrs Campbell sat in the corner opposite to him, pale, but composed in her aspect; and the motion of the carriage, and the air together, as they went on, seemed by degrees to refresh and revive her. Sarah, quite recovered from her panic, sat beside them prattling all the way; – the sun shone bright from the western sky upon the wide beautiful valley; the noble river winded gently and calmly far below, and a pervading breath of cheerfulness was everywhere above and around them. There was nothing of the boisterousness of glee; but I believe they were all in that quietly happy state of mind to which boisterous glee is as inferior a thing as possible. – During the most part of the ride, both Charlotte and Mr Blair kept their eyes on the fine landscape, but every now and then they exchanged silent glances of gratitude and gratulation.

The sun had just disappeared from the edge of the horizon as they reached Cross-Meikle; and when they left the carriage, every thing was so beautiful in earth and heaven, that neither of them could think of going into the house. A happy woman was little Sarah, when she was desired to go in and prepare matters for serving up tea out of doors, while Mr Blair and Mrs Campbell, without thinking of the odd dresses in which they were arrayed, sat down together in a low garden-chair, beneath the ancient and celebrated hawthorn tree, which stands (or stood) in the centre of the little green before the door of the Manse. This was by far the finest thorn in the whole vale, and its beauty had always been a matter of great pride both with Mr Blair and his wife, – and indeed with every body who had lived there. A few dozen yards off, one might easily have taken it for a small oak, it was so round in the head, so dark in the foliage, so straight and massive in the trunk, and so considerable in stature; – but at this time, it was in full blossom, indeed so much so, that it had, at a little distance, the appearance of being quite covered with a feathering of snow-flakes. Nothing could be more charming than the perfume exhaled from this fine tree all around it; and every time the breeze passed through the boughs overhead, the richest of odours and of garlands came raining down together upon the place where they were sitting. The fervours of the day had gone by, but the reflected glow that still lingered upon the surface of nature, was sufficient to make them relish the exquisite coolness of a spot which had been all day long sheltered and shaded from the sun's rays; – and so there they sat together, side-by-side, in silence, enjoying, in a sort of half-languid mood, the calm, and the beauty, and the fragrance, of the lovely evening.

Neither Mr Blair nor Mrs Campbell were aware of any body being near where they were sitting, until they were addressed in a pitiful tone of voice by an old man, clad in very tattered garments, who had walked over the turf towards them, and was now standing but a few paces off, with his head bare, and in an attitude of supplication. Mr Blair was familiar with the faces of almost all the beggars who were used to make their rounds in that district of the country, so that he was a little surprised with finding himself addressed in this manner by a person whom he could not recollect ever having seen before in his life. But there was something in the appearance of the old man which might have commanded some attention, even in a place where mendicants were many and their visits frequent, and which could not therefore fail to procure him kind looks and words in such a region as this – above all, from such people as he was now addressing. He was a singularly fine-looking old man; he was lame in one leg, and had a crutch which he handled with the air of a halberdier; and besides, though his raiment was poor enough, it was not arranged without something of that sort of neatness, which commonly distinguishes your old soldier from most other persons in the lower ranks of life.

He stood bare-headed, as I have said, before them, and while a few thin grey hairs were blowing back and forwards about his bald temples in the breeze, began to tell all the long story of his griefs and sufferings. His tone was querulous, and his voice feeble; but while he spoke of the scenes through which it had been the fortune of his manhood to pass, it was easy to see that all his enthusiasm had not been banished by the sense

of age, infirmity, and poverty. There was still lingering
about his aspect –

> 'Something that spoke of other days,
>   When trumpets pierced the kindling air,
> And the keen eye could firmly gaze
>   Through battle's crimson glare.'

After he had ended his tale, and received their alms,
the old man bowed himself once more on the green
before them. 'God bless you, sirs!' said he; 'God bless
you, my bonny lady! – You and your young goodman
will no sit there beneath your auld tree together this
bonny gloamin the less pleasantly for having helped a
puir body in his need; no, nor yet when night comes, will
ye sleep the less soundly, wi' your head in his bosom,
because you have gotten an auld man's blessing wi' you.
Be happy, be happy, sirs, while you can. I mind the
day when I had a canty wife o' my ain, and a bit garden
too, and a bower, and a tree, and a' the lave o't in a puir
way; but that's lang gane by, sirs, and happy as ye be,
you'll maybe live to see that there's a dark face of things
as weel as a fair one. Good night, my bonny lady, I wish
you baith a sweet sleep, and braw pleasant dreams.
Take care ye dinna stay out ower lang, now the sun's
gane down.'

'Good night, good night, old man,' said Mr Blair,
rather hastily; and then he added, after a little pause,
'we're not man and wife, as ye take us to be, friend – but
we are not the less obliged to you for your good wishes.'

'I crave your pardon, sir,' said the old soldier, bowing

himself very low; 'and I crave the bonny lady's pardon – I am sure I meant nae harm; but,' – (and the old man smiled as he spoke,) – 'but I see I have waukened mair blushes than I should have done, and I'm very sorry if I've said any thing that's disagreeable. But though you're no man and wife now, ye'll maybe be sae ere yon braw thorn shakes down a' its white blossoms; and then ye'll no hae ony leisure to be angry at the auld man's mistake. Good e'en again I wish you both, and God bless you for your kindness.'

So saying, he turned from them, and walked slowly, leaning on his crutch and staff, towards the village. Mr Blair followed him with his eyes for a minute or two, for there was something or other that made him avoid encountering Mrs Campbell's looks just at that moment. Sarah joined them immediately, however, and then that feeling, whatever it was, passed away. If Charlotte had indeed blushed while the old soldier was speaking, there was no blush upon her cheek now; nay, in truth, she was paler than she had been even during the former part of the afternoon. She sat sipping her tea for a long while in perfect silence, and trifled with the spoon after the cup was empty, not heeding, as it seemed, one word of all that little Sarah prattled at her knee. Mr Blair watched her looks, and perceiving that she shivered once or twice, as if from cold, said, he was afraid she might injure herself by sitting out any later. She rose when he said so, and that so feebly, that it seemed as if she should scarcely be able to walk even the few paces to the door without assistance. He offered

his arm, therefore, and he felt her trembling and shivering more than ever, as she leaned upon it across the
green. On entering the house, she said, in a faint tone
of voice, 'I believe I have really had my nerves shaken
a little to-day. I think, Adam – I think I had much
better go up at once to my own room.'

'I think so too,' said Mr Blair; 'and I hope you will
go to bed immediately, and Sarah and I will try to
make a glass of white-wine whey for you, and you will
be quite well after a sleep.'

'Thank you, thank you both,' said Mrs Campbell;
'but if you will only lend me your arm till I get up
stairs, I believe I shall be better without any thing.'

She walked up stairs, therefore, still leaning upon
his arm, and they had both entered her bed-room before
Mr Blair was aware whither she had led him. When
he had seated her in the armchair by her bed-side, and
looked round, and perceived that he was in the forbidden chamber, which he had never entered since the
night before his wife's funeral, he started suddenly, as if
from a dream, and with one hurried 'good night,'
walked as hastily as his feet could carry him out of the
room. He met one of the female servants on the stair,
whispered to her that she had better go and attend to
Mrs Campbell, and then taking his hat, passed out into
the open air, and walked away from the house, without
casting one glance behind him.

He did not approach it again until the moon was
risen; nor even then did he for some little time enter the
Manse. He sat down by himself under the old haw-

thorn, and continued there, leaning on his elbow, with a very listless air, till one of the servants came out and told him that supper was on the table. Little Sarah had, of course, retired to rest for some time, so that he sat down quite alone, and it was the first evening he had done so ever since Mrs Campbell's arrival at Cross-Meikle. I believe he did not taste a single thing but a glass of water; and in the course of a few minutes, he was heard going very softly up stairs to his bed-room. His servants were waiting, in the expectation of being summoned, as usual, to prayers; but when they found he had left the parlour for the night, they took it for granted he had been afraid Mrs Campbell might be disturbed.

Chapter

II

—••⋲)(⋹••—

It was long ere Mr Blair fell asleep that night, but exhausted nature at last sunk under the burden of reflection; and, for several hours, he lay buried in slumber as
profound as had ever visited his eyelids.

He awoke, sitting bolt-upright in his bed, his hands
clenched violently together, his night-cap off, his hair
on end, and the sweat standing in big and palpable
drops upon his forehead, and the sound of his own
screaming voice in his ear. He clasped his brows, and
staring wildly about him in the dim chamber, strove
instinctively, rather than consciously, to retrace the outlines of what he now felt to be nothing but a dream,
although he was still too much agitated with its delu-
sions to be able to enjoy the sense of reality and repose.
Everything, however, as he looked back, seemed to become darkened the moment his mental eye approached
it; – every strong and distinct image seemed to vanish,
and leave but a vapour behind it, and it was in vain he
endeavoured to make out any consistent or intelligible

notion of what had passed – although a sort of confused and distorted 'cloudland' of terrible things still continued to lour above the whole surface of his imagination——The black river – the sob of his child – the water gushing into his eyes and ears, and then closing with a rushing sound over his head – the agony of mortal terror – the joy of sudden deliverance – the tears of joy – these had all been with him, and he felt that they had been with him as vividly as during the waking hours of the eventful day before. But other images had followed these, some of them as dark and as terrible, but the whole texture of which seemed now to elude the grasp of his remembrance. He had a sort of obscure sense of having been fighting, wrestling, combatting fiercely, hand in hand, with some strong adversary; – whether he had stood or fallen he could not tell, but there was such a mixture of the feelings of wrath and sorrow, that this was as nothing: –

> 'Fantastic passions! maddening brawl!
> And shame and terror over all! –
> Deeds to be hid which were not hid –
> Which, all confused, he could not know
> Whether he suffer'd, or he did: –
> For all seem'd guilt, remorse, or woe –
> His own or others', still the same,
> Life's stifling fear – soul stifling shame.'

What did not diminish, but much increase and strengthen the pain and horror of all this, was, that a sort of voluptuous, languid, sultry air, seemed to hang over the whole mass of the retrospect: Red setting suns –

broad, calm, purple skies – mighty trees, loaded with leaves and blossoms – these were the strange accompaniments – strangely jumbled together and ill defined, it is true – of screams, and battles, and headlong peril, and blood, and death, and misery. Beautiful women's shapes, smiling eyes, and burning blushes, darted in glimpses here and there from amidst the thickest of tumults. Every thing was waxing every moment obscurer and dimmer, as he gazed back upon it. – He leaped from his bed, flung aside the window curtains, and the last faint traces seemed to vanish before the first gleam of the open day light.

He leaned over the window to inhale the refreshing breath of the morning air, enriched as it came to him through the sweet briars that clustered all about the window; and while his eye wandered away over the bright fields, on the face of which every tree had flung its long westward shadow, or rested on the grey sky which was swiftly clearing and kindling into splendour as the sun advanced, the memory not only of his troubled visions from which he had so recently started, but even of the pain they had left behind them, passed far away into the back ground, and mingled with the thousand and ten thousand dreams that had sent their shadows thither long before from hours both of sleeping and of waking life.

He had continued for a long time in the same posture, and his thoughts were gradually becoming serene, like the face of nature before his eyes; when, suddenly, he heard the sound of Mrs Campbell's voice. She was singing in a clear and beautiful tone, by herself, at the window of the adjoining apartment. The strength of her voice was such, that he felt she must have perfectly recovered from all the agitation of nerves which had been perceptible in her demeanour on the preceding evening; indeed, though he had often heard her sing the same song before, it appeared to him that she had never sung it with the same effect. It was the well-known old ballad, 'Saw ye my father,' and she sung it on as far as the verse –

'The cock proved fause, and untrue he was,
For he crew an hour too soon;
The lassie thought it day when she sent her love away,
But it was but a blink of the moon.'

He had heard out the stanza, and was listening quietly for the next, when his servant tapped at the door of his room, and came forward to him with a letter in his hand, which he said had just been brought by a servant from a neighbouring gentleman's seat. Mr Blair broke the seal, which displayed a very comely coat of arms, rather encumbered with excess of quarter-ings, and found the communication to be from one of the last persons he should have thought of – his old acquaintance Duncan Strahan, now a thriving solicitor in Edinburgh. It ran as follows: –

'Rev. and Dear Sir,
'I have come thus far from Edinburgh on my way to your residence, for the purpose of transacting some

business with Mrs Campbell of Uigness, who, I understand, has been for some time living in family with you.
I should have given Mrs Campbell more timeous notice had it been in my power, but it was only the day
before yesterday that I received Uigness his letter, which
caused me set off without delay, as the business it concerns is of urgency. Therefore, I hope the blame of
arriving so suddenly will not be laid at my door.
Hoping to find all with you well, I remain, Rev. and
dear Sir, with esteem, your obedient servant,

'DUNCAN STRAHAN.'

This letter was written on very fine paper gilt at the
edges, and in a hand-writing, more particularly the
signature, by no means destitute of pretension. These
circumstances, together with the heraldic emblems on
the seal, and the laconic and somewhat dignified strain
of the epistle itself, could not fail to make Mr Blair cast
an eye backward to the days when Duncan Strahan
spent twelve hours out of the four-and-twenty, on a tall
three-legged stool in the most dismal corner of old Mr
Monypenny's writing-chamber, and thought himself
a fortunate man if he could command cash enough to
console the evening of his busy day with a welsh rabbit,
and a pint of very small twopenny at THE COFFIN
IN THE WALL. 'Most wonderful,' quoth he to himself,
'most wonderful indeed it is how these Edinburgh
writers do thrive!' But part, at least, of this not unnatural, nor, to say the truth, very original exclamation,
might perhaps have been spared or altered, had Mr

124

Blair known that Duncan Strahan, who had received his first pair of shoes and stockings from Mr Monypenny's bounty, and in the sequel risen to be his master's partner only through the continued exercise of great generosity and kindness on the part of that old gentleman, had, about six years before, seen his benefactor's head laid in the grave, and proceeded to shew his respect for his memory by devising and executing a scheme which terminated about two years after in the total ruin of his son and family. Taking advantage of the youth and inexperience of his old patron's representative, he had prevailed on him to consent to some alteration of the terms of the co-partnership, and the upshot was, that 'Monypenny and Strahan' soon became one of the firms that had been, while 'Duncan Strahan, w.s.' was blazoned in single brightness on door, ledger, and strong-box. Young Monypenny having ere long become food for gun-powder on the banks of the Rhine, he and his story had, of course, passed speedily together into oblivion; while Duncan Strahan, ascending gradually but surely in the scale of his professional honours, had already become laird of the very acres on which

—— 'The braw bairn
Had of old tended sheep in the county of Nairn;'

and begun to regard it as the reverse of improbable that he might end his days in the 'otium cum dignitate' of The Clerk's Table.

Such was the great man whose arrival was scarcely announced at Cross-Meikle, ere it actually took place.

For Mr Blair, not expecting Mr Strahan to come before breakfast, did not think of communicating the intelligence he had received to Mrs Campbell until she should have quitted her bed-chamber; and, in fact, she had just entered the parlour, and was in the act of perusing the letter in question, when a sharp rattling of wheels was heard in the lane, and forthwith up drove a tolerably smart chariot, containing the important person of Duncan Strahan, w. s.

Duncan had not fed on the fat of the land for ten years, without exhibiting the natural effects of his cheer in his countenance. Instead of a pale, yellow-faced youth, with fustian sleeves, there stept forth a portly, rosy-faced gentleman, clad in a handsome suit of sables, with lace ruffles, and a neat tie periwig.

He desired the postillion to put up his horses in a voice of great authority, and then approached the door of the Manse with not a little of that condescending air which great men are sometimes good enough to display when they enter the dwellings of people whom they are pleased to consider as their inferiors.

He was received by Mr Blair with the civility due to old acquaintanceship, although the minister, from observing the countenance of Mrs Campbell, while she was reading the letter, had already formed no slender suspicions that the visit boded no good to her, – and was therefore far from being gratified with its occurrence. Mrs Campbell, on her part, was so much a woman of the world, as to be able to suppress her own private feelings on such an occasion as this, and she met Strahan's courteous, perhaps even fawning salutation, with all the apparent ease of a person having no reason either to hope or to fear anything from his arrival. Breakfast being served up almost immediately, there was no opportunity for entering at once on business, and the meal passed amidst a succession of such common-places as usually fill the room of conversation between people who have been long acquainted with each other, and never dreamed of being friends, – and who meet after years of separation, rather with the feeling that something ought to be said, than with any particular predilection in favour of one topic of table-talk more than another.

The dulnesses of Edinburgh and the middle Ward of Lanarkshire having been exchanged, and the proper quantity of boiled eggs, oat-meal cakes, and honey-comb consumed, Mr Strahan kept his seat in silence for a few seconds, and then rising, said with a low bow, that he had to crave the honour of a few minutes' conversation in private with Mrs Campbell. 'Certainly, oh certainly!' answered the Lady, in a tone of great indifference; 'I shall fetch my bonnet, and, if you please, we may walk round the garden together.' Having said so, she tripped out of the room, and returned bonnetted and shawled, although not perhaps quite so quickly as might have been expected from the style of her exit. She had also a long black veil in her hand, and it did not escape Mr Blair's notice, that although this formed no part of her usual walking costume, it had been arranged very deliberately, so as to cover the whole of her face and neck, before she and her attendant had proceeded more than three steps over the green.

Mr Blair followed them with his eyes, until the thick and high beech hedge which surrounded the garden, concealed them from his view. While they continued within sight, their pace was leisurely, and they seemed, so far as he could judge, to be saying little to each other, and that little without emotion; – yet, when they had disappeared from his view, he could not help being filled with a sort of heavy presentiment that all was not right, and that Charlotte would not return from that walk so happy as she had begun it. The manner of the Solicitor had been, during the hour of breakfast, smooth of the smoothest, and no syllable had escaped his lips that could be supposed to have any relation to any subject of the painful order. Nevertheless, he had once or twice observed in Strahan's eye, when it happened to rest upon Mrs Campbell, an expression of a mixed sort – an indefinable gaze of conscious power, – and he could not but suppose, of conscious mischief – which had not struck him the less for being followed by the blandest of smiles. In Mrs Campbell's demeanour, on the other hand, cool and indifferent as it had been meant, and as on the whole it appeared to be, there had not escaped him a little occasional flutter – a hasty glance now and then of something between fear and scorn. Altogether, that instinct by which the movements of the stronger passions are detected, in spite of all the art that may be used to conceal them, had done its duty: – and Blair, during the time they remained together in his garden, would have betrayed, had any one been there to notice him, by every gesture of his body, as well as by every motion of his features, a sense of painful perplexity, totally different from, and not in the least to be mistaken for, the common workings of curiosity. He continued a long while walking backwards and forwards in the parlour, and casting an anxious glance from the window every time he passed it. Little Sarah spoke to him over and over again, without being able to get any answer from him, more than an indistinct *hem*, or a hasty pat on the head as he walked by her, – and, at last, the servants having taken away the breakfast-apparatus, the child also had retired, leaving her father alone to the meditations in which he seemed so loath to be disturbed.

Meanwhile, Mr Blair began, as anxious people will do, to overcalculate the lapse of time. They had not been away ten minutes ere he thought half an hour had passed; and when half an hour had elapsed, it seemed to him as if the whole day were about to wear away before their return. He opened the parlour door, looked at the clock in the lobby, and re-entered; walked six or eight times more up and down the room, re-opened the door, re-examined the clock, and again resumed his walk.

In short, his fretfulness was great, and increasing momently, when he at last saw Mrs Campbell walking alone towards the house with rapid steps; and Strahan, who had lingered behind her, leaning with his elbow, in a thoughtful attitude, on the garden wicket. He had his fingers instantly on the handle of the door, and was in the act of opening it, when he heard Mrs Campbell run along the passage, and up the stairs, her dress rustling as she moved, so as to shew that she was in great haste. He opened the door more deliberately than he had intended; and walking forth slowly from the portico, directed his steps towards Mr Strahan, – who, on his part, although he was evidently aware of Mr Blair's approach, did not in the least alter his position, but remained as if waiting for him; and this with an air of the most perfect composure, – except only, that he once or twice bit his lips; which, after all, might have been a matter of mere habit.

Mr Blair had come within a very few steps of Strahan ere he made any alteration in his leaning posture. He then exchanged it for one of at least equal *nonchalance*. He balanced himself in a careless way on his left foot, his right shuffling back and forwards behind it, thrust both his hands deep into his breeches' pockets, and looking into the clergyman's face, with a smile of the calmest self-complacency, 'Mr Blair,' said he, 'you have really got a very snug little shop here; upon my honour, Blair, I half envy you your retirement; a perfect bird's-nest of a place! – By Jove, I don't know but you demure-looking fellows in the country here understand life, after all, as well as your neighbours. – How much may the thing be worth? – Come now, ha! speak honestly, what may you touch in a fair average year, Blair? A rich country, a very fine rich country this! pray, how long may it be since you had your last augmentation, Blair?'

'Five years come Michaelmas,' answered Adam; 'but oh, Mr Strahan,' he proceeded more rapidly, 'what's this that's going forward? – Nay, you need not put on that look, Mr Strahan. I'm sure you've given Mrs Campbell some ill news, and whatever they be, I must e'en hear them – I got but a glimpse of her face as she passed the window, but that was enough. – What *is* it, Mr Strahan, that you should be so unwilling——'

'Then you did not speak with Mrs Campbell,' interrupted the Writer; 'then she has not informed you of her purpose to set off with me immediately?'

Blair, starting back, said, with a half incredulous waive of his hand, 'Set off immediately, Mr Strahan? what? and with *you*?'

'Yes, with *me*, sir,' resumed Strahan, and speaking very quickly indeed; – 'with me, sir, and with whom else should she go, when Uigness has sent his commands for her to submit herself entirely to my conduct? – You may stare as much as you please, Mr Blair, but I suppose it is not the first time I have been trusted with as delicate pieces of business as this comes to, even take it at the worst; – which I am by no means inclined to do; – although, by G——, sir, let me tell you,' and his colour rose as if to set off his oath, 'I can't say that most people would be more likely to put the most charitable construction on things, for having seen what I have seen this morning in the lady – no, nor (damme! why should not I speak it out?) for what I have seen in yourself.'

He ended with a very firm compression of his lips,

and pointing his eyes like two darts upon Mr Blair's face, said, or seemed to say to himself, that he had given the minister his *quietus*. Blair gazed back upon him for a moment or two in silence, and this with an air of such simple surprise, that he began to doubt the penetration of his own craft. The instant after, however, a deep flush of indignation, or some other fiery passion, rose in Mr Blair's face to the very eyes, and the Writer no doubt mistook what he saw for the livery of shame and guilt, for his countenance immediately relaxed into a grin of superior delight. He whistled a few notes of *Tuttie Tattie*, and then said in a half whisper, 'Come, come, Mr Adam Blair, you entirely mistake my intentions. I see how it is, but upon my soul you are safe – perfectly safe, damme! We're all flesh and blood: a minister's but a man after all, and Charlotte is *un peu passée*, to be sure, but a fine woman still, a fine woman, a very fine woman still, 'pon honour. Damme, don't be afraid, man, snug's the word with Duncan Strahan. I would not expose you, man, although you had kissed half your parish; cheer up, Blair, we are off immediately, for Campbell gave me no law in the business: she must just put up with the old tower till Uigness comes home, and who can tell but they may come together and be very happy again, once this new suspicion has got time to blow over.'

'Sir,' said Blair, as pale as marble and as immovable, – Sir, – Mr Duncan Strahan, – I tell you, sir, your suspicions, or his, or whosever they be, are false, foul, black as hell! – I call God to witness——'

It was Sarah that interrupted him. She came, moving as swiftly as her feet would carry her, over the green, and catching her father by the hand, cried, 'Papa, Mrs Campbell's up in the room packing her trunk. Come away, papa, and speak to her – Mrs Campbell will no say a word to me.'

The moment the child began to speak, Mr Strahan turned upon his heel, and walked into the garden with a firm and deliberate step, whistling to himself as he went. Mr Blair suffered his daughter to lead him towards the house, but made no answer to the innumerable questions she kept putting to him all the way. She kept her hold of his hand, and conducted him up stairs. The door of Mrs Campbell's room was wide open, and he saw her with her back turned towards him, kneeling on the floor over a large travelling trunk, into which she was flinging gowns, petticoats, linens, in haste and manifest disorder. She did not seem to be aware of their presence, until the child went round and knelt down before her on the other side of the trunk; and then turning suddenly, she shewed a face of steady, glowing scarlet, but filled with such a mixed expression of anger, scorn, and sorrow, as he had never before seen on any set of human features. She looked at him for a moment, and then waving her hand to him to retire, stooped down again to her work with greater pertinacity and zeal than before. He turned away, and as he descended the stair, heard her sobbing bitterly and the child crying.

He remained under the porch for some minutes in a

state of much bewilderment, until the carriage was driven round, and drawn up close by where he stood. Strahan issued from the garden the moment he heard it, and walking over the green rapidly, began to talk aloud to the postilion, but avoided even meeting Mr Blair's eyes. The next moment, the servants brought down Mrs Campbell's trunk, and Strahan was busy in helping the man to fasten it behind the carriage. The cords were just tied, when Charlotte herself was heard running down the stair. She stooped and kissed Sarah beneath the porch, and had her foot on the step of the chaise ere Mr Blair caught her hand to assist her in entering it. He would have saluted her, but, though salutes in those days meant nothing but common civility she drew back her cheek, and pulled her veil over her face ere his lips touched her. She squeezed his hand with hot and trembling fingers, at the same moment sprung into the carriage, and flung herself back in the corner of it. Blair stood in silent confusion, gazing after her. Strahan, uncovering himself, bowed very respectfully, but still without looking Blair in the face, – and, calling out, 'To Glasgow, Thomas,' – took his place instantly by Charlotte's side.

The horses were turned, and had rattled half way down the lane, ere Mr Blair took his eyes from off the vacant space which the carriage had filled before the door of his Manse.

Chapter
12

——•°⟨⟩⟨⟩°•——

A deep shade of gloom continued all that day to linger upon Mr Blair's countenance. He retired immediately to his chamber. Sarah, after a while, dried her tears, and followed him thither; but she heard her father's voice as if he was speaking earnestly within, and knowing that nobody was in the room with him, she was afraid to open the door. In a few minutes he came forth: he started on seeing the child, kissed her hastily, and without saying a word to her, ran down the stairs and passed into the garden.

He paced, for some time, back and forwards with rapid steps, uncovered, in the sun: then entered the house again, and taking his hat and his fishing-rod, walked along the village lane in the direction of the mountain-stream, which not far from thence mixes its waters with the Clyde.

He soon reached the wood of Cartriecraig; and sitting down on the brink of the shaded bank, began to arrange his fishing tackle. He dropped his line upon the surface of the pool, and kept his eyes fixed upon it, as it floated hither and thither with every creeping motion of the water-breeze, amidst the innumerable green and shining insects which were sporting in the cool shade. Any body who had seen him would have said, 'there sits a very personification of the *quiet delight* described by old Isaac Walton.'

And yet the listless and indolent attitude, and calm face of Mr Blair, were but the mask of a spirit labouring under the fever of as many restless and painful thoughts, as could well inhabit together within an innocent bosom. The scorn and wrath with which he had met the first insinuations of unmerited suspicion had indeed subsided; but the less he thought of himself now, the more was his leisure to think of poor Charlotte, suspected as basely and as foully as himself, and unlike him, compelled to endure the presence and the power of the very person whose suspicions had insulted her. When he pictured her to himself, sitting all day long, shut up in a carriage with that rude and heartless man, obliged to listen either to his odious sneers, or his more odious flatteries, and prevented by the natural timidity of her sex from saying or doing any thing to defend her; or, when looking further on, he thought of her left all alone in a desolate place, by the sea side, to brood over the ungenerous treatment with which Campbell had requited her affections, and from weary day to day to contrast her situation at Uigness with the cheerful society she had just abandoned – he could not help being filled with regret, that she should ever have come to Cross-Meikle. But then, all the long pleasant walks they had taken together – the interesting conversations which had been held – the conscious restoration of his own mental serenity – the charming, kind looks of Charlotte – and last, not least, her heroic resolution exhibited but the day before – all these images rose again fresh on his memory, and he sighed as he thought within himself how many delightful weeks would have, but for Charlotte, passed on in the same dreariness and desolation with those that had preceded them.

The longer he mused on all that had happened, the more pensive he became, and the more hopeless for poor Charlotte – while as to the rest, he could not help accusing himself of having behaved in a most unmanly and foolish manner, in not having come to some open and distinct explanation with Strahan, ere he suffered Mrs Campbell to quit the protection of his roof. 'Child! fool! coward,' said he, 'that I am! what occasion had I to be thrown off my balance by a few words of mean and knavish insult, uttered by a man whom I despised from the moment he entered my house? What prevented me from making him speak out all he had to say, and compelling him to listen to me fully and leisurely in return? What made me flush into crimson – for I felt my cheek burning – instead of looking at him with the stedfast and unshrinking eye of scornful innocence? What kept me from withering the scoundrel by a single glance? Why did I suffer *her* to endure, for one needless moment, the visible torture under which her spirit writhed as she bade us farewell? Had I acted like a friend, like a man, I might have arrested him in the midst of his vile triumph, I might have forced him to kneel in the dust before the presence of the innocence he had insulted, I might have made him turn away – yes, even *him*, with a blush, a burning blush. Poor Charlotte! she does not blame me, but well might she do so if she knew what a dastard I have been. Poor beautiful Charlotte, alas! what a dark fate seems to hang over the whole of an existence that seems as if it had been formed for happiness! What rivers of tears have been shed by those lovely eyes! How gaily they would have sparkled had she found a tender bosom to recline upon!' – A thousand thoughts – sorrowful, affectionate thoughts – floated after each other over his mind as he continued gazing on the face of the water; and he was roused, at last, from a reverie of hours, by the splash which his fishing-rod made in dropping from his fingers into the dark pool far below him.

The abruptness of the bank just there, rendered it necessary for him to make a considerable circuit ere he could reach the edge of the river, and by that time the fishing-rod had drifted far away into the stream. He followed it along the brink from pool to pool, and stream to stream, and at last, after wandering the better part of a mile, he came up just in time to see it enter the smooth glassy current above the small cataract of Craigtrie-fall, and then disappear over the rocks amidst the shower of spray that rises eternally from the boiling basin underneath. He strained his eyes, but could not descry the least fragment on the surface of the wide dark stream, in which the river rolls on after its fall; and after staying till his ears were half stunned, and his eyes giddy in his head, he at length bethought him, from the appearance of the heavens, that the day must be well nigh spent, and began to retrace his way homewards with slow and cheerless steps.

He found Sarah sitting on the turf at the end of the lane which leads to the Manse, and John Maxwell standing beside her. The child sprang up, and ran forwards to meet her father as soon as she saw him approaching, while John, taking off his bonnet, said, 'Oh, sirs! Mr Adam, ye've gi'en the puir bairn a fright, I trow. Whare hae you been a' day, sir? I'm sure its lang since we've heard of you trying the fishing, and this was a bonny-like day to begin the trade again, when the waters are as clear as a drop in a glass, and there's no a fish would think of rising that had sense enough to ken its head frae its tail. But ye've left your rod behint you. I dare say ye thought better when ye got to the water-side, and layed it by at Tam Ogilvie's.'

Mr Blair told John what had been the fate of the fishing-rod. The old man smiled as he heard him, and said, shaking his head, 'Weel, Mr Adam, I'll lay a saumon to a par, that I've read your thoughts for you. It's nae wonder that ye took nae tent to the bit fishing-rod, when ye had sae meikle to think about. I'm sure it's been a wae heart to me to hear the puir bairn – and I dinna doubt ye're amaist as vexed yoursel as she is wi' the loss o' yon canty cheerfu' face, that did a' body meikle good to see it – to say nothing of you that had

mair of her company. Mr Adam, I hope she'll soon be
back again amang us. But there's my callant that has
been down at Glasgow, has just come hame, and he
has brought a letter for you; – he tauld me she gied it
to him wi' her ain hand, just as she was setting off for
Greenock. She'll be gaun back to the Highlands, I'se
warrant – nae doubt her goodman will be some of the
Argyll's folk.'

John had been fumbling all the time he was speaking
about his great black leather pocket-book, and at
length, having succeeded in extricating it from amidst
I know not how many Aberdeen almanacks and
market-bills, he presented the letter in question to Mr
Blair. He received it eagerly; looked for a moment upon
the scrawled and blotted address, pressed the seal to his
lips, and tore open the envelope. He began to read
immediately, but had walked away to some little distance from John and Sarah, ere he came to the end.
The letter was as follows:—

'Glasgow, Friday afternoon.

'I cannot think, dear Mr Blair, of leaving this town
without saying a word on matters which I could not
speak of when I was leaving you this morning, and
which, perhaps, I could not speak of now, were I restored to the protection of your roof at this moment. Do
not suppose that I can think without horror, as well as
shame, of the misfortune to which you have been exposed, in consequence of your great and truly Christian
kindness to the most unfortunate of women. For me, I
have been well used to the misery of distrust and in-

justice, and any new insult of that sort rather sickens than irritates me, as far as myself am concerned. But when I think of you, and of what I have brought upon you, God knows how unsuspectingly, I cannot find words to express what I feel. It is my consolation that the world will give to you what it has long denied to me, and that the insults of a fool and a knave together, cannot possibly be productive of any lasting injury to *you*. Mr Strahan, I think, says he informed you that it was his orders to carry me to Uigness – nothing less it seems will satisfy Mr Campbell. I once went to Uigness with a light heart, but I left it with a heavy one, and I go back as I left it. One thing comforts me, that when I am there I shall at least be delivered from this base man's presence. Every word he says, is, in one way or another, an insult to me; but his flattery and fulsome smoothness are far the worst I have to bear with. Dear Mr Blair, I think it proper to say, that it is my opinion you should see Mr Strahan as soon as possible; he talks of going to Edinburgh as soon as he has seen me at Uigness, and I really would humbly suggest that you should go into the town on purpose to see him. There is no saying how far such a man may suffer himself to proceed, unless something be done in proper time to stop him. I hope you will soon see him, and I am confident he will be humbled when he hears what you say, more quietly than could be expected even from you this morning.

'I hope you will write to me, if agreeable, and let me know how my dear little girl is, and how all things continue at dear Cross-Meikle. Dear Cross-Meikle I may well call it, and you may be assured that I shall think, if I may not speak of it. Little did I think, when we were sitting together beneath that beautiful tree – but why should I think of such things. Mr Blair, I am much to be pitied, but I hope I shall be strengthened to bear what bear I must.

'Your humble and affectionate servant,

C. C.'

I have said, that Mr Blair had walked to some distance from John Maxwell and his daughter ere he had finished the perusal of this letter. He stood still, and read it over again from beginning to end, thrust it into his bosom, and proceeded straight towards the Manse, without turning round to them. They followed him, and found him seated at the table, where the servants, who had seen him from the window, had already served up the long-deferred meal. Little Sarah took her place opposite to him, and John, who had dined many hours before, stood by the window which looked out upon the green. Mr Blair had been for some minutes eating rapidly, apparently without knowing well what he was swallowing, when John stopped him, by saying, that he saw the Semplehaugh coach turning down the lane.

Mrs Semple had taken an evening airing in that direction, with the view of making her inquiries after Mrs Campbell and little Sarah, who, she supposed, might have caught cold from their wetting of yesterday; and Dr Muir and his daughter, who had staid all night at Semplehaugh, now accompanied her in her visit to the Manse. It may easily be supposed that they expressed not a little surprise when they found that Mrs Campbell had taken her departure in such a sudden and unexpected manner. Dr Muir threw out several hints, which told pretty plainly that he wished to hear a little more than had been mentioned about the cause of an event so unlooked for: but Mrs Semple had *tact* enough to perceive that Mr Blair had no inclination to be very communicative on this head, and politely gave the go-by to the subject, by engaging Dr Muir in conversation touching the relative merits of the gooseberry wine of Cross-Meikle, and the liquor of the same denomination manufactured by the fair fingers of Miss Anne at Cambuslee. The Doctor, filling his glass to the brim, discussed that ever grateful theme for some minutes with his usual zeal, but stopped, unlike himself, in the middle of a sentence, on observing that Mr Blair was paying no attention to what he was saying. He rose from the table, and, hearing Mrs Semple say something about the propriety of taking leave, whispered into Blair's ear that he wished to have a moment's talk with him in private, if agreeable, before quitting the Manse.

Mr Blair immediately conducted him into his library, and the Doctor, seating himself in an elbow-chair by the fire-side, coughed twice or thrice by way of preparation, and then proceeded to business upon the old rule of *in medias res*. 'Mr Adam,' said he, 'my excellent young friend, Mr Adam, ye'll not, I am very sure, take any thing amiss from an old friend, who means nothing but your good. I see well enough that Mrs Campbell's off-going in this hasty fashion has made every thing look a little dull at Cross-Meikle, and your own face among the rest. Now, look ye, Mr Adam, I hope it's no offence, but I really must say, as a friend and a brother, that I am heartily glad the bonny lady is gone. A bonny lady she is, and, I hope, a good one, which is better; – but, – and really Mr Adam you must not look glum at me for saying it, – there are folk in the world who make no bones to lightly her a little: and what with her being away from her ain goodman so long, and what with your solitary condition here, I would fain say it as decently as I can, but i'faith, man, there was twa or three ill-tongued bodies about the country that had begun to make some bits of jokes about you and her; and meikle as I despised them and their jokes, we a' ken fu' weel that siclike stories are never tardy travellers; and, not to mince the matter, I'm just as well pleased that Mrs Campbell's off and away, which will put an end to all their clishmaclavers. Sae pluck up your heart, my man, and put on your ain face again, and beware o' sinking back into your dumps, and gang about your work and among your folk as usual, and, take my word for't, ye'll no repent it in the long run. – Oh, man,' he continued, in a lower tone of voice, – 'Oh, man, I can take my laugh like other folk, and I ken I've been often abused for liking my bit joke better than I should do; but really, Adam, it makes me sick at the heart to see the cauld-rife fashion this world gangs on in.— Oh, man, this is a poor world, and a heart-broken man has nae want of excuse, if he sometimes thinks to himself that it would be a braw thing to be out o't altogether.'

Mr Blair heard the old man out in perfect silence. When he had done speaking, he said to him very seriously, 'Dr Muir, I thank you. I perceive what you mean, and I won't be the fool to deny that I do so. God knows, sir, how little I have deserved such suspicions as you allude to. I trust I shall be able to bear this as I have borne other things.'

'Spoken like a man,' said Dr Muir; 'dinna be angry now, Adam, but I tell you ye've gien me mair pleasure with the twa or three words ye've just been saying than I can weel express. I see it is as I thought, and said, and was sure it was. But there's an awful text says, 'Let him that thinketh he standeth take heed lest he fall;' and God forgive me, man, but I'm rejoiced to the very heart. Good e'en, good e'en, Mr Adam; I hope you and your bairn will come ower to Cambuslee, and we'll see what we can do to divert the lassie for a day or twa till she's gotten used to the want of her cousin.'

So saying, the old gentleman walked down stairs again, and the evening being already on the decline, the whole of the party were soon on their way back to Semplehaugh.

Mr Blair was left in a strange and perplexed state of mind to muse over the letter he had received from Mrs Campbell; the friendly and well-meant, but painful communication of Dr Muir; and the whole of the events from which both of these had originated. He retired earlier than usual to his bed-room, and lay for an hour in the dark buried in meditation. He tossed from side to side in a fever of doubt and irresolution, viewing and reviewing every thing in every possible point of view; and the end of it was, that he got up and summoned his old serving-man, who had not yet gone to bed, to attend him. James, with the utmost surprise, received his master's command, first, to fetch a light to his bed-chamber, and secondly, to saddle his horse. He stared with a blank face upon Mr Blair after he had executed the first part of this commission, as if not able to believe in good earnest that his ears had played him no trick as to the second. The command was repeated, and James, shaking his head as he went, proceeded to the stable.

Mr Blair got up immediately, dressed himself, and sat down at his writing-table. He wrote and sealed a letter for Mrs Semple, another for Dr Muir, and a third for Mr Jamieson; and ere he had finished all this, he heard James walking his horse up and down before the door. He wrapt his cloak about his shoulders, and with his candle in his hand, entered softly, and on tiptoe, the room in which Sarah slept. He stood for a few moments by the bedside gazing on the beautiful creature, as she lay half uncovered before him, and smiling in her sleep. 'God bless my orphan child,' said he, stooping to kiss her brow; and then left the apartment as silently as he had entered it.

When he came out, James did not assist him to

mount his horse without expressing his astonishment at a journey begun at such an hour. Mr Blair made no answer to his interrogations, except that he expected the letters he had left on his table should be delivered before breakfast on the following morning. He then rode off at a leisurely pace, which, however, James could ascertain to be considerably quickened ere the horse's tread was beyond hearing.

The moon was already set, or at least the drifting clouds concealed her, but it was still a fine, bright, star-light night, with a high and whistling wind. The minister of Cross-Meikle, pushing his mare into a good round trot, was soon far beyond the reach of his servant's ears. 'He'll be in Glasgow in no time,' quoth James to himself, as he shut the door; 'I never heard him ride at sic a rate, and at sic an hour too! Good guide us, I'm sure the minister has heard some black news.'

—••₤ ⅜ ₃••—

It is unnecessary to trouble the reader with transcribing
the three letters which Mr Blair's servant delivered next
morning at Semplehaugh house, when the family were
seated together at the breakfast table. Dr Muir having
laid down his with a face of utter astonishment after he
had read it, turned to Mrs Semple, and saw on her
countenance the expression not of astonishment merely,
but of astonishment mingled with regret, sorrow, perhaps something of indignation to boot. He rose from
table, and drew the old lady into the deep recess of a
window, too much darkened with heavy and loaded
emblazonments to contribute much of light to the
apartment. They conversed there in whispers for some
minutes, and when they rejoined the party, Mrs Semple's
face had recovered its usual benignity of expression, although it was still sufficiently evident that her surprise
had not altogether subsided. The carriage was ordered
immediately after breakfast. Mrs Semple drove to Cross-
Meikle Manse, and made little Sarah dry her tears and

accompany her back in it. Dr Muir and his daughter took leave early in the day, and the child found herself established amidst the usual domestic quiet of the household of Semplehaugh, where all her days she had been accustomed to enjoy the ease and the kindness of a second home.

The minister of Cross-Meikle had performed a journey of no inconsiderable extent ere these arrangements took place among the friends he had left behind him.

The first grey light of the dawn found him already several miles below Glasgow, riding at a pace of undiminished celerity close by the river's side. All night long there had been a high wind, and the voice of the breeze, and the perpetual racking of the clouds overhead, had conspired with the murmuring of the great stream rolling near him, to keep up that spring of mental as well as animal excitement, under the influence of which he had quitted his home at the hour of – to all but him – repose. The animal he rode seemed to feel the inspiriting breath of the chill atmosphere, and the roar of the winds, amidst the starry and clouded sky, as if in sympathy with his master, and neither horse nor man had ever for a moment paused or flagged. Swiftly they passed through the blackness of the ancient pine woods which here and there skirt the margin of the river. Swiftly they pursued their course over moor and meadow; but most swiftly of all did they hold on their speed when the opening Clyde gleamed broader and broader on their right, beneath the reddening morning beams, and the mighty mountains of the west rose before them from among the dispersing mist and haze in which their huge summits had hitherto been enveloped. For the last six or seven miles the path lay along a narrow stripe of sand, which intervenes beneath the river and its high and craggy bank – where the spray now and then rose, and flashed about the horse's hoofs as the tide was gaining rapidly upon the sand. Blair sitting back firmly in his saddle, kept his eyes fixed vacantly upon the brightening waves, while from time to time his lips uttered an unconscious echo to the hollow sweepings of the breeze among the tall ferns that flung themselves out from the face of those rifted and half impendent rocks.

He reached the Bay of Greenock about seven o'clock; and having put up his foam-covered horse, and swallowed some glasses of wine and a crust of bread, walked down immediately to the shore to inquire when any vessel or boat was likely to set sail for any part of Loch-fine. In those days, no regular packets, (far less steam-boats,) rendered the coasts of those Highland arms of the sea at all times accessible to the traveller; – but it happened that after some search, Mr Blair discovered a small wherry, the master of which had come to Greenock with a cargo of fish, and said, that although his business was not quite completed, he would, as the gentleman seemed to be in a hurry, oblige him by setting off immediately on his return to Inverary, – provided the gentleman had no objections to remunerate him adequately for any loss he might sustain from departing under such circumstances. Mr Blair was in no mood for being startled with trifles, so a bargain was soon struck; or rather, an instant assent was given to the by no means over-modest proposals of the skipper. Four stout lads, all clad in the same dark tartans of the Maclachlan, were ere long assembled by the whistle of the master. Blair took his place near the helmsman, who offered him an enormous boat-plaid to wrap himself in; and the sudden transition he had so lately made from violent exercise on horseback, to a naked beach and a sharp sea-breeze, might well render this courtesy acceptable.

Covered over with the coarse and thick garment, he reclined himself at all his length upon a layer of chests and barrels, with which the stern part of the boat was filled; the sails were hoisted swiftly to receive the favouring gale; and the small bark was soon dancing gaily over the green and shining billows, while the helmsman began to chaunt in a hoarse deep voice, one of those rude ancestral ditties with which the strenuous boatmen of the Gael are accustomed to sooth the Genius of the Deep. The younger mariners joined in the chorus, and every slender plank in the bounding wherry seemed to quiver like human pulses beneath the stirring music of their 'Echinafoam.'

Mr Blair, unused to the motion of a boat at sea, was soon rendered not sick but giddy, by the swiftness with which the keel glanced over the surface of the waves. The want of sleeep, and the strong circumstances of excitation under which he had performed his land journey, conspired perhaps to make him less capable of resisting what he could not have been expected under any circumstances to resist effectually. His eyes reeled in his head, amidst the countless glitter of the waters; and he lay in a state of mingled stupor and bewilderment, and not without occasional flashes of a dizzy delight, all the while that they were running right before the wind to the headland of Dunoon.

He recovered by degrees the full possession, but not the tranquillity of his senses, as they coasted the bold and beautiful coast westwards. The rich and verdant Island of Bute on the left, contrasted itself with the bare healthy hills of Argyll on the right, and the sea, locked in on every side between gigantic cliffs and wooded promontories, displayed not the general aspect only, but the smooth and glassy surface of some mighty lake. Calmly and sweetly the heavings of the water bore them onwards; and Adam Blair, lulled insensibly by the gentle rippling of the transparent waves, and the singing voices of his unwearied boatmen, had passed several hours in deep and refreshing slumber ere the breeze deserted him, at the mouth of the loch for which their course was bound.

He was roused by the bustle of furling the sails, and unshipping the oars; and saw the wide arm of the sea gleaming beneath the radiance of a splendid sunset, as it wound away up before him among the black shadows of the mountains.

All around was silent as the grave, except the regular dash of the oars, and now and then some white sea-mew screaming as they passed it, where it floated with the wave, or the far-off cry of the unseen goat, borne shrill over the waters from the echoes of his solitary rock. The scene surpassed all he had ever beheld, or conceived, of the still beauty of nature. Here, tall yellow crags, lashed by the sweeping waves, shone bright through the spray that foamed against them, and tinged the rising and falling sheet of vapour with all their own hues of richness. There, some fragrant grove of birch nodded the fresh green of its foliage over the very bosom of the waters which seemed to linger beneath the soft shadow, as if enamoured of the perfume it exhaled. Beyond, some gently-retreating bay received the advancing billows upon a shore of smooth golden sand, or glittering pebbles; while here and there an old mouldering oak cast its image for a moment upon the varying mirror beneath, as if to reproach the assailant that had so smilingly undermined it. The eye found repose on all sides amidst the purple hills, which seemed to swell away in interminable succession, ridge beyond ridge, into the heart of the Highland solitudes, or on the remoter wastes of water over which their eternal shadows lay brooding and blackening into deeper and wider gloom, as the last crimson line of sunset kept sinking down lower and lower in the western horizon.

Daylight was all but gone, and the moon had already begun to shine feebly through the fleece of white clouds which rested on the summit of the hills eastward, when, as they were gliding along close to the shore, Mr Blair, who was standing upright in the stern, contemplating the magnificent scene of repose around him, was startled by the loud laugh of a voice, which at the moment sounded to him as if he had certainly heard it somewhere before. Casting his eyes upwards on the beach, he saw a horseman on the brink of the rock scarce twenty yards off, and was satisfied that the laugh proceeded from him. The boatmen too rested on their oars, as if in expectation that the stranger would address them, but the moment they paused, he turned his horse's head, and rode some paces in the direction opposite to that in which they had been moving. Blair looked anxiously and keenly; but it was impossible for him to distinguish the person, although he still imagined that he could not have been mistaken in having conceived himself to be acquainted with the voice. The boatmen, after the pause of a few moments, resumed their labour, and the boat was again in motion. The stranger hearing the dash of the oars, turned again, repeated his laugh more loudly than before, and then clapping spurs to his horse, vanished among the trees. The boatmen talked earnestly together after he had disappeared from view, but they spoke Gaelic, and Blair of course understood nothing of what they said. He could easily comprehend, however, that they were all of them not a little surprised with being hailed in such a rude fashion by a person who apparently had no wish to say any thing to any of the party. He, on his part, being neither conscious of evil, nor suspicious of evil, soon resumed his cloak and his reclining posture, and dismissed the incident from his thoughts.

The moon had been for some time shining in all her beauty on the waters around them, and his eyes had been feasting on the new loveliness of the landscape under the influence of that softer light, when the helmsman ran the boat under a low reef of black rocks which projected from the shore, and told him, pointing to a solitary tower on the height above, that he had reached the place of his destination. Blair, starting up, paid his fare, and prepared to leave the boat. One of the young sailors leaped up to his middle in the water by the prow, and having taken Mr Blair in his arms as easily as if his weight had been that of a child, waded about a dozen yards with him, and landed him in safety on the beach of Uigness.

Blair sat down on one of the large fragments of grey rock, which lay tumbled on the beach as if they had lain there ever since they had been shattered from the brow of the impending rock by some primeval convulsion of nature. He gazed after the boat which had conveyed him thither, until it had disappeared from his view behind a low neck of wood-covered land which runs far out into the sea some space farther up, and even then he continued in the same posture, listening to the sound of the oars until their last retreating echo had quite died upon his ear. It was then that he arose from his seat, and began, though with slow and lingering steps, to ascend the narrow path which the moonbeams shewed him winding up the face of the cliff. Often he paused, and turned round again to the sea, and once or twice he felt as if he would fain follow the boatmen and abandon the object of his voyage at the moment it was within his reach. These, however, were but the passing tremours of a mind somewhat shaken by so many un‐wonted species of excitement. The purpose for which he had come, he said to himself, was both an honest and a kind one; and why should he fear to act that which he had not feared to plan? He approached, at length, the gate of the tower, and knocked upon it with a firm hand.

No answer was made to him, although he repeated the signal more than once. At last he heard distinctly the opening of a door, and the tread of a foot within the house, and knocked again more loudly than before. Immediately afterwards, a window over his head was drawn up, and he saw a naked arm stretched out, and a weapon of steel flashing bright in the moonlight. 'Who is there?' cried a voice, – and he knew the voice to be Charlotte's, although he had never heard it in the same tone before; – 'Who is there? If you be come back to insult me, to torment me farther, look up, scoundrel, dastard, and see that I am armed. Go, fly, base‐born villain, and tempt not too far blood that is already too hot for fear.'

Mr Blair was so much astonished at the words he heard Charlotte utter, that he could not, for a moment, say any thing to interrupt them.

'Charlotte,' he said at length in a calm voice, 'in the name of God, what say you? It is I, Charlotte – It is your friend – it is Adam Blair that has come to see you.'

She leaned over the window, and, clasping her hands

together, lost her hold of the weapon, which fell close to him on the pavement of the court. She screamed aloud as her eye followed the falling sword, and drew back with a shudder when she saw how nearly it had escaped him. A moment after, the bolt was withdrawn; the door sprung open, and Charlotte, rushing out half naked as she was, had flung her arms around his neck, and buried her face in his bosom, ere he was able either to meet or to reject the proffered embrace.

She drew herself back, gazed upon his face through visible tears, and then again folded herself round him. 'Oh, Adam,' said she, 'God has heard my prayer – God has not deserted me – but now I was alone – now I have you with me, and I shall fear nothing.' She uttered a short convulsive laugh, and added in a whisper, 'No, no, I shall not be afraid of an hundred Mr Strahans now.'

'Be calm, be calm, dear Charlotte,' said Blair, 'what have you to fear? what have you to dread? Why should you be thus discomposed? I am here – your friend – your brother is here. I pray you be comforted, be composed, there can no evil befall you. Let us go in,' he added, 'the night is cold, Charlotte – I shall reproach myself if you be the worse for this.'

'The worse for this!' cried she, 'the worse for this, Adam! – do you say it is cold? – I feel none, – but you shall soon be warm. – Come in, come in, Adam, you shall soon be warm, very warm.'

She laid her arm round him, and drew him into the house, and up a dark flight of stairs which led to an upper chamber, in which a single taper was burning faintly. She seated him by the fire-side, and immediately began piling up logs of turf and timber above the embers of the hearth: then stooping on her knees, she blew, and the flame was easily excited, and the chamber was filled with the ruddy light. She turned round, seized his hands, rubbed them between hers, and drew his chair nearer to the fire; and then, as if for the first time remembering anything of herself, hastily covered her person as well as she could, and ran out of the apartment.

She re-entered after a little time, arrayed in her dressing-gown, the long folds of which swept the floor as she trod, and bearing in her hands a small tray, which she placed on a table, and drew it close to Mr Blair. 'Come, Adam,' said she, 'you were cold but now, and you must be hungry too. Eat and drink, dear Adam, we shall have time enough for talking and thinking hereafter. Drink, Adam,' and she poured a large glass from a flask of wine as she spoke, 'drink, drink, dear Adam, and I will pledge you, I will pledge you gaily – Come, drink, Adam, for your own sake, or for mine.'

Mr Blair swallowed the wine she poured for him, and she poured glass after glass, and would take no refusal; and whether from that, or from the great heat of the fire she had kindled, in a room that would at any rate have appeared warm to him after being so long exposed to the sea-breezes, or from whatever cause, it seemed to him, in a moment, as if he could not breathe without difficulty. He rose and threw open the window of the apartment, and leaned over it to inhale the freshening breeze. She followed him, and resting her head upon his shoulder, gazed out along with him upon the wide silver lake, stretched out far below, and the glorious moon, which had now risen high in the heavens, and was beaming resplendent amidst all her attendant millions of twinkling stars. While they gazed, a white radiant cloud floated nearer and nearer, and at last gathering over the face of the beautiful planet, blotted her light from heaven; assuming, at the same time, a dark and frowning hue, as if mourning over the obscurity of the very luminary its own veil was concealing. The sky was darkened, and the sympathetic lake seemed to lie like a sea of ink spread out wide and far, with scarcely one solitary star here and there reflected on its surface. The winds too seemed all to have subsided; and, for a moment, earth, sky, and sea, were alike black and alike silent.

Mrs Campbell took Blair's hand and withdrew him from the window. She re-seated him by the table, poured another glass of wine, and again forcing him to swallow it, began to tell him, in broken syllables, the story of her insults.

Had she never told that story, perhaps Adam Blair had never been a fallen man – nor

> 'The moon hid her light
> From *his* heaven that night.'

Chapter

14

———•◦❁◦•———

```
*       *       *       *       *       *       *
*       *       *       *       *       *       *
*       *       *       *       *       *       *
*       *       *       *       *       *       *
```

*   * The wind rose higher and higher, and the roaring waves lashed far up against the black rocks of
Uigness, and the wild voice of the tempest howled
deeper and deeper along the forest ridges, and over the
waste moors. They heard not the uproar of the elements,
or if they did, it accorded but too well with the tumults
of sense and passion throughout that long dark night, –
the morning of which dawned upon slumbers, hot,
feverish, but deep, nevertheless, and lasting. An old
Highland crone, the only other inhabitant of the tower,
after waiting many hours beyond the time when she
expected to be summoned, entered the chamber, and
having been in bed long before Mr Blair's arrival the
night before, it may be more easily imagined than de-

scribed with what surprise she beheld her mistress asleep in the arms of a man – and a stranger.

She stood for some minutes as if unable to believe her eyes, and at last, seeing Blair toss his arm aloft and turn himself on the couch, she withdrew hastily, and the massy door swung after her with a heavy slap when she quitted the guilty chamber.

The noise of this shook slumber from Blair's burning eye-lids, and he started at once from the couch of Charlotte as if he had been wreathed in the coils of a serpent. He rushed to the window, and threw it open, and looked forth upon the sea, once more calm and glassy, and the sky glowing with the still and sultry fervours of a summer noon. Every thing was in repose except the bosom on which anguish, remorse, despair, sat like midnight demons, flapping in unison their cold and mighty wings.

Suddenly there came wafted from afar-off the echo of a bell tolling slowly, every note of which seemed to pause upon the surface of the smooth waters over which it was borne. The remote solemn music summoned Christian worshippers from many a lonely glen, and many a boat glided swiftly at its signal from the neigh-bouring creeks and bays. To one only, of all that listened, those holy sounds, floating gently over the deep, sent no message of peace and gladness.

The muffled knell, that announces to the felon the hour of his mortal doom, fell never with a more thrilling sweep of horror than did the simple melody of that Sabbath-bell upon Adam Blair's shrinking ear. – The pulse of human agony was never stirred with a deeper throb.

He clad himself hastily, and without casting more than one hurried glance upon the sleeping partner of his guilt, walked out of the house, and followed, with trembling step, the path which wound up the face of the wooded hill immediately behind it. He turned back when he had reached the rocky summit, looked down once more for a moment upon the shining loch and its magnificent shores, and then rushed with the speed of a maniac into the gloomy and deep glen which sinks beyond. When he stopped, he threw his eyes round him, and saw nothing but a narrow circuit of heathy and stony desolation; and in the centre of the barren amphitheatre a small dark mountain tarn, the still waveless waters of which reflected nothing but the surrounding gloom – and that so truly, that he stood almost on the margin ere he had discovered that there was any thing but heath below him.

This melancholy tarn, formed where three hills descend into the bosom of the earth together, is of such depth that no plummet could ever sound it, and it shelves from the very brink sheer down into this unfathomable blackness. The sea-mew rests her weary wing there, when driven by the fierce tempest from the breast of ocean; the wild-deer, that has escaped from the hunters of some distant forest, pants in security on the untrodden heath beside it; the eagle, sailing far overhead, casts a passing shadow upon its surface; the stars visit it with their gleams – long before any human eye can distinguish their presence in the heavens from the brow of the neighbouring mountain. But no living thing was near, when Adam Blair took his seat upon one of the great shapeless fragments of stone that here and there gird the heath, and lean their bare masses over those dismal waters – and though the bright sky of noon-tide hung far above in its beauty – the black mirror below him reflected nothing of its azure.

Blair sat there gazing upon the pool, with his arms folded on his breast, until the multitude of his agonizing thoughts had totally perplexed the clearness both of his mind and of his vision. Once and again he strove to frame his lips to prayer, but the syllables stuck in his throat, and he gasped for breath, as if a great weight had been squeezing in his bosom. At last, he knelt with his fore-head low down in his hands upon the stone, and struggled inwardly till every limb of him shook and quivered; but still no drop of tears would gush from his throbbing eye-lids, no Christian ejaculation would force itself through his dry and parched lips. He felt as if he were wrapt in some black and burning cloud, which would not let in one ray upon his misery of thirst and scorching, and became at last utterly be-wildered with a crowd of the most horrible phantasies. The anguish of his remorse clothed itself in tangible forms, and his spirit shrunk amidst them, as if he had been surrounded with the presence of real demons. Black loathsome creatures seemed to sit close beside him on either hand, polluting the breath ere it reached his nostrils, scowling upon him with faces of devilish

163

glee, pawing upon his head with hot talons, fanning his temples with wiry pinions, which stirred the air, but lent it no coolness. Wide glaring eyes fastened upon him, and held him fixed as their prey. – At one moment it seemed to him as if the church-yard of Cross-Meikle were the scene of his torments. He saw the tomb of his father, with filthy things crawling up and down upon the face of the marble; while he himself lying prostrate upon the grave of his wife, heard the poisonous breath of fiends whistling in his ear above her dust. He saw his living friends; old Maxwell was there, with fierce angry eyes. Little Sarah stood close by him pale and motion-less; farther off, the whole of his congregation were crowded together about the door of the church, and he heard the voice of scornful curses muttered everywhere round about him, by lips that had never been opened but to bless him. These vanished as if some spell had wafted them far away beyond the clouds, and he felt, with a sort of sense of relief in the midst of his despair, as if he were once more alone with the ill-favoured attend-ants to whom he knew himself to be abandoned. He gazed back again with sullen dead eyes upon their gleaming countenances of wrath and joy, distorted and intermingled together. He frowned upon them, as if daring them to do their worst. They screamed aloud with harsh horrid voices – pounced upon him – lifted him up into the air, and then flung him down again, as if in sport, and he their plaything. He strove to utter the name of his Maker, but ere he could open his mouth, the holy name itself passed away from his recollection, and they stooped nearer and nearer to him, and peered into his eyes with looks of triumph, as if they had read his thoughts, and knew he was baffled from within – without their working.

In his agony, he shook the stone beneath him, and it heaved on its crumbling foundation. A spasm of natural terror made him spring to his feet, and he leaped backwards upon the heath. The big grey stone, its motion accelerated by the action of his leap, loosened itself the next moment, and tumbled headlong into the dreary waters over which it had toppled perhaps for centuries. Down it went with one heavy plunge; for the ear that followed it instinctively strove in vain to catch its meeting with the bottom of the tarn. Ring after ring circled and glistened wider and wider on the face of the black mere, and all was again black, motionless, silent as before.

Mr Blair devoured with his eyes the heavings of the water until they were no more, and then stretching forth his hand above his head, cried out, with a voice of piercing horror, 'My God, my God, hast thou deserted me utterly! Why leaped I back from the trembling rock? Why is that saved once more, which is useless, worthless, miserable, lost, lost for ever! God, God, look down in compassion! – my misery is greater than I can bear!'

He was in the very act of springing – the next moment would have been his last, when he was seized firmly from behind, and the voice of Charlotte thrilled in his ears.——

'Stop, rash man! what dost thou? Wilt thou slay thyself? – Look back, faint heart! Look back on me! Art thou alone miserable?'

Blair turned round and met her wild eyes; – 'Lost woman,' said he, shaking himself from her grasp, 'what dost thou? What brings thee here? Wilt thou not leave me to myself – to my misery? It is all thou hast left me.'

'Adam Blair, what hast thou left to me?'

'To fly, woman, to repent – to weep, – perhaps, not to weep for ever. For thee there may be hope.'

'For me! why not for thee?'

'Torment me no farther. I preached to others – myself am an outcast. Once more leave me. – Farewell.'

'Adam Blair, your hand burns; your fingers burn like a coal.'

'My heart, my heart burns,' cried Adam, smiting his breast. A moment after, he covered his face with his hands, kneeled at Charlotte's feet, and wept audibly.

'Go, go, I beseech ye; yet forgive me before you go – say that you forgive me, Charlotte, before we part for ever!'

'I forgive? Is it for *me* to offer forgiveness? Oh, little do ye know my thoughts. Would I could forgive myself!' – and she knelt on the heath beside him, – and their tears mingled as they rolled down upon the ground.

'My God!' said Blair, 'my God! bruise me no farther. – Oh Isobel, my Saint, my wounded Saint, my Isobel! Wife of my bosom! my only, my virgin love! look down in pity, if thy pure eyes behold me! Look down in pity, sweet Saint, upon frail, sinful dust and ashes! If angels weep, weep for me, my Isobel!' ——

Charlotte sprung up, and dashing the tears from her eyes, said, 'Adam Blair, we part, and part for ever! – But I go not until you have promised – until you have sworn by the God, who said, "Thou shalt not kill," that you will do yourself no harm. Selfish man! would you heap sorrow on sorrow, till the heart break beneath its burden, with all its guilty blood unpurified within it? Speak – promise – swear, while you are on your knees before me, – and remember that God is present to hear you – even here in this wilderness ——'

'I swear,' he said, casting his eyes upwards, but without looking on Charlotte, 'I swear that I shall wait God's time. God grant it be not long. God shield me from presumptuous sin.'

When he had uttered these words, he stooped his head downwards again, and remained for some moments with his eyes fixed upon the ground, – but without any motion either of sobbing or of weeping.

When he rose again, his face was filled not with the turbulence of contending passions, but with a fixed and desperate calmness. 'Charlotte,' said he, 'we should part in sorrow, not in anger: Let each keep for solitude, what in solitude only is fitting. – Farewell, Charlotte, – go, and sin no more, – once again, farewell, and for ever!'

Charlotte's tears burst once more over her burning cheek, as she answered, 'Farewell!' She extended her hand towards him, but instantly drew it back; and stood with her eyes fixed upon the water, while he, with quick and violent steps, walked away from her along

the rugged margin of the tarn, and then up the face of
the heath, in the direction opposite to the path by which
he had come thither from Uigness.

He had proceeded at a rapid though uneven pace
for a considerable way up the steep side of the hill, ere
Charlotte withdrew her eyes from the water, and with
a sudden start of emotion, gazed wildly after him over
the gloomy space he had traversed. She saw him distinctly labouring up the ascent many hundred yards
above, and followed him with her eyes, until his figure
was shut from them by the projection of a crag, behind
which his course lay. She still gazed for a moment, but
he did not re-appear – and then at last she sat down
among the heather, and clasping her hands together in
her bosom, wept bitterly and silently. The sense of utter
desertion, for the first time, mingled with the pangs of
contrition; and her woman's breast panted beneath the
burden of hopeless misery. 'Alone, alone, quite alone,'
said she to herself, 'alone as in the grave. No last look of
love to dwell with me – alas! not one. I am pitied – ha!
perhaps I am scorned, – perhaps I am hated. – Love!
Oh, I was never loved. Even now, – it is but of Isobel
Gray he thinks; – he prays to her spirit, – he wastes no
thought on the living heart that is broken. – Oh! that it
would break! Go, Adam Blair, – go, weep, and dry
your tears, and mingle with man and woman, and find
other comforters. Misery is with you now; but what is
your misery to mine? – to my utter misery? Oh, God!
dark and inscrutable are thy ways; if indeed thou re-
gardest us; if indeed it be true that the doings of earth

are heeded from above? – Is there indeed an above? – Is there indeed a God? – Are we more than clay – than dust? – Shall we indeed be more than dust hereafter? Alas! Oh God! all is blindness – blackness – utter blackness. – God have mercy upon me, a sinner. – God have mercy on me, there is no other eye to pity. – Great God! look down upon me, in compassion. – Jesus, Saviour, gentle Saviour, pity me – hear the cry of a bruised heart!'

A momentary pause took place among the troubled workings of her mind, and then her thoughts flowed in quite another course. She took up one stone after another, and hurled them from her into the pool, and listened to the splashing sounds she was herself creating. Suddenly she stopped, and began to speak aloud amidst the silence of the desert place, with a voice of more energy than she had ever addressed to the ear of man. 'Wretch,' said she, 'oh, wretch that I am! Is it for me to conceive reproachful thoughts? Is it for me to brood in bitterness over that which, but for me, could never have been? Is it for me – me miserable – to complain of him that I have ruined – undone – undone perhaps for ever? Calm and pure was his spirit, – calm, even as those waters, till my hand stirred their depths. Would to God his calmness could be restored like theirs! For a moment I can wound and disturb that glassy surface, and in an instant it slumbers over the unfathomed depth below, as smoothly as before my rash hand did its deed. But oh! what time, what healing length of time shall be able to sooth the spirit I have tortured from its repose? Pure spirit! – blessed spirit – I came to comfort; – of what have I not robbed thee? – Isobel – sainted Isobel – thee too have I injured – thee too have I robbed. If sorrow can reach the abodes of the departed, I have sent sorrow to thee. Poor innocent orphan, I thought to love thee like a mother – What a mother! A fiend came to the dwelling of sorrow and innocence when I came to theirs. When shall that lowly roof hang again over untroubled heads? I have spoiled them of all, of every thing: and yet I reproached Adam Blair – yes, I reproached him with my eyes, and he turned from me as if I, not he, had been the victim. Cruel, heartless, selfish wretch! He went from me – he has gone from me for ever, and I never knelt – his eyes never saw me kneel in the dust before him. I bandied words with him – I intruded on his solitary anguish – I disturbed, I tormented him anew. I saved him, yes, I saved him – I saved his life – Yes, but I spoke to him as if it had been mine to speak and his to hear. Oh God! I cannot bear this thought. I will fly after him. I will fly rapidly after him, over hill and heath. I will find him – I may yet find him in the wilderness. I will kneel to him ere he goes. I will rain tears upon his feet. I will bid him farewell, not with words, but tears: they fit me better. I will arise and follow Adam Blair. God strengthen me! God strengthen my feeble feet!'

Chapter
15

❖

Feeble indeed she was, but the stung mind lent its vigour to the sickly frame as she followed the path which Blair had taken up the steep and shaggy precipice before her. She never relaxed her speed, except now and then for a moment, and then she resumed her way with additional impetuosity. The strong wiry fibres of the untrodden heath tore her ankles until the blood burst through her stockings – but she never heeded the smart.

At length she gained the brow of the hill, and cast her eyes around her to consider in which direction he had most probably taken his course. Her eyes wandered wide over a sea of purple mountains, divided everywhere by deep and rocky glens, down which, in every direction, the Alpine streams were flowing – but nowhere, though she strained her vision to the utmost, could she descry any human dwelling, far less any human form. 'I shall never see him,' said she to herself, 'I shall never see him more – he is lost to me for ever – I shall never find him among this labyrinth of mountains.' And so saying, she plunged more rapidly than ever down the shelving bank, and ran on in that sort of blind agony until her course was arrested by a brook, which had been swollen into a torrent by the storm of the preceding night.

She followed its course, having no power to cross its waters; nor, if she had been able to do so, any predilection for one path more than for another. It soon conducted her into a black rocky pass, through which the tumbling waters forced themselves, leaving barely room for any human foot to partake the passage they had opened for themselves in the winters of ages. Just there, however, Charlotte descried the mark of a man's foot as if recently stamped on the wet sand, and she knew it was Blair's, and went on, with new strung nerves, although it was sometimes necessary for her to leap from one wet stone to another, on footing as uncertain as might have arrested a hunter in the full career of the chase.

The dark pass opened upon a little hitherto-unseen glen, down the purple waste of which a green line winding from side to side, and here and there a solitary birch tree, marked the progress of the streamlet. At the further extremity, perhaps a quarter of a mile off, her eye discovered a little desolate shieling perched on an elevation of rock over the margin of the brook. A pile of dried turf stood immediately beyond, and was only to be distinguished from the human dwelling by the want of the heavy wreath of smoke, which was seen issuing from the centre of the roof beside it. A bare pine-tree, with a few ragged branches, leaned over the shieling; and a little patch of broader verdure on the other side of the brook, betokened the scanty agriculture of the Highland shepherd who tenanted that remote abode.

The shadows were, by this time, beginning to fall eastward, and it immediately occurred to Charlotte, that, in all probability, Mr Blair would not think of going beyond this place until the return of day-light; or at least that, if he had passed onwards, the people of the cottage would be able to give her some information of the direction in which he had bent his steps. The shieling, therefore, was her mark, and she continued to move towards it by the side of the stream; but insensibly, as she drew nearer to it, her pace was slackened, and she lost that spring of excitement which had hitherto carried her bounding over bog, rock, and heath. Slowly, and with lingering steps, she went over this last part of her way, and she paused entirely, and sat down by the side of the brook when she had reached a point from which her eyes could see, with distinctness, the low door of the shieling – its solitary milk-cow grazing on the small space of grass in front of it – and an old bearded goat reclining on the turf of which its roof was composed, and nibbling the few ears of barley that had found room to grow there among the layers of heath.

She kept her eyes fixed upon these poor symptoms of human habitation, endeavouring in vain to summon up courage enough to carry her into their presence. At last, however, an old woman came out to carry in fuel, and, as she was about to stoop and re-enter the house, it happened that she threw her eyes up the glen. It may easily be supposed that she started on seeing a lady clad in white, sitting by herself close to the margin of the water.

The old woman paused for a moment at her door, flung down her bundle of turf, and began to walk as nimbly as her age permitted, towards the place where Mrs Campbell was sitting. Charlotte, in the meantime, perceiving her approach, rose from the stone on which she had been sitting, and advanced, though still with slow steps, to meet her.

The shepherd's wife at once recognized the Lady of Uigness, although she had not seen her for many years, nor heard any thing of her return to that part of the country: but although the courtesy of her salutation needed no aid of language to make itself understood, as Charlotte knew no more than a very few words of the Gaelic, their communication was at an end almost before it could be said to have begun. The old woman, however, found means to make Charlotte comprehend distinctly that there was something wrong in the shiel-ing, and that the lady would confer a favour by im-mediately entering it along with her. The anxious pointing of her finger, and grasping of her garments, told the tale plainly enough, and Charlotte, not with-out some suspicion that Mr Blair was already there before her, summoned up all her lost energies, and readily accompanied the motions of her guide.

She followed her over a rude bridge, constructed from two half-mouldering pine-trunks, and was very soon at the door of the hut, from which, as well as from every crevice in the frail walls, wreaths of smoke came forth, eddy upon eddy, and curl upon curl. She stooped after her and entered; but, for a moment, the dark atmosphere within, and the pungency of the turf-smoke, rendered her eyes quite incapable of discovering any object in the interior.

She rubbed her smarting eyes and saw Blair lying prostrate on the floor, with a plaid wrapped over part of his figure, close to the fire, which blazed under its canopy of smoke in the centre of the place. One of his arms lay stiffly by his side; the hand of the other covered his eyes and forehead; he seemed to be in a state of stupor, but every now and then all his limbs quivered and shook beneath the folds of the garment which enveloped them. Charlotte stood in silence by the old woman, who kept pointing towards him with her finger, and whispering all the while into her ear discordant and unintelligible sounds of alarm and fear. After a pause of some minutes, during which nothing indicated that Mr Blair was aware of any one being near him, she at last spoke these words in a whisper, 'Adam – Adam Blair, you are sick, you are ill. Do not shrink from me; alas! you need not; look up, and speak to me, and tell me what you feel.'

Mr Blair uncovered his eyes, looked wildly through the smoke, and, uttering a deep hollow groan, turned himself with his face towards the earth on the floor of the shieling.

Charlotte stood for some space in the same attitude in which she heard his groan, and then perceiving that his silence was either obstinate or involuntary, she drew near to him, knelt down beside him, and seized one of his hands in hers. The moment he felt her touch, the sick man started to his feet, and leaped backwards from the place where she was kneeling.

'Off, off – torment me not – woman, torment me not! – Wilt thou never leave me? Shall the curse cling to me for ever?'

He said these words in a tone of voice, low indeed and feeble, but nevertheless quite distinct and fervid, and then made an effort as if he would have escaped towards the door; but the exertion was beyond his strength: he reeled, he staggered, and sunk once more to the ground, on which he would have fallen with all his weight, had not Charlotte been there to receive him in her arms, and support him gently into the plaid upon which he had before been stretched. She wrapped its folds once more over him, and he seemed to coil himself up in a knot below them, while a spasm of more convulsive shivering agitated the whole of his body. He stretched forth his hand at the moment when all his limbs were shaking with violence, drew one of the corners of the mantle right over his face – and, in a moment, lay at her feet as motionless as a log.

Charlotte watched him for a few minutes in silence – and then flinging herself on her knees again beside him, uncovered his face, and gazed upon his closed eyes and pale features. She took his hand, now unresisting, lifted it up, and pressed it to her lips, and when she quitted her hold of it, saw it drop down as heavily as if it had been part of a dead man. With that she sprung up, and seizing a wooden vessel which lay near, ran out swiftly from the shieling. She returned, and kneeling down again, began to lave water on his face. He opened his eyes heavily on feeling the coolness; but instantly the lids relapsed, and not one word or motion farther attested his sense of her presence.

She was still in the same posture, when, after the lapse of half an hour, the old herdsman entered the hut along with one of his sons who had been out with him all day on the mountain. Charlotte recovered herself the moment they entered, and addressed them with an earnest interrogation, whether it were not possible to make a sort of litter and carry Mr Blair as far as Uigness. The young man, as it happened, understood a little English, and as soon as he had comprehended the purport of her speech, he said something in Gaelic to his father, and they both quitted the place immediately, making signs that they would be back again ere long.

They had not been long away, when Mr Blair shook the plaid from above him, and sat up supporting himself on his hands. He regarded first the old woman, and then Charlotte, with his dull eyes, and said to the latter, in a low and broken whisper, 'Charlotte, I have used you ill – even now I have used you unlike a man. Forgive me, Charlotte, I feel that my mortal offences will soon be over – I feel that within which cannot deceive me. I am sick, I am sick to death. Farewell! for God's sake leave me. I shall die here; I shall be buried here in this wild place. Let no one know where I have been buried.'

Her tears flowed abundantly as she listened to these calmly spoken words; but a moment afterwards his cheek began to glow again, and his eye to flash, and another ague-like shivering passed over his whole frame, and he sunk prostrate once more on the ground, apparently as helpless as before.

It was just then that the young man re-entered the shieling, and invited Mrs Campbell to come and look at the litter they had formed. It consisted of three or four pieces of timber wattled together with withs plucked from the low green willows, which here and there grew among the rushes by the side of their brook. A layer of heath was arranged over this rude frame; and Charlotte having seen her own shawl, and the mens plaids added, desired them both to come in and lift her friend.

They obeyed her, and Blair seemed to be quite unconscious of what had happened, until they had borne him out into the open air. He then opened his eyes again, and looked about him for a moment, but still without appearing to take the least notice either of the men or of Charlotte. They laid him at length on the litter, – wrapped the plaid over him, and began to bear him like a child along the path which both he and Charlotte had already traversed. He lay as they walked, with closed eyes, and Charlotte began to hope that the motion had perhaps lulled him into a slumber, that might in the end prove salutary and refreshing.

These mountaineers, burthened as they were, moved on so nimbly over their native heaths, that Charlotte had some little difficulty in being able to keep up with them. They were too well acquainted with those glens, however, to follow throughout the same track by which she had penetrated into their retreat. A much shorter cut over the hill brought them, in not much more than an hour, to a summit from which the expanse of Lochfine could be descried; and, in half as much more time, Charlotte could see the old tower of Uigness breaking the outline between [them] and the bright waters. When they had reached the lower eminence immediately above the house, she hastened her steps, passed the swift bearers, and had gained the door of the tower before they had finished the descent.

Mr Blair never opened his eyes until the litter on which he had been conveyed was let down on the floor of the chamber which Charlotte had already prepared for his reception. It was then that he started up from his prostrate posture, and gazing wildly round him, seemed to be waking as from a dream. Charlotte motioned to the men, and they began to undress him; but although he kept his eyes open while they were obeying her directions, he appeared to have as yet no knowledge either of where he was, or of what they were doing with him. In silence, he suffered himself to be stript, nor did he offer any sort of resistance when they lifted up and bore him

179

towards the bed which had been made ready to receive him. A moment after, he sat upright in the couch, and fixing his eyes on the window, which was wide open to the air, seemed to be agitated all over with some new and sudden shudder of bodily anguish. He leaped from the bed with the activity of a man in full health and strength, escaping, or striving to escape, from a mortal foe – rushed towards the window – leaned over it naked as he was, and groaning over the beautiful prospect which lay spread out below him, sunk backwards upon the floor of the chamber.

He was quickly lifted up again, and borne back towards his bed, but when his hand touched the sheets he wrestled so violently, that the men were compelled to lay him down upon the ground. 'Not *there!*' he cried with a voice of thunder – 'not *there* – no, no – not *there!* Spare me that last agony, ye avengers of guilt – spare me, spare me, lay me anywhere but *there!*'

With these words he had exhausted his energy, and he lay once more feeble and helpless as an infant before them. But Charlotte dashed away the tears that had sprung into her eyes, and motioning with her hand to the bearers, led the way into an upper chamber, where another bed was hastily prepared. He tossed from side to side fiercely, stared round and round him with glazed, hot, burning eyeballs, but neither spoke a word after he had been laid there, nor made the least effort to lift his head from off the pillow.

The moment Mrs Campbell felt satisfied that he was too much weakened to attempt any farther violence, she dispatched the younger herdsman to Inverary, having desired the father on no account to quit the tower. She made every one leave the room, and closing the windows against the bright moon-light, she took her place in silence, and in darkness, beside the couch of Blair.

Chapter

16

———••§)(§••———

It was about noon, on the seventh day from that in which these things happened, that Adam Blair opened his eyes after being buried for fifteen hours in a deep sleep, and gazing about the chamber in which he was lying, began to make his first faint endeavour towards consciousness. He was so feeble that he could not lift his head from the pillow without being oppressed with a dizziness, under which he was immediately compelled to submit, and it was not until after many efforts, that he so far recovered himself as to be sensible that he was lying alone in a half-darkened room, and that many days must have passed over his head since any distinct image of any kind had been retained by his memory.

A dim, confused, languid, dream of interminable duration, seemed to have been hanging over his faculties, and even now he could scarcely satisfy himself that its oppression had passed away. During that long dreary night, what sufferings had he not undergone? Whither had his spirit wandered? Whence had it returned? Pain had been with him; burning pain had racked every thew and sinew of his frame. Chill icy pangs had been with him also; even yet his limbs were stiffened with the sense of cold, creeping anguish. But over all alike what a cloud of blackness, utter impenetrable blackness, had been wrapped and folded! Troubled visions had passed before him, glaring through the enveloping darkness – strange unearthly sights, mixed up with human faces he knew not of whom – strange hollow whispers, hands grasping him, and blindness, and helplessness, and dumbness, and deadness, suspended all the while like weights upon his bosom. His feeble brain reeled under the exertion his faculties were making to retrace something of what had been during this blank interval, and he closed his eyes because the lids felt so heavy that it was a pain for him to keep them open. Body and mind had been alike shaken, alike unstrung, by the fever through which he had passed; and he lay in a state of total languor, as if expecting some new assault of a mighty foe whom he had no longer either the power or the hope, or even the desire of resisting.

Suddenly, there came to his ear the echo of mournful music; and although it seemed to him at the first moment, as if it were produced quite close to him, he became sensible, after listening for a few moments, that the notes came from some considerable distance.

It was a wild, plaintive strain, played, as he fancied, on a single pipe – and he could not help imagining, that the same sounds had been heard by him more than once

183

during the long trance from which he had just been roused. Never was such a deep melancholy clothed in sweet sounds; never was melody so fit for feeble dying ears. The breath of it seemed as if it were wafted from some world of unearthly repose, some sphere of pensive majesty – above joy, too calm for sorrow. The tears flowed softly, slowly, healingly, over the sick man's cheek as he listened to those sounds, which seemed to be every moment receding farther, and dropping fainter from the wings of the light breeze that bore them.

The music stopt as suddenly as it had commenced, and Mr Blair felt as if all his illness were returning with its cessation. He, after one or two vain attempts, at last succeeded in quitting his bed, and finding that he could by no means support himself on his feet, he crawled like an infant towards the window. With much difficulty he opened a little piece more of the shutters, but shrunk back from the increase of light, as a strong man does from a torch held close to his eyes.

By degrees, however, he could not only endure the light, but as if moved by some strong instinctive thirst for the fresh air, he opened the casement also, and admitted the healthful breeze to play upon his worn and wasted frame. The balmy breath of Nature did not come to him in vain: it calmed his fluttering pulses, soothed every racked and wearied nerve, and sent renovated life into every exhausted vein. Nevertheless, the exertion he had made, had, for the moment, overtasked his forces, and I believe he would have sunk to the floor in a faint, when a new impulse was lent to his efforts by the recommencement of the same melancholy music, which had already enticed him from his bed of sickness.

He leaned his elbow on the stone frame-work of the window, and bent his eyes in the direction from which, as it appeared to him, the music proceeded: but he saw nothing except a single boat rowing away outwards into the Loch. A moment after, two other boats followed from behind a projection of the shore, not far from the place where he himself stood; and when he perceived that they were all moving together, he was satisfied it was in one or other of them that the musician was playing.

Slowly he followed with his heavy gaze the retreating course of the three boats, but he was altogether unable to distinguish any thing either of the number of persons in them, or of their quality. At last he saw them glide one after the other close upon the little islet of Inchree, which lies nearly half way between Uigness and the opposite coast of Lochfine. He observed, that none of them emerged again upon the water beyond the wooded island, and concluded that their object had been to fish under the shelter of its rocks. A moment after, however, it flashed upon his mind that he had once heard some dark and mournful story, the scene of which was laid in that desolate land. Who had told him that story? – Strange to say, it was so that the first idea of CHARLOTTE was that day excited within his mind; but, oh! with that idea what thousand thoughts of grief, shame, terror, misery, floated into his bosom, like the black lashing waves of some returning and irresistible sea.

In an instant, the whole mystery of his malady lay clear before him; he remembered every thing that had happened on the day after that night of darkness as if it had occurred but a few hours before; he remembered the image of the distant glen, and the black shieling, and Charlotte there bending over him unexpectedly, and the bier on which he was carried, and the motion of the bier, and the faces of the men that conveyed him. He remembered his being carried into the house; – his spasm of horror when he felt himself on the bed of Charlotte, seemed as if it had scarcely left his bosom. Then he remembered something more confusedly, of drink being administered to him by Charlotte, and of his dashing the cup from her hand, and lying before her, burning with thirst, cursing her with his eyes. Then it seemed as if she had kissed him where he lay motionless with cold lips, which glowed at the touch – and then, all at once, she vanished, and there was nothing behind except one mingled mass of dream and delirium – dull dreary images, all huddled together, alike obscure, alike painful. Where was Charlotte now? – What had become of her? – Why had she deserted him? – Had he driven her from him in anger? – Had he in madness insulted her? – Had she fled from him in wrath? – All these thoughts, and hundreds more, flashed in rapid succession over his mind; and the weary body, yielding at last to the unequal conflict, sank altogether helpless, and almost as insensible as helpless, upon the floor.

He was lifted from it again after the lapse of a few moments, and once more recovering himself, he found that he was in the arms of an old woman, and of a young man clad in black, and having something the appearance of a gentleman.

He said nothing until they had laid him on his couch, and folded the bed-clothes over him; and then he asked feebly for something to drink. The old woman reached a glass to him, and he drank abundantly, and felt refreshed to the core as he closed his eyes.

Chapter

17

—••€ ❳❲ Ʒ••—

Exhausted nature asserted her privilege, and once more
Mr Blair's senses were steeped for a long succession of
hours in the profoundest forgetfulness. The clamour of
turbulent voices, with which the chambers below him
resounded, during a great part of the evening of that day,
had no power to rouse him from this deep and motionless slumber; and when he at length awoke again about
the rising of the moon, everything about him was silent,
his brain felt cool and composed, and he fixed his eyes
stedfastly upon a human figure kneeling alone at the
foot of the bed on which he was lying. The feeble twilight was not enough to shew him anything more than
the general outline, and he continued gazing on it, for
some time, without betraying, either by word or gesture,
that sleep had deserted his eyelids.

At last he said, 'Friend, who are you, who is here
with me?' in a whisper; and the moment he had said so,
the kneeling man arose slowly, and bending over him,
and taking hold of his hand, made answer also in a

whisper, 'It is I – it is John Maxwell – Heaven be praised that you see me!'

Mr Blair drew his hand from between the old man's clasping fingers, and pulled the sheet over his face, and replied, groaning deeply, 'John Maxwell, John Maxwell, you know not what you do, you know not whom you bend over, you know not for whom you have prayed!'

'Dear sir, dear Mr Adam,' replied the old man, 'I pray you be composed; look at me, and you will know me well: I am John Maxwell, and you are Adam Blair, my friend, my minister – you have had a sweet sleep, and all will yet be well again.'

'Oh, never!' the sick man groaned from underneath his bed-clothes, 'Never – never – never more! Leave me, good John, leave a sinner, an outcast, a wretch abandoned of the Almighty. I pray you, leave me to myself! – Against you also have I sinned.'

'Sir, dear sir, you wander; your mind is not yet restored; your dreams and visions yet hang about you. I pray you let me feel your hand – it is burning hot again, and yet now it is cool. – I pray you shake these terrible fancies from you, and know yourself and me. We are here, we are both at Uigness; but all is well at home, and you will be strong again, and we shall soon return together to Cross-Meikle.'

'Home! – Home! – Cross-Meikle! return together to Cross-Meikle! – My God spare me!'

'The Lord's will be done, Mr Adam; you must not forget that blessed text: "The Lord giveth, and the Lord taketh away.' This is not the first awful bereavement you have undergone. Hitherto, the Lord hath holpen you; yet, again, you shall be strengthened with strength that is from above.'

He paused for a moment ere he made answer. 'Bereavement! – of what speak ye? – Surely, my spirit wanders indeed. Of what thing is it that you speak to me?'

'Oh! sir,' said John, 'if you knew it not before, I have done much amiss.'

'Speak out – let me hear – have you brought me evil tidings of my child? I charge you speak out. I am prepared for all things! – what blow can be too great?'

'God be praised, the bairn was well two days ago, and I trust is so now. – It was not of her that I spake.'

'Of whom spake you?'

'Oh! sir, you terrify me with your groans. Listen to me more composedly else I cannot speak. – I spake of her whom we have this day buried. – I spake of Mrs Campbell.'

At that word Mr Blair threw the bed-clothes from off his countenance, and sitting upright, gazed stedfastly upon the old man's face, on which by this time the moon-light was streaming clearly. 'What say you of burial? – of death? – Let me hear you speak. – I pray you, let me hear it all.'

'Ah! now sir, this is like yourself; it is so we should hear of what it has pleased God to do. But surely they told you before how the fever had wrought with her.

Surely, they said to me that you had seen the boats as they were rowing off for Inchree.'

The remembrance of the solemn music, and the three boats, floated over Mr Blair's mind when he heard this. He remained in silence for a few moments, and then flung himself back upon his pillow, and weeping aloud, cried, 'Oh God! oh God! not one hour for repentance! not one hour for tears! oh God! why sparest thou the blacker sinner? – why lie I here to be told of this? – I remember it all, I remember it all clearly now. I remember her watching over me, I remember my spurning her away! – Yes, yes, I see it clearly; from me, from me she caught this malady! – Great God, in darkness thou workest! Terrible Maker, all is night around thee.'

With these words of anguish, Mr Blair once more covered his face, and for a space of many minutes, John Maxwell could not prevail upon him to make answer to any thing he said. The old man stood all the while leaning over his couch in a state of painful suspense, but, after a time, he desisted from addressing him. He had been silent, therefore, for a little space, when Blair suddenly started up again, and said in a tone, the composure of which, following as it did so many broken and groaning ejaculations, thrilled him even more than any voice of violent emotion could have done, – 'John Maxwell, I am faint at heart, I would fain have food. Get me something speedily that I may eat and drink. My fever has left me, and deep weakness is all that remains.'

'Thank God,' said John, 'thank God for that word I have heard. Be calm, dear sir, and I shall return to you immediately.'

So saying, the old man left him, and after a few minutes, came back with a salver of bread and honey-comb, and a large basin of milk. Mr Blair turned away his face, while the old man pronounced a blessing upon what he had brought, and then recovering all his composure of look and gesture, began to swallow eagerly whatever was prepared for him. 'So,' said he, after he had ate and drank abundantly, 'even so. The frail body will soon be able to sustain the needful pains that are before me. Once more, good old man, I thank you – I thank you – unworthy though I be of your kindness, God will not disdain it.' And he added, after a pause, 'John Maxwell, come to me early in the morning; but leave me now, for I feel that I shall sleep once more, and when that is over, I shall be better able for that which must be said and done.'

The old man smoothed his pillow, saw him stretched in the attitude of perfect repose, and then obeyed him by quitting the chamber. He went no farther than the door, however: having taken his seat immediately behind it, he lighted his taper, and prepared him to watch there, lest his Minister should have any occasion for his services during the night.

Blair, meanwhile, strong in resolve, even in the midst of misery and weakness, conquered the thousand thoughts that would have banished repose, and slept on, perhaps, with such deep and death-like slumbers as visit the eyelids of hopeless men, who know that, sleep they or wake they, death awaits them on the morrow. – Nor was it anything wonderful that the wearied old man slept soundly too, although he had resolved upon watching. He had been for two days a traveller, and had not enjoyed anything more than hasty and broken slumbers ever since he set out from Cross-Meikle in quest of his Minister.

—••E)(E••—

Mr Strahan, repelled in the ruffian insults with which he had ventured to harass Mrs Campbell, quitted Uigness, it may be supposed, on his return to the Low Country, in no very enviable state of feeling. He was riding rapidly, like a man capable of any thing but repose – (for the shame of detection was to him in the place of the shame of guilt, and scorn of what he conceived to be an injury done to himself, was blended with many uneasy anticipations of what he might have to suffer from the merited anger and scorn of Captain Campbell, his employer, whose trust he had so foully betrayed,) – when his notice was attracted by a boat moving, as it seemed, towards the tower he had just abandoned: And when he recognized the form of Mr Blair, it was with a fiendish, and, at the same time, a cowardly joy that he did so; for it immediately flashed upon him that the Clergyman had followed Mrs Campbell thither by her invitation, and under the intoxicating influence of a guilty passion; and secure in the sense of having at least ascertained, (for so he thought he had now done,) the justice of his own and Captain Campbell's original suspicions, he, from that moment, discarded the troublesome meditations which regarded himself more personally, and continued his journey in a mood almost as triumphant as malignant.

His surprise was great, when, on reaching the inn at which he generally put up when in Glasgow, he heard himself suddenly called to from a window looking out upon the court-yard, in a voice which could belong to no one but Campbell of Uigness himself. It was not without a considerable struggle, though brief in duration, that he contrived to smooth his brow sufficiently for entering the room in which the Captain was waiting for him; but he was relieved once more from his trepidations, when Campbell, receiving him with all his usual cordiality, said simply, 'Strahan, I was astonished at not hearing from you; and besides, I thought this was a piece of business I had done wrong in devolving upon you or any man, when I was in a condition to execute it myself. So, I e'en put my foot in a vessel that was a-sailing for Leith, and here I am, so far on my way in quest of this unhappy woman. Not finding you in Edinburgh, and hearing that you had gone westwards, I took it for granted you had set off for Uigness. – Is it not so? – speak: tell me all that has happened – tell me all you know; I am prepared for every thing. You can at least have nothing to tell that will *surprise* me.'

Mr Strahan replied by a brief summary of all that he himself had done. When he came to the end of the story, however, he found himself a little at a loss to account for his having suffered Mr Blair to approach the house of Uigness, without having taken care to provide proper evidence of the fact of his coming thither, and remaining there, alone with Mrs Campbell, under such circumstances of suspicion. He stammered for a moment, when this idea crossed his mind, and then concluded his speech, with saying very boldly, 'I thought it was of no use, sir, to go about the matter, when it had come thus far in any thing but the most deliberate and accurate manner. So I took boat, and came thus far, that I might procure the assistance of two or three people of respectability, personally acquainted with this Blair, with whom it was my attention to return to Uigness tomorrow, and so put an end to the whole affair at once.'

'Right, right, quite right,' muttered Campbell, with a sullen and dogged sneer; – 'but I believe there is no great need for all this now, – I know Charlotte better than you do. I shall go and see them myself, – and trust me, there will be no need for any more witnesses. But, to-morrow, as you say, will be time enough; i'faith, there is no fear of their parting so soon after they have taken so much trouble to meet. This is Sunday, is it not? damme, you may swear he'll take the week out at Uigness ere he thinks of coming back to his psalm-singing. – I have just ordered some dinner, ——, we'll join our messes, and make a night on't; and now I think on't, I have not tasted your right rum-punch for these five years. – Geneva! by Jove, you can get any other schnaps

where you please, but I never tasted rum that was worth
the name, except either over the herring-pond, or here
in this pretty town. What signifies being in the dumps,
Strahan; – and about a woman? Oh fie! a false judge
of a woman – Why, what says the old song? – I'll sing
it: – by Jove, I'll sing it, below their window.

> 'Your most beautiful bit,
>   That hath all eyes upon her,
> That her honesty sells
>   For a haut-gout of honour;
> Whose lightness, and brightness
>   Doth shine in such splendour,
> That none but the stars
>   Are thought fit to attend her, –
> Though now she be pleasant
>   And sweet to the sense,
> Will be damnable mouldy
>   *A hundred years hence.*'

Pooh! pooh! Master Duncan Strahan, my very good
friend, you shall give me the grace-cup of salt and water,
if you see me flinch once for all that's come and gone.'
    Duncan Strahan drew his chair, and caroused till
cock-crow with the valiant Captain; as it is like enough
many brothers of his trade had done before, and have
done since – with clients, who would have broken
their heads had they known all the services they had
received at the hands of these smooth-faced bottle com-
panions. A few short hours of feverish slumber were
sufficient to make Captain Campbell himself again,

and after breakfast they parted, Mr Strahan proceeding in his own course to Edinburgh, and Uigness committing himself to the fortunes of a Lochfine boat, which he had discovered at the Broomielaw.

Mr Strahan, in his way eastward, halted for a few hours at the house of a gentleman who resided in the parish immediately adjoining to Cross-Meikle, and took occasion, with infinite dexterity, as he thought, to insinuate all his own notions concerning Mr Blair's conduct, and the motives of his absence from his own residence. Dr Muir, the minister of the parish where this took place, happened to call in the course of the morning, and received the scandal from the lady of the mansion, at which Strahan had dropt it. He, with great indignation, took up Blair's defence; but having, as he thought, effectually undone the evil in that quarter, he could not help riding over to Cross-Meikle, ere he returned to his own house, for the purpose of making some farther inquiries, either among the Semplehaugh family, or the domestics at the Manse. In the course of his ride, he fell in with the elder, John Maxwell, whose friendship for Mr Blair, as well as his influence in the parish, were both so well known, that the Doctor did not hesitate to enter into some conversation with him upon the subject that occupied his reflections. The result of this conversation, whatever it might be, was, that next morning, honest Maxwell took his staff in his hand, and commenced the longest journey he had undertaken for more than a score of summers – to Lochfine side.

He did not reach the place of his destination, however, until long after Captain Campbell, who had at command much greater personal vigour, to say nothing of other appliances to boot, had once more gained the shore of his native loch.

As he sailed up the strait, on the evening of the second day after his parting from Strahan at Glasgow, and saw, at last, before him, the tower of Uigness, with all its woods and rocks – Campbell, who had hitherto performed his journey in a mood of sulkiness, almost of indifference, felt his bosom kindled with a savage and yearning rage. – He leaped on shore the moment his boatmen halted on their oars, and without saying a single word to any one of the crew, rushed swiftly up the rocky path, to his mansion. His hand was on the hilt of his sword when he stepped over his threshold, and entered his long deserted hall: – and his face glowed with the stern scarlet of revenge.

He had not time to penetrate into the inner part of the house ere his motions were arrested by the young gentleman who has already been mentioned. Seeing that his dress was black, he never doubted that he was in the presence of Blair, and the first words he uttered were, 'Kneel, rascal! kneel, holy rascal, and say your last prayers, and let them be the sincerest you ever said, as well as the shortest!'

The young man started backwards from the furious man, and answered calmly, 'My name is Campbell; I am a surgeon at Inverary; I have come hither, because I was sent for: I have done what I could, although I came too late: what is it that you or any man has to say to me?'

Captain Campbell put up his weapon in great confusion, and having craved pardon for his violence, passed at once into the extreme of cool civility. The surgeon, on his part, lost no time in informing him that he had been sent for to see a strange gentleman, who had been taken violently ill at a cottage in a neighbouring glen, and conveyed to Uigness by the attention of Mrs Campbell – that he had come, accordingly, two days before – that the gentleman, after great sufferings, had at last begun to give hopes of overcoming the disorder; but that Mrs Campbell had caught the infection, and already yielded under the violence of the fever. 'God knows,' added the surgeon, 'what is now to be done? There is no one here but a single old woman, and a couple of ignorant herdsmen, and I know not who is the person that ought to be sent for in the absence of Uigness.'

'I am the man,' answered Campbell in a low and broken voice – 'I am James Campbell of Uigness. – My wife is dead?'

The young man bowed in great confusion, being quite shocked with the thought of having communicated his fatal intelligence in a manner so abrupt.

Campbell stood before him for some time with his eyes fixed stedfastly on the ground, and then motioned to him to lead the way up stairs. The young man made an effort to restrain him, but perceiving that this was in vain, he obeyed, and threw open the door of the chamber, wherein the remains of Charlotte had already been stretched forth in her winding-sheet. – Campbell signed for the surgeon to leave him the moment he entered the room.

He passed an hour there by himself, for aught that was known, in total silence; and came out with no trace of tears on his cheeks, but with an air of melancholy and depression, such as would have not a little surprised any one acquainted with his character. He conversed calmly with the surgeon; desired him to do all he could for Mr Blair; gave directions about his wife's interment, for which he fixed the proper day and hour; and then took leave, saying, that he must needs go and warn some of his relatives in person, but that he should take care to be back at Uigness the morning of the day on which the funeral was to take place.

When he returned he found John Maxwell in attendance upon the sick man along with the surgeon, and having heard who he was, and what was his errand, he received him with much courtesy. He made John sit in the boat with him as he went over to Inchree, where the ancient burial vault of his family was situated; and, in like manner, when, after Charlotte had been laid in the dust, he rowed back again from that desolate island to Uigness. His company, according to the custom of the Highlands on such occasions, sat long and drank deep, but he had not failed more than once to make inquiries after the condition of Mr Blair in the course of the evening. On the whole, as John himself had as yet entertained no belief in his Minister's guilt, so he had as yet found no reason to suppose that Captain Campbell had the least suspicion, of the sort with which his mind was in reality but too deeply filled: and the good old man slept that night beside the door of the sick man's chamber – alas! with more serenity than he was destined to know for many a long night thereafter.

Chapter

18

—••◄❊►••—

Long before Mr Blair awoke next morning, Captain Campbell had again quitted the house of Uigness, nor did he again return thither until nearly two days had elapsed.

The truth is, that no man's mind ever underwent a more sudden and remarkable change than his had done, in consequence of the events which have already been narrated. He had originally married Charlotte merely because he admired her beautiful person, and pitied her for the hard treatment she had received at the hands of young Arden; but after the lapse of a short time, the facility with which she had hearkened to his own addresses, came to be thought of by him in a manner of which there have been, and it is to be feared, at all times will be, but too many examples among our ungenerous sex, and the very circumstances which had, at first, afforded gratification to his vanity, furnished, in the sequel, food to that suspicious and jealous temper by which his character, like that of very many vain men, was distinguished. In short, ere they had lived together for many months in their Highland solitude, they had mutually become very sensible to their unfitness for each other: but, it must be admitted, that while Charlotte controlled her high spirit, and strove to the utmost to appear an affectionate wife, Mr Campbell had either less pride or less art, and very soon gave up any attempt to conceal his real sentiments. When they left Scotland, and mingled again in the world, Charlotte's naturally lively disposition led her to make up to herself, by a large participation in all the pleasures of social life, for the long restraint and solitude of her residence with her husband at Uigness; while he, bringing with him into the open scenes of life all that suspiciousness which had been too well nursed in his retirement, watched every ebullition of her thoughtless glee and vivacity with an eye of predetermined evil, and caused her to chequer her hours of gaiety by many bitter tears shed in moments of secrecy. Their mutual dislike was at last brought to a point, which rendered it next to impossible for them to remain any longer together, by some circumstances trivial enough in themselves, and with the relation of which I shall not therefore fatigue the reader's patience. Charlotte left Holland, and came to Scotland by herself. The first news Campbell received of her was through the channel of Mr Strahan; and we have already had abundance of leisure to observe what consequences were produced from the malicious view he had given of Charlotte's residence under Mr Blair's roof at Cross-Meikle.

But when Captain Campbell received the sudden intelligence of his wife's death – and the moment after, contemplated with his own eyes the cold remains of the beauty he had once worshipped – a crowd of thoughts which he had for years banished, and which had never been so utterly alien to his mind as they were but a few seconds before, rushed into a bosom not by nature entirely devoid of generous feelings, nor incapable of reflection, and overcame and vanquished all the fiery passions with which his soul had been so deeply and so recently filled and agitated. In a single moment, the image of all his own early conduct to this unfortunate woman rose clearly on his memory; the harsh, and causeless, and visible transition from love to aversion, by which he had chilled and checked all her young affections, was, for the first time, remembered with a self-reproaching acuteness; and Campbell bending over the lovely corse, smote his bosom, and accused himself of having been the true cause of too many of her worst errors. The feelings of shame and sorrow which mingled in his breast left little room for anger, and this very moment, when, for the first time, he was certain of having been injured, was also that in which he, for the first time, felt himself to be capable of forgiving an injury.

The favourable accounts he had formerly heard of Mr Blair's character, even from Mr Strahan himself, recurred to his mind, softened as it was by these feelings; and when he had conversed with John Maxwell, and so ascertained to what a depth of veneration the regard of Mr Blair's parishioners for their minister in reality amounted, we must do Mr Campbell the justice to say, that he began to contemplate even the guilt by which his own honour had been wounded, with emotions rather of sorrow than of wrath. Aware as he was that a blot which the world would have thought comparatively little about in any other man, could not be discovered in the character of a minister of the Church of Scotland, without bringing along with it utter ruin, both of reputation and of fortune, and having no longer any personal advantage to expect from proving the guilt of his wife, but rather good reason to wish that all her faults should be buried in oblivion, Mr Campbell's feelings were entirely adverse to any public exposure of Mr Blair. He was a hot, a violent, a vain, and in many respects a rude man, but we must give him credit for both feeling and acting on this occasion, in a style of which a great many more polished characters might have been altogether incapable under similar circumstances. He determined to have some private conversation with Mr Blair, as soon as he should be so far recovered as to be able to listen to him without bodily harm, and then having delivered him from those fears, with which he naturally enough supposed he must be labouring, to dismiss him from Uigness in safety. And as soon as he should have done this, it was his intention once more to quit Scotland, and rejoin his regiment abroad.

Mr Blair, on the other hand, had been led to conceive, from the report John Maxwell made of Captain Campbell's behaviour, that his suspicions had either been originally less violent than Mr Strahan had represented them to be, or that he had dismissed them from his bosom, in consequence of some circumstances to himself unknown. With such feelings, we may easily suppose how Mr Blair's sensitive mind, more especially now, enfeebled as it was by bodily illness, shrunk and recoiled from the idea of meeting the man he had so deeply injured. But, to say truth, there was so great a cloud of deeper sorrow on that anxious and shaken mind, that this was rather an occasional visitant than one of its continual burdens.

With the restoration of his bodily health, he recovered, of course, in some measure, his command over his conduct; but while there was that in him that made him feel every kind confiding look the good old Maxwell threw upon him as if it had been a dagger thrust into his heart, he was nevertheless as yet quite incapable of summoning up the courage requisite for a solemn and deliberate confession of his guilt. Hour after hour, while the pious old man sat reading aloud by his bed-side, he lay brooding over his own unseen miseries, and striving to nerve himself for disclosing what he could not endure the thought of keeping concealed. Yet, whenever he had framed his lips for uttering the fatal words, his heart died again within him, and he was fain to defer the effort, even although he in part felt that the longer it was deferred, it would in the end be the more painful.

Perhaps this continual uneasiness, harassing as it was in itself, might nevertheless be of some advantage to Mr Blair's mind, by breaking the tenor of those profounder meditations of misery, to which the writer of such a story as this can venture no more than an allusion; – the secret miseries of a soul prostrate under the sense of spiritual abandonment. Had there been no thoughts of a less awful, however painful, nature, to disturb the deep flow of that stream of mental anguish, who shall say whether a mind such as his might not have sunk into that utmost abyss, on the brink of which he too often hovered? The weight of human sorrow, like that of human power, is broken by being divided – and in the midst of his chastisement, mercy was present with him.

Such is a very slight and superficial sketch of the state in which these two men's minds were, when they met for the first time in their lives. Mr Blair was walking very slowly on the smooth sand by the sea-shore, supported by John Maxwell's arm, and listening not to the words of comfort which the good man was whispering into his ear, but to the deep and hollow rush of the waves, in their advance upon the beach, – when suddenly the sound of a horse's hoofs was heard behind them, and John, looking back, told Mr Blair that here came Uigness himself. They halted, and Captain Campbell, slackening his pace as he approached, saluted Mr Blair with very grave courtesy. Blair, on his part, with some difficulty uncovered himself to return the salutation, and displayed to Mr Campbell's eyes, a head, the hair of which had, in the course of not many days, been changed from black to grey, under the mingled influences of mental and corporeal sufferings. The suddenness with which this change had taken place, was of course unknown to Mr Campbell; but even without being aware of that, there was enough in the appearance of Mr Blair's countenance as well as figure, to astonish one who knew the shortness of the period during which he had been confined. His mind became inconsciously more and more softened as he gazed on the wan and wasted form before him, and that face on which the darkest melancholy seemed to sit enthroned in the midst of languor and feebleness; and he felt so much compassion, that he certainly would have passed on without speaking, had he not believed that what he had to say must tend to restore something of the tranquillity, the absence of which was so visible.

He dismounted, and placing the rein in John Maxwell's hand, requested him to pass on with the horse to a little distance, as he had something which he must say in private to Mr Blair. John, though hesitatingly, obeyed his direction; but not until he had spread his plaid on a large stone, and seen Mr Blair seated there in safety.

As soon as John had walked fifty yards off, Captain Campbell, who had hitherto looked downwards, fixed his eyes on the pale countenance which Mr Blair had not the power at that moment to avert from his gaze, and broke silence in a tone but little above a whisper.

'Mr Blair,' said he, 'seeing you so imperfectly recovered, I should scarcely have stopped you, unless I had hoped to give you in so far relief. I am perfectly willing, sir, to give you my solemn assurance, that I shall not only do nothing against your character, but that I shall do whatever I can in your behalf, if need be.

– Sir, you are a young man, and I believe you have already repented of your offence. I forgive you, – I forgive you, freely, sir. Go back to your own country, and guard yourself better. The grave has swallowed up all my resentment. – I hope *you* have not had so near a look of it for nothing.'

Mr Blair shook from head to foot like a child, and kept his wide eyes fixed stedfastly on Campbell while he was saying this; and when he stopped, he gasped and gazed on, without being able to utter a single word.

Captain Campbell paused for a moment, and then resumed, 'Sir, I am afraid I have agitated you more than I thought for. When you are left to yourself, you will remember what I have said; and remember that you may rely upon it, as much as if I had sworn by the God – who hears us, whether we swear or not. Sir, I hope you will recover yourself, and not betray anything of this new emotion to your old friend when he rejoins you. – I have ordered a boat for you, according to what the Doctor said, and it will be ready in the morning. I wish you health, sir. – Farewell.' –

With this, Campbell parted from Mr Blair, remounted his horse, and returned to the place from which he had come. John Maxwell led his trembling Minister into the house again, not suspecting any thing more than doubting that the increased agitation he observed had been produced by the sight of a person, whose appearance could not fail to be instantly associated with the image of the buried lady. And, indeed, after a little time, Mr Blair recovered his composure in a singular degree, and gave directions about preparing all things for the voyage of the morrow, in a manner so quiet, and distinct, that the kind old man heard him with feelings of refreshed hope – I had almost said of cheerfulness.

Little did John Maxwell, – little did Captain Campbell suspect what were the secret workings of Adam Blair's mind, during the last night he spent in the tower of Uigness.

Chapter
19

—••⁑••—

They embarked next day, beneath a warm atmosphere and a bright sunshine; and perhaps it was so much the better for the convalescent man, that there was not wind enough to fill the sails of the boat in which he lay. Slowly they made their progress by the strength of oars; and with difficulty, reached Rothesay-bay ere the evening closed. It was another long day's voyage to Greenock; and during the whole of the time, Mr Blair had reclined in the stern of the wherry, wrapt up from the air of the sea, and preserving the same aspect of silent dejection with which he had quitted the shore of Uigness. Nor after a time, did his aged friend interrupt his meditations by many words; for he perceived, that any answers he could extract, were things uttered merely at random, and rightly judged, that whatever disease remained was in the mind, which must slowly work out its own cure for itself.

The third day, Mr Blair took his station in a passage-boat for Glasgow, after committing the care of the horse, which had been left all this time at Greenock, to the charge of John Maxwell; – He, on his part, rode on early in the morning, that he might reach the city in time to prepare accommodations for his Minister.

Mr Blair held little communication with any of the persons who travelled in the passage-boat along with him; and indeed, after a little time, shut his eyes as if asleep, that he might the better escape from their notice. As the river narrowed before him, however, it was evident that he partook in that sort of excitement which is generally diffused over any set of people, when they feel that their journey is nearly at an end. He did not, indeed, mingle in the conversation which was going on round about him, but he sat up in the stern of the boat, and every now and then fixed his eyes eagerly in the direction of the city to which he was approaching. He saw at length, the high towers of the Minster rising far above the woods which clothe the left bank of the stream; and from that moment, he never ceased to gaze towards them. Once or twice he rose from his seat, sat down again suddenly, and then rose again, all in the space of half a minute; insomuch, that the man beside him, who had the direction of the helm, was obliged to request him to lessen his impatience, lest he should injure the balance of the boat, adding, that in a very short time he would be able to see the Broomielaw, without stirring from his seat.

And they soon reached that little hamlet by the riverside, which the progress of half a century has converted into a crowded line of quays in the heart of a great city.

John Maxwell was already waiting for them on the pier; and as soon as Mr Blair had stepped ashore, he informed him that he had provided a bed for him at the house he generally frequented in the High Street; and in the meantime, ordered some dinner, which would be ready by the time they should have walked through the town. John added, that he suspected it was a Presbytery day, for that he had passed more than one of the neighbouring ministers, although none with whom he was personally acquainted. Mr Blair leaned strongly on his arm when he heard him say this, and began to walk towards the city, at a pace which, though unequal, was on the whole so rapid, that it a good deal surprised the old man.

Mr Blair was obliged to sit down and rest himself more than once before he reached the heart of the old town of Glasgow; but ascended the long street with which his journey terminated, even more swiftly than he had begun his walk. After he had entered the inn, his first questions to the landlord were, whether or not this was a day on which the Presbytery had a meeting, and if he had seen any thing of Dr Muir of Cambuslee. The man replied to both in the affirmative: he added, that the old Doctor had proceeded up the hill to the High Church some hours before, and that he expected him and the rest of the clergymen to dine in his house after their business was concluded.

The remarks which the publican and his wife made in relation to the 'awful shake' Mr Blair had evidently had while he was in the Highlands, were in number, and perhaps in expression, such as might have been expected, but it did not escape Mr Blair's notice, that the looks with which these people regarded him had, in their turn, undergone some change also. The landlady in particular was visibly fluttered, and there was a chillness over the whole surface of her civility, altogether unlike what he had ever observed before in the same quarter. Mr Blair eyed the pair keenly and in silence, while he sat for about ten minutes by their fire-side, and then rising once more, said to Maxwell, 'Come, John, I must have your assistance yet a little farther. I must go up the hill to the Presbytery.'

'If it be not for the length of the walk,' said John, 'I'm sure ye'll be meikle the better for seeing your friends all about you again; and I'm sure they'll be as glad to see you, as ye can be to see them.'

With this they were leaving the inn; but just before they passed out into the street, the landlord ran after them, and drew back John Maxwell, whispering into his ear, that he had something particular to say to him. John followed the man to a little distance, conversed with him in whispers for a few minutes, and then rejoined his Minister. When he did so, there was a burning spot on each of his old cheeks, and his lips were white as marble; but Mr Blair took not, or seemed not to take any notice of all this, and once more leaning upon his arm, began to walk up the steep hill on the brow of which the cathedral is situated – although not with quite the same celerity of motion which had excited John's surprise a little while before. As they walked on, several persons stared very much at Mr Blair, and many stood still to look at him after he had passed them, but he met no one who seemed to be personally acquainted with him, until he had reached the great and spacious church-yard, which lies stretched for many a rood round about the cathedral.

As they were passing over the tomb-stones towards the eastern gate of the edifice, two or three beadles and church-officers crossed their path, and Mr Blair, when he perceived how much they stared at seeing him, could not help observing to his attendant, 'Surely, John, this illness has sorely changed my aspect. These people scarcely seem to know me again.' But it was now John's turn to give answers wide of the mark, and he replied, lifting his eyes hastily from the ground, ''Tis a grand place, sure enough, a very awfu' place; but I like our ain kirk at Cross-Meikle far better, though it be nae bigger than ane of the side aisles here.'

In those days, the ecclesiastical courts of that district were still held in the ancient Chapter-house, a chamber of very lofty proportions, situated close to the eastern extremity of the nave, and approached through what was formerly the Lady-chapel, immediately behind the great altar of the Cathedral of Glasgow. In this now deserted chapel, serving as a sort of anti-chamber to the Presbytery, a number of the ecclesiastical attendants were pacing backwards and forwards when they reached it; while two or three seemed to be listening at the key-hole of the Chapter-house door. There was an evident confusion among the whole of these persons when it was discovered that Mr Blair was in the midst of them; and when he motioned to the man nearest the door, that he wished to have admittance, this confusion rose so high, that any one must have perceived on the instant, there was some particular circumstance at the bottom of it. One or two hands were stretched out as if to prevent him from approaching the door; but when he laid his hand on the bolt, and was just about to throw it open, one of the men drew close to him with an eager face, and whispered something which John Maxwell, although he was standing immediately behind, could not hear.

'I know it well,' was Mr Blair's answer – and the words were uttered in a voice perfectly calm as well as distinct – 'I know it well; for that very cause am I here. Do you open the door for me.'

The man at last obeyed; Mr Blair, as he was turning the key, grasped John Maxwell's hand fervidly, although without looking back to him. The moment after, the door closed again, and John was left alone with these attendants.

Chapter
20

When the clergymen composing the Presbytery found themselves assembled that day, it would have been evident to any one who might have been present, that their minds were occupied with something very different from the ordinary routine of their ecclesiastical business. The clerk read his minutes without being listened to by any body, and while many little matters were being arranged in the usual manner, among the usual functionaries, the different members of the court were seen forming themselves into knots, and whispering together low and anxiously in various corners of the Chapterhouse. At length one of the members, a tall, thin, elderly person of very formal aspect, moved that the court should be cleared, as he had to call the attention of his brethren to a subject, which, in its present state, ought to be discussed with closed doors.

When this clergyman, by name Stevenston, was satisfied that all strangers had retired, he addressed the chair in a long and elaborate speech, for the tenor of which almost all who heard him were sufficiently prepared before he opened his lips. He expatiated at great length on his own unwillingness at all times to open his ears to scandal, more particularly against the character of any of his hitherto respected brethren; – explained, however, that, under certain circumstances, it was every man's duty to overcome his private feelings; – and then entered into a serious, circumstantial detail of the many rumours which had been for some time afloat, concerning the conduct of Mr Blair of Cross-Meikle. He concluded with moving a string of resolutions, which he held written out on a card in his hand – the general purport of which was, that the scandal concerning this member of their court had already amounted to what, in the ecclesiastical phraseology of Scotland, goes under the name of a *Fama Clamosa;* and that, therefore, it was the bounden duty of the Presbytery to take up the matter *quam primum*, and appoint a committee, with powers to commence a *precognition* – and that such and such persons ought to constitute the committee in question. His motion was instantly seconded by another person on the same side of the house, who, however, in doing so, expressed his own firm belief that there was no foundation whatever for the foul allegations too publicly circulated against Mr Blair, and that, on a proper investigation (which, for the sake of Mr Blair himself, ought to take place without any further delay) it would become manifest to all, that a few casual imprudencies, misinterpreted by the malicious, were all that could be laid

218

to his charge. He concluded with a eulogium on Mr Blair's previous character and conduct, both of which, he said, had always been regarded with the deepest respect, even by those who differed most widely from him in opinion as to matters of inferior moment – and by none more so than himself.

When this speaker sat down, there ensued a pause of some moments, during which, those on the opposite side of the room (the same among whom Mr Blair himself usually sat) were seen consulting among themselves, as if anxious, and yet hesitating, to make some reply. Dr Muir, who happened to be the Moderator of the Presbytery, and of course had his seat apart from any of the other clergymen, continued for some time looking towards them, and at last he rose up, and requested one of their number to relieve him, for a moment, from the duties of the chair.

As soon as he had quitted the desk, the old man, still standing in the open space in the centre of the room, threw his eyes eagerly round him, and began to speak of the matter which had been brought before their notice, characterizing as rash and imprudent, in the highest degree, the conduct of those who had broached such a subject in the absence of the person most immediately concerned in it, and fervidly expressing his own utter contempt of the rumours they had heard of, and his most sincere conviction, (for such it was) that the pure and stainless character of Mr Blair had been assailed in consequence of nothing but the malice of one individual, whose name need only be mentioned in order to satisfy the Presbytery with how much caution they ought to proceed upon this occasion. – He then sunk into a lower but not a less serious tone, and – after desiring his brethren, with the authority which years and superior talents alone can bestow, to banish all thoughts of party in considering an assault which might have been made with equal success, as well as, he firmly believed, with equal justice, against any one of all who heard him – the old man proceeded to relate the substance of the conversation he had himself held with Mr Blair the night before he left Cross-Meikle, and the solemn denial of the alleged guilt which he had then received from the lips of his young friend. Dr Muir himself felt, as he went on, that what he said was producing a powerful effect, and he therefore opened himself more and more freely, and reviewing the whole course of Adam Blair's existence, dared any one present to avow his belief, that even if he had been capable of offending in the manner imputed to him, he could have been so of telling a deliberate and an uncalled-for LIE. 'Sirs,' said he, 'I put it to all of you, whether you do not feel and know that Adam Blair is innocent; and is it thus, that while we are ourselves convinced of his innocence, we are rashly, hastily, sinfully to injure our brother, by countenancing the clamours of the ignorant, and the malicious, and the ungodly, in his absence? Would to God that he were present with us this day, that he might have done for himself effectually, what a feeble old man has rather the will than the power to do for him!'

Dr Muir was speaking fervently in this strain, and the visible emotion of a man who generally controlled and concealed his more ardent feelings, was kindling even the coldest who listened into the same congenial warmth, when the door of the Chapter-house opened, and in walked Adam Blair himself. Every eye being fixed stedfastly upon the impassioned speaker, the entrance of a stranger was not for a few moments observed by a single person there; and indeed Dr Muir himself never suspected what had happened, until the pale and altered man was standing at the distance of three or four paces right in front of him. He stopped in the midst of the sentence, and gazed for a moment in silence, first upon him, and then upon the audience – and then suddenly resuming all the fervour of his tone, said these words, 'I thank my God! – Adam Blair, speak, look up, let them hear your voice. Speak solemnly, in the hearing of God and your brethren! – Adam, are you guilty, or not guilty, of this uncleanness?'

The unhappy Blair, laying his hand upon his breast, answered quickly and clearly, 'Call me no more your brother – I am a fallen man. – I am guilty.'

Every pulse shook beneath the tone of that voice – but Dr Muir groaned aloud, ere he made answer. 'Fallen, indeed, Adam Blair, – woe is me – doubly, trebly fallen! Do you remember the words you said to me when I spake with you in private?'

'I do – and they were true. *Then* I deceived not you, but myself. *Now*, no one is deceived.'

The old man covered his face with his hands, and

flung himself backwards upon his seat, while all the rest continued silent, speechless, staring upon the countenance of Blair.

It was he himself who broke once more the silence of their assembly: 'I call you no longer my brethren – let me still call you, though unworthy, my friends: let me still partake your prayers. – Pray for me; – I dare not pray for myself. The God that hath abandoned me will hear your prayers.'

At these words Dr Muir uncovered his face, and fixing his eyes once more on the unfortunate, continued, for some moments, to regard him in silence, like all the rest. A big tear rolled over his cheeks, but he brushed it hastily away ere he said, 'Adam Blair, you have been ill. You have been ill in the body. But a few days ago your hair was black, and now it is as grey as mine; your cheek is white, your strength is gone.' He started to his feet as he continued – 'Our brother has been visited with much sickness. Perchance his mind also has been shaken.'

'It has, it has,' muttered several voices.

Mr Blair looked all around him, and, for the first time, the water stood in his eye, as he replied, 'Body and mind have been shaken, but it is not as you would too kindly persuade yourselves. Oh, sirs! – I have spoken the truth. I came hither to speak it. What hope of peace or mercy could I have until I had spoken the truth, and resigned my office into the hands of God's servants? – I do now resign it. – My ancestors were peasants, and I return to their lot – would I were worthy of them! –

Once more, I demand your prayers. Refuse not my parting request.'

The whole assembly remained, once more, fixed in silence. Dr Muir, still erect in front of Blair, surveyed them all round and round; and then saying, 'Brethren, I read your thoughts,' fell down upon his knees. They all knelt at the same moment; and Blair, weeping like an infant, knelt also in the midst of them, and stooped his forehead to the dust.

Chapter
21

···⋅⊱✦⊰⋅···

The reader who has followed me thus far, must be contented if I trace with a much more rapid pen what yet remains to be told of the story of Adam Blair: but, indeed, he who comprehends what has already been said, will easily dispense with much of detail in the sequel.

Those who know what were the habitudes and feelings of the religious and virtuous peasantry of the west of Scotland half a century ago, can need no explanation of the immediate effects of the things which have been narrated in the last chapter, upon the inhabitants of Cross-Meikle. A deep and painful shock was given to every simple bosom among them, and the fall and deposition of their minister were things of which all thought, but of which very many were never heard to speak. The service of the church was, of course, suspended during a considerable series of weeks; and thus the chief opportunity which the country people commonly had of meeting together in numbers, was taken away from them. As, however, the very particular circumstances which had attended Mr Blair's degradation, were soon as universally known as the fact of the degradation itself having taken place, there can be little difficulty in supposing, that, in spite of all the horror with which that primitive people regarded the offence of which their minister had been guilty, there gradually mingled in their feelings as to himself, a large share of commiseration – not to say of sympathy. Nor can it be doubted that the manner in which John Maxwell hesitated not to express himself whenever he was compelled to speak (and it was then only he would speak) upon the subject – venerable as this man was in years and character – exerted a very powerful influence over the minds both of those with whom he was personally intimate, and of others who heard the report of his conversation.

Meantime, there was no one in the parish who knew, or seemed to know, for a considerable time, what had become of the unhappy man himself. He had avoided being seen by any one who was acquainted with him during the evening which followed his resignation of his office; and although several made inquiry after him next day, at the place where he slept, the people of that house could tell nothing, but that he had sold his horse to the landlord, and gone off alone, and on foot, they knew not whither, at an early hour of the morning. This sudden and unexplained disappearance excited many anxious thoughts among those who, notwithstanding his fall, still continued to feel some interest as to the fate of Blair; and these, it has already been hinted, were far from being few.

There was but one person in that neighbourhood who was really aware of Blair's place of retreat, and of the nature of the plan which he had sketched out for the future course of his life; – and that person (it was no other than Dr Muir) had received, along with the information he possessed, the strictest injunctions to keep it as far as was possible to himself. – Mrs Semple of Semplehaugh, indeed made no secret that she had received a letter from Mr Blair, dated at Glasgow the same day he had appeared before his Presbytery; but as to its contents, she made no communication, even to the members of her own family. The daughter of the deposed clergyman remained, however, under her roof, and continued to be treated with the very same marks of kindness as before. There were not wanting some ladies, and gentlemen too, of Mrs Semple's acquaintance, who thought fit to express some little surprise, – perhaps even some little indignation, when they were informed of this last circumstance; but none of these persons were so bold as to say a word of the matter in the presence of the good Dowager herself. The innocent child herself, was told by the old Lady, that her papa had been very unwell, but that he was getting better, and she should soon see him again; and, of course, suspected nothing of the true cause of his continued absence from Cross-Meikle. By and bye, however, it became necessary that she should be farther informed; and she was by degrees led to believe, that her father had sunk into a state of health so feeble, as to render it unlikely that he should be able to resume the duties of his clerical office. Often after she had been made to understand this, the poor child would be found weeping alone in some remote corner of the house; and in truth, it was more easy for Mrs Semple to weep along with her than to bid her dry her tears.

The excellent Dr Muir was, in the meantime, not negligent in complying with the requests with which Blair had ventured to trouble him. He disposed of the furniture of the Manse to Mr Jamieson, who, it was soon announced, had received Mr Semple's presentation to the living – retaining nothing but a few of the simplest articles, and some two or three dozens of volumes out of the library. He paid off and dismissed the other servants; but transferred to his own household the old man who has already been mentioned, and who had spent the greater part of his life in the service of Mr Blair and his father.

These arrangements it was easy to make without attracting much notice, except among the persons more immediately concerned in them; but Dr Muir had other matters to attend to, which could not fail to excite the curiosity of Blair's late parishioners in general.

It has already been mentioned more than once, that Mr Blair's grandfather had lived the life of a peasant in the parish, of which two of his descendants became ministers in the sequel. The two or three acres of land which had formed this old man's patrimony, and by the cultivation of which he, like all his forefathers, had subsisted, had still remained in the possession of the family; but for a long time they had been let to the occupier of a considerable farm immediately adjoining; and the humble cottage, which stood among five or six ancient ashes and willows in the midst of Blair's paternal field at Sargard, had for many years been uninhabited, and all but a ruin. Now, however, it soon became known that the farmer had given up the remainder of his lease into Dr Muir's hands, and that, under the Doctor's directions, the walls and roof of the old cottage were about to receive some repairs. And from the time when these circumstances transpired, it came to be pretty generally surmised, that the fallen man intended either soon, or at least at some future period, to take up his residence in the long deserted dwelling of the old Adam Blair.

It was a simple matter to restore that lowly dwelling to all that it had ever been. In the course of a very few days, a new roof of thatch replaced that which had for years become pervious to the rain; the crevices in the eastern gable were filled up, and the windows, which had been wide to the blast, received new casements. The interior accommodation consisted of but two very small apartments, the one opening off the other; and these perhaps had never been so well furnished as they were now, when the few things which had not been disposed of to Mr Blair's successor had been removed thither from the Manse of Cross-Meikle. As Dr Muir was riding over one day to inspect what had been done in these matters, it occurred to him, for the first time,

that he had neglected to give any orders about re-
digging and re-inclosing the little old garden behind
the house. But when he reached the place, he found that
some one had anticipated all his wishes. The hedge
had been trimmed, and all its gaps filled up. The whole
of the soil had been carefully trenched; the turfen walk
down the centre pared and shaven; the deserted willow
arbour, at the extremity nearest the stream, had once
more resumed its shape; and many new slips of such
plants as in those days constituted the wealth of the Scots
cottar's *potager*, had been recently arranged by the hand
of some experienced gardener. The Doctor inquired by
whom all this had been done; but all the people who
had repaired the roof could tell him was, that none of
them had meddled with these things. He called, on his
way to Cambuslee, on the farmer who had tenanted the
field, and asked him also whether he had done any
thing as to the garden. The man replied that he had not
done so, nor heard of any thing being done: – but
added, after a pause of a few moments, that he had seen
old John Maxwell the Elder passing his door of late
very early in the morning.

The truth is, that John and his son had risen before
the dawn of day for some seven or eight mornings, and
laboured together in a work, of which, although they
wished to do it in secret, they neither were nor had any
reason to be ashamed.

One evening, about the close of the autumn, Dr
Muir came to Semplehaugh-house, and having said a
few words in a whisper to the old lady, took little Sarah

Blair in his hand, and walked with her towards the cottage of Sargard. He prepared the child – as they went, for meeting her father – knocked at the door – saw her enter – and withdrew without witnessing their interview.

By this time, Mr Jamieson had been, for several weeks, exercising the office of the ministry at Cross-Meikle; and although neither his personal manners, nor his style of preaching, were exactly of the sort most likely to be in favour with the country people, the events which had happened in that parish had taught some lessons of humility to young and old, and the new clergyman was, on the whole, meriting and receiving the respectful attention of those committed to his trust. The circumstances under which he had come to the living were such that he must have been a very foolish man indeed, had he not been modest in all his demeanour. And Mr Jamieson, though by nature a person neither of warm feelings, nor of very profound understanding, had both feeling and sense to conduct himself quite as he ought to have done in a situation which we must admit to have been of very extraordinary delicacy.

Next day being Sunday, the Minister of Cross-Meikle walked as usual through his congregation in the churchyard, and they had all followed him into the church and taken their places, and he had just begun to read the words of the Psalm, with which the service was to commence, when Adam Blair, with his child in his hand, entered by a side-door, and walking forwards slowly, without once taking his eyes from off the ground, seated himself opposite to the Clergyman, in the darkest and remotest corner of the western aisle. Every eye followed him to his place; and not a few of them were suffused with tears, as the fallen man was seen turning, with an unsteady hand, the leaves of his Bible, and pointing out to his daughter the passage the Minister was reading. But, after the first moment, – such is the grace of that natural courtesy which politeness never surpasses, and seldom equals, – there was not one grown-up person there who did not endeavour to avoid looking towards the corner in which Adam Blair had taken refuge. The children only of the congregation, kept gazing all the while upon him – and there was a superstitious terror in some of those young eyes, which shewed how deep an impression had been made by the few broken and mysterious hints they had heard – about the guilt, the punishment, the penitence of him, whom from infancy they had been taught to look upon as the pattern of all excellence.

Adam Blair sat with his head bowed down; but when they began to sing, he was heard joining in the Psalm, with low and trembling notes, while the clear shrill voice of his child rose from beside him in a stream of gladsome melody. It is difficult to say which of those sounds sent the deeper thrill into the ears that heard them.

In like manner, throughout the whole of the service, Mr Blair continued to keep his eyes fixed upon the ground. When the final blessing had been pronounced, he sat down again in his place, and remained there until the last of the congregation had quitted the church, and then walked out with his child in his hand as he had entered. In general, it is the custom of the Scots peasantry to linger a good while together in their churchyards after the termination of public worship, – and here, as elsewhere, the practice uniformly prevailed. That day, however, this custom lacked observance. When Blair and Sarah came forth, young and old had already passed beyond the elms which encircle the burial-ground. The child gazed round, as if wondering that no one drew near to speak to them, and instinctively she led her father a few steps in the direction of the Manse. But Mr Blair said to her, 'My love, we are going the wrong way: we must go home to Sargard.'

'Papa,' said she, 'I like the Manse better. The Manse is a far bonnier place, and what for should we no gang back to the Manse?'

'My poor bairn,' he replied, 'you cannot understand this. I am not the same man that I was.'

'But you'll soon be weel again, papa, and we'll gae back to the Manse when the bonny summer days come round again.'

Blair allowed the child to prattle as she pleased; halted with her for a moment beside her mother's tomb, and then walked slowly, and with a composed aspect, along the narrow and winding lane which leads from Cross-Meikle to the banks of the streamlet on which Sargard lies.

After his child had gone to rest that evening, he laid down the book he had been reading, and walked forth by himself in the twilight. I know not whether, when he passed his threshold, he had made up his mind as to the direction in which he would go; but so it was, that he wandered over the fields until he had come very near the place where John Maxwell lived.

In those days it was the custom of many of our godly peasants, and among the rest it was the custom of John Maxwell, to pray aloud, out of doors, morning and evening. The smallness of their houses, and the impossibility of finding places of retirement within these, had probably led at first to this practice, and it did not then enter into the mind of any body to connect its observance with any notions of pharisaical display.

When Mr Blair, therefore, had come within a few paces of the old beechen hedge at the foot of this man's garden, it was not with surprise that he heard his voice among the shade. He knew, from the low fervid solemnity of the sounds he was uttering, that they were addressed to no human ear, and he drew back to some little distance that he might not be, by accident, an intruder upon the secret of that privacy – but stood still, within reach of the sound, until he was satisfied that the good old man had made an end of his prayer. He then approached more nearly, and opening the wicket, had gone up close to John Maxwell ere he was aware of his approach.

The old man gazed in his face in silence for some space, and then received him in his arms – 'My son,' said he, 'God hath chastened severely. – You have kissed the rod.'

'I kiss the rod,' answered Adam Blair; 'this day my

bosom hath shaken off something of its load. I have at last been seen by the eyes of my people. I have sinned against them, yet I see that they pity me.'

'We have all wept for you, Mr Adam; – this day, I hope – almost, I rejoice.'

'Some light at length breaks my darkness. – John Maxwell, you are my friend, what must I do?'

'My son, God will enlighten; his Word is our only lamp. Hitherto you have done well.'

So saying, the old man led Mr Blair towards the door of his house, and he followed him beneath its roof without hesitation. Young Maxwell and his wife received him at first with some awkwardness; but the humbled man constrained himself, and after the first barriers were broken, the conversation flowed easily, although he modestly spoke far less than the rest. He knelt with them at their social devotions, and shared their meal, and said, as he rose to withdraw, 'My friends, I thank you for your kindness. Would I were worthy to live among you as my fathers did!'

The next morning's sun had scarcely sent its first rays into the valley ere Adam Blair was up and in the field. He laboured for many hours alone, and ate and drank cheerfully at evening with Sarah – his only hand-maid – his only house-hold. The fire was then blown into a blaze upon the hearth, and the father resumed his old occupation and delight in hearing and instructing his child. The toil of the day had prepared him for repose, and he retired early to bed, where once more healthful slumbers awaited him.

Humble, silent, laborious, penitent, devout – it was so that Adam Blair began the life of a peasant. Seldom, except on the Sabbath day, did he for many months quit the narrow precincts of the field to which he had returned. He was poor, but his hands could win him bread; he was fallen, but he repined not at his fall. His former associates came not near him, but he had reason to believe that they did not stay away from unkindness. His beautiful child smiled upon him in his solitude; and from day to day his heart acquired strength to endure all the bitterness it had pleased God to mingle in his cup of existence.

Chapter

22

—••⋘⋙••—

Let the reader imagine for himself what might be the natural effects of this lonely life of penitence and labour, persisted in, without deviation, during a period of ten long years – and then come with me to the conclusion of this story.

By this time Sarah Blair had ripened into woman-hood, and was the most beautiful girl in that part of the country. She was seldom seen beyond the little valley in which her father's cottage was situated, and almost never apart from her father, to whom she was evidently devoted in the whole depth of her affections. It has already been said, that she was his only hand-maid: throughout all this course of years she had performed the humblest offices about his humble habitation: nevertheless, her mind had been cultivated and improved, it is not improbable, much beyond what it might have been, had she lived in the midst of the society of which she seemed to have been born to form the ornament; and her demeanour, amidst an excess of bashfulness, betrayed abundantly the elegance of her mind. She was extremely shy and reserved if, at any time, she was thrown under the observation of strangers: but at home, when alone with her father, a sober maiden-like cheerfulness sat on her brow. In solitude, she was a melancholy girl – and no wonder – for, by slow, very slow degrees, as her understanding opened with her years, and the power of observation grew along with the capacity of feeling, Sarah, pure and innocent as she was, had divined something of the cause of her father's altered condition in life. One of the first discoveries she had made, and indeed she had made this long before she ceased to be a child, was, that the mention of a certain name never failed to produce a momentary shudder in Mr Blair's bodily frame, and she had very soon desisted from doing what she found to be invariably connected with this painful consequence. Her father's own broken and mysterious expressions of humility had, by some accident, come to be linked in her mind with the idea of that forbidden name; and, perhaps, in the course of so many years, she might casually have heard something drop in conversation from some of the neighbouring peasantry, sufficient, if aught was wanting, to supply the defect in her own train of associations. A pensive gloom, therefore, hung upon her lovely countenance – and was dispelled only when she exerted herself in presence of her father, or constrained herself before the eyes of others.

Adam Blair, on the other hand, had for a long time recovered, amidst the healthful exercises of the field, the original strength and activity of his person. His hair, which had become tinged with untimely grey (like that of the Royal Sufferer of Carisbrooke) had now become almost entirely white: beneath the sun and the wind, his countenance had assumed a hue of deep rustic brown; but his eye had recovered, if not all its youthful bright-ness, at least all the serentiy of his earlier manhood. His dress had long been the same with that of the people into whose rank he had descended; but the suit of village grey he wore, was always perfectly neat; – every thread of it had been woven by his daughter's fingers, as she sat by his side, during the long days and nights of the dark and solitary season of the year. In all his outward appearance, Adam Blair was a peasant living among peasants.

After two or three years of his penance had gone over his head, he received a letter from Mrs Semple, inviting him to come and see her, with his daughter, at Semple-haugh. He handed the letter to Sarah, and after she had read it, said, 'My child, I see what you would say: I shall write to Mrs Semple immediately.' – He did so: he expressed great gratitude to the Lady for the return of her good opinion – and the deepest sense of all the kindness he and his family had in former days received at her hands; – but concluded with requesting, that he and his daughter might be excused from again ming-ling in society which no longer became their condition in life. – The Lady of Semplehaugh appreciated Blair's humility; and though she subsequently took many ways to shew that she still kept her eye of kindness upon them

both, she never afterwards obtruded any offer of personal communication upon them. She respected them
and their lowly retirement, and said to herself, that the
time had not yet come.

Several years had elapsed after this communication
took place, when Mr Blair, as he was digging one
beautiful spring morning in his garden, received a message from his ancient friend Dr Muir, which immediately
stopt him in his labour. The old man had for some
months been unable to leave his own house; but although Mr Blair was aware of the increase of his infirmi-
ties, he was not prepared for hearing, as he now did,
that the last energies of nature were at last entirely exhausted; and that neither he nor his medical attendants
expected he could outlive two days more. The dying
man expressed an earnest desire to have some conversation that morning with Adam Blair; and he, under
such circumstances, was not likely to require a second
bidding.

He quitted his spade, therefore, and having told the
news he had heard to his daughter, immediately accompanied Dr Muir's servant to Cambuslee, which lies at
about the distance of six miles from Sargard on the other
side of the river.

When he approached the Manse, he saw Mrs Semple's
carriage in waiting near the entrance, and his first impulse when he observed it, was to walk aside for some
time, and defer his visit until hers should have been
finished: and indeed he had already turned himself
from the house, and begun to retrace his steps towards

the neighbouring wood, when he heard himself called upon by name from behind. It was Mrs Semple herself, who was looking towards him from one of the upper windows of the Manse, – and she instantly repeated her address in a tone which took from him all thought of disobeying it. Slowly, therefore, he drew near; and when he had stepped over the threshold, the same domestic who had conducted him beckoned to him from above, and led him on to the door of the chamber in which her master was lying.

When he entered it, he found himself not in a dark place, as chambers of sickness are used to be: the windows of the room were both of them wide open, not only to the light but to the air. Mrs Semple was alone with the old man, sitting by the side of his bed, and watching over him while, as it seemed, he slept. She extended her hand to Mr Blair, and he advanced treading softly, no longer hesitating to receive the symbol of kindness. Dr Muir opened his eyes at the same moment, and fixing them upon Mr Blair, while a faint smile passed over his lips, said in a low but audible whisper, 'This is right – this is quite right. I bless God that I have lived to see this day. Adam Blair, my son, draw near, and kiss my lips ere I die.'

He obeyed in silence, and immediately the dying man resumed: 'Adam, your two old friends have been both thinking and speaking of you this morning ere you came. It has pleased God to be very merciful to you and to us all. You must promise not to resist in that which we have designed for your good, and the good of many.

You must come back to the vineyard. You will be a better labourer in it now than you were in your best young days.'

'I am not worthy,' said Blair, – 'I am contented where I am – I fear change.'

'Adam Blair, I shall not see yon sun go down. I would fain leave my people in your hands.'

Mrs Semple whispered earnestly into his ear at the same instant, 'Yes, Mr Blair, the time is come: you will not hang back when all unite in entreating you.'

Mr Blair bowed himself low, and answered – 'You are both too good – too kind: but I know myself, and I know my place. Permit me to die in my humble cottage. I have tried both, and that lowly life is the better for me.'

Having said this, he withdrew towards the window and seated himself there, apart from his friends. Dr Muir kept his eyes upon him for a moment, and then whispered something he could not hear to Mrs Semple. She replied, and they conversed together for some time in the same manner. After which, the old man beckoned Mr Blair once more to approach his bed – and when he had done so, he made him kiss him once more, and then said, 'My friends, you must now leave me. Adam Blair, there is one thing you will not refuse me. My child is far away from me. I have no kinsman near – you will lay my head in the grave.' He added, after a brief pause, 'I see you will obey me – and now, God bless you, God bless you both – I would fain turn my face to the wall. *Now* I fain would be alone.'

They left the good man, as he desired, and waited in silence together below, until it was announced to them that all was over. Mrs Semple stood by Blair, while he closed the good man's eyelids, and then leaving him in charge of the house, set off on her return to Semple-haugh.

Chapter
23

—••E)(E••—

Mr Blair discharged the duty bequeathed to him by this venerable man's parting breath, amidst a numerous assemblage of the neighbouring gentry, and of the whole members of the Presbytery, to which the parishes of Cambuslee and Cross-Meikle belonged. He received their salutations with modesty, but without any apparent awkwardness; and parting from them at the church-yard, walked home to his cottage.

His daughter and he were sitting together quietly by the fireside the same evening, when a knock came to the door. Sarah rose and opened it, and in a few moments, the cottage was quite filled with the same clergy-men who had been present at the funeral. Mr Blair stood up to receive them; but he had not time to ask them the purpose of their visit ere the eldest of those who had come, addressed him in these words: –

'Mr Blair, your brethren have come to speak with you on a very solemn subject; but there is no occasion why your daughter should not hear what we have to say. It appears that our departed father, Dr Muir, had expressed a strong wish, that you, being reinstated in the ministry, should succeed him at Cambuslee, – and that the family who have the patronage of that parish, were exceedingly anxious that his dying request to this effect might be complied with. You, however, have declined to accede to their wishes. We, your brethren, have this day held a conference with the family at Semplehaugh; and another arrangement is now proposed to you by them through us. If Mr Jamieson becomes Minister of Cambuslee, will you return to your own old place? – Will you once more set your hand to God's work here at Cross-Meikle?'

Mr Blair's daughter turned aside and wept when she heard these words; but he himself stood for a moment in silence before them. – It was then that John Maxwell, who had been bed-rid for three years, was borne in a chair into the midst of the assembly, and said, 'Mr Blair, we, the Elders of Cross-Meikle, are all present. We are all of the same mind. Oh, sir, fear not! we have all witnessed the purification! let me not die until I have seen you once more in your father's place!'

The tears at length gushed over a face that had been long too calm for tears; and Mr Blair, altogether over-powered, submitted himself to the will of his brethren. His friends perceived that he would fain be left alone, and they all departed. Sarah rushed into his arms and wept, but not bitterly.

A moment afterwards, she also withdrew, and Blair was left alone to meditate upon his pillow concerning all these things, and concerning more than these.

CONCLUSION

—••ᘓ✕ᘓ••—

Shortly after, the necessary formalities having been complied with, Mr Blair resumed his office, and he continued, during a long series of years, to discharge all its duties in the midst of an affectionate and confiding people. He did so, however, with a modesty – a humility, such as became one that had passed through such scenes as I have attempted to narrate; and one thing, in particular, did not fail to make a very strong impression among the people of his flock.

In those days, persons guilty of offences against the discipline of the church, were uniformly, after confession, and expression of penitence, rebuked from the pulpit after divine service on Sunday in presence of the congregation. Whenever Mr Blair had occasion to discharge this duty, which is perhaps, under any circumstances, one of the most painful that fall to the lot of the parish-priest, he did it with deep and earnest simplicity: but he never failed to commence his address to the penitent before him, by reminding him, and all present, of his own sin and its consequences. I have said that this produced a strong and powerful impression on the minds of his people; I might have said, with equal truth, that it exerted a most salutary influence upon their conduct. That primitive race were generous enough to sympathize with generosity, and I believe not few among them found an additional safeguard against guilt in the feeling, that by their guilt, the old but deep wounds might be re-opened in the bosom of a man whose own errors, fatal as they were, and fatal in their effects, they had unconsciously come to look upon somewhat in the light of a mysterious and inscrutable infliction, rather than of common human frailty.

In the midst of this kind people, Mr Blair at last closed his eyes upon all earthly scenes, after he had laboured among them during a space of not less than twenty years after his restoration. His daughter, fair and lovely as she was, had, in her time, received the addresses of many wooers, but she never would listen to any of them – continuing to devote herself in all things to her father. Soon after his death, she retired once more to the Glen of Sargard, the lowly cottage of which she had not ceased to visit from time to time, with a view, it may be supposed, to that which she executed in the sequel.

Sarah Blair spent the evening of her days in calmness, meriting and receiving every species of attention at the hands of her late father's parishioners. Not many years have passed since she died. With her, the race of the Blairs in that parish ended – but not their memory.

I have told a TRUE STORY. I hope the days are yet

far distant when it shall be doubted in Scotland that
such things might have been.

> 'Stranger! henceforth be warn'd, and know that pride,
> Howe'er disguised in its own majesty,
> Is littleness. That he who feels contempt
> For any living thing, hath faculties
> Which he hath never used: That thought with him
> Is in its infancy. The man whose eye
> Is ever on himself, doth look on one
> The least of Nature's works, one that might move
> The wise man to that scorn which Wisdom holds
> Unlawful, ever. O, be wiser thou!
> Instructed that true knowledge leads to love;
> True dignity abides with him alone,
> Who, in the silent hour of inward thought,
> Can still suspect and still revere himself
> In lowliness of heart.'

THE END

PRINTED BY R. & R. CLARK, LTD., EDINBURGH